Bridget finished doctoring her Quarter Pounder with three packets of ketchup on each side of her burger. "I wish I had better eating habits," she admitted. "My parents didn't let us have much candy either, but that didn't help me once I got out on my own."

She took a big bite out of her Quarter Pounder and within seconds a huge dollop of ketchup fell on her shirt. Bridget set her burger down in horror as she looked down at the mess on her chest. *Why didn't I see that coming?* she thought as she grabbed for some napkins. Her eyes opened wide with surprise when Gwen reached over with a French fry and dabbed it in the ketchup on Bridget's chest.

"No sense in wasting it."

Bridget looked down at her shirt again and laughed when the second fry gently plunged into the bright red glob on her chest. Her irritation and embarrassment slowly turned into light amusement as they both sat there dipping crispy fries into the concoction prominently displayed on the right side of her shirt.

Visit

Bella Books

at

BellaBooks.com

or call our toll-free number

1-800-729-4992

MIDNIGHT RAIN

PEGGY J. HENDERSON

Bella
BOOKS
2005

Bella Books, Inc.
P.O. Box 10543
Tallahassee, FL 32302

Printed in the United States of America on acid-free paper
First Edition

Editor: Anna Chinappi
Cover designer: Sandy Knowles

ISBN 1-59493-021-X

For Stormy

Acknowledgments

I would like to thank Frankie J. Jones, always my first reader. I depend on your impressions and insight. You've never failed to help me write a better book.

I want to thank Martha Cabrera for the brainstorming sessions over fried chicken. I look forward to having many more of those!

Thanks to Robert B. Rylander Jr. and friends for the car chat. It was fun and you know your stuff! I appreciate your support and enthusiasm for my work.

A special thanks to Laverne Bell. I adore you. Don't ever change.

About the Author

Peggy J. Herring lives on seven acres of mesquite in south Texas with her cockatiel, hermit crabs and two wooden cats. When she isn't writing, Peggy enjoys camping, fishing and traveling. She is the author of *Once More with Feeling*, *Love's Harvest*, *Hot Check*, *A Moment's Indiscretion*, *Those Who Wait* and *To Have and to Hold* from Naiad Press and *Calm Before the Storm*, *The Comfort of Strangers*, *Beyond All Reason*, *Distant Thunder* and *White Lace and Promises* for Bella Books. Peggy is currently working on a new romance titled *Shelter from the Storm* to be released in 2006 by Bella Books.

Chapter One

Two months ago, 2 a.m., West Side Laundromat

Lupita Ochoa took the last of her clothes from the hot dryer and began folding them neatly before placing them in the basket. The hum of an anonymous washer on the other side of the room gave the place a semblance of personality that she hadn't noticed before. She squinted over at the huge clock on the wall—her left eye was only partially swollen shut today. Lupita was also reminded once again of the pain in her back and the stiffness in her neck. She buttoned the top of her sweater and gently touched the bruises on her throat where he had tried to choke the very life out of her several days before. The memory crept away much slower than it had arrived.

She finished folding the clothes and tucked the small box of detergent snugly in the basket among the rest of her things. Digging in her pocket for bus fare to her sister's house, her fingers still hurt from slapping at him, and her back ached where he had thrown her against the wall in their small apartment. Lupita vowed to work two jobs and save her money—three jobs if she had to. Never again would she be put in this position. Never.

She caught her reflection in the door of the dryer and looked away quickly. *How thick can a person pile on makeup without looking like a freak? And how can I go to work with a face like this anyway?*

She picked up the basket and felt another pain in her side. As every second ticked away, her body seemed to be shutting down and turning against her. If her back and ribs continued hurting this way, she would have to call in sick at her new job, and she couldn't afford to do that right now.

Shuffling across the floor, scattering candy wrappers and fuzz balls with each painful step, Lupita pushed the heavy door open with her sore hip and breathed in the chilly October night air. The sidewalk and parking lot pavement were wet, and the absence of traffic on the usually busy street added an extra sense of eeriness to the night.

She was halfway across the empty parking lot before she realized he was there. She sensed his presence moments before seeing him. Fear paralyzed her as Rudy grabbed her from behind. Lupita dropped the basket and tried to scream, but nothing came out of her mouth. His thick hairy arm was squeezing every last wisp of air from her lungs. She tried to bite him and flung her arms about wildly. He would kill her this time. She would die here in a Kwik Wash Laundromat parking lot.

Dark clouds had moved in, covering the moon and stars. The empty bus stop on the corner, at this point her only possible means of escape, could have been a thousand miles away for all the good it was doing her. Rudy loosened his grip for only a second and yanked Lupita around by the hair. With a gasp she clutched her throat and tried to scream again, but failed miserably as she started to cough. She threw her hands up to protect her face when he started hitting her. Still hurting from her last beating, Lupita had no strength left. How she was still standing was a miracle in itself. Each devastating blow he landed now helped merge the pain into

2

one massive burrow of darkness. Somewhere through the deep hollow of fear and pain, Lupita heard squealing tires close by and then a car door open. Her heart fluttered at the possibility that she was no longer alone with him.

The massive fists eventually stopped punching, but Rudy grabbed her once more around the neck and squeezed hard again for good measure.

"Let her go," she heard someone say.

Rudy tightened his arm around her, pulling her closer up against him, but took his other hand away from her throat. Lupita was finally able to breathe again and was suddenly nauseated by his sour whiskey-breath and huge sweaty body. She tried to bite his arm again, but didn't have the strength to pry herself away and carry through.

"I said let her go," the voice uttered, ringing out into the night. It was a cool, even voice. A woman's voice. The voice of an angel. "Let her go *now!*"

Rudy yanked Lupita around beside him. "Mind your own business, bitch!"

Through the blood oozing from a cut over her already swollen eye, Lupita could see the woman still standing on the driver's side, towering over the jet-black sports car, one arm casually resting on its low roof. A moment later Lupita saw the pistol in the woman's hands, pointed at him, and heard that wonderful deadly click of the hammer.

Rudy let go of her, raising his hands up slowly as Lupita crumbled to the ground.

"Don't shoot," he said.

"Move away from her."

"It's OK," Rudy said, putting his hands down. "It's OK. She's my wife."

There was a loud piercing sound that boomed into the darkness. It was then that she heard screaming—Rudy's screaming. It stopped almost as abruptly as it had started as he stood there shaking with his hands up in front of him.

"There's a bullet hole through the top of your cap," the woman said calmly. "Next time you won't be quite so lucky. Now move away from her like I said before."

Rudy scrambled several yards to the left, holding his hands up over his head. "Don't shoot!"

The woman kept the gun pointed at him and came around the back of the car. She was dressed entirely in black—soft leather boots, black leather pants, a black long-sleeved silk shirt, and black scarves rolled up and neatly tied around her arms. She was tall and elegant, the gun huge in her hands.

"Get behind the car," the woman said, motioning with the weapon. Rudy stumbled over in that direction, keeping his hands above his head.

Lupita tried to sit up so she could see better. She watched as the woman opened the trunk of the car and again motioned with the gun.

"Get in."

"Get in?" Rudy repeated dumbly, his voice rising an octave. "Get in where?"

Lupita heard that sound again, the cold click of the gun being cocked.

"Get in," the woman said simply, motioning toward the opened trunk of the car.

"No way, lady! Are you nuts?"

She raised the gun to his head, further encouraging him to climb into the trunk. Lupita watched with delight as his knees began to knock against each other. If her mouth hadn't been so tender, she would have smiled at the sight.

"What are you gonna do with me?" Rudy asked. "I won't hit her no more, OK? I won't hit her no more!"

The woman slammed the trunk shut on his muffled pleas. Without Rudy's shouting, Lupita could finally hear the wail of a siren in the distance. As she lay there on the pavement, scared and shivering, bleeding from her nose and the gash over her eye, there was a feeling of being totally safe . . . that warm, secure feeling of someone taking charge and making things all better. The woman in black knelt down beside her and gently brushed the damp hair away from Lupita's eyes.

"Everything's fine now," the woman whispered. She unzipped a small pocket at the knee of her black leather pants and took out a white card. She gave it to Lupita and then stood up. "The police and an ambulance will be here soon." She quickly moved around to the side of her car and opened the door.

Lupita could hear Rudy pounding on the inside of the trunk, yelling and cursing in muffled hysteria. Lupita tried to sit up again, but the pain in her back and ribs was excruciating. She rubbed her throat and coughed.

"Wait," Lupita said, her voice no more than a raspy croak. "Who are you?" she managed to ask.

"That doesn't matter."

"Please," Lupita said. "Who are you?" Her throat felt like it was swelling shut. In a near whisper she said again, "Who are you?"

The moon broke away from behind the clouds and revealed a kind, gentle smile from across the top of the car.

"I'm a friend," the woman said above the shrieking sirens only a few blocks away. "He won't hurt you anymore. I promise you that." She got in the car and the passenger's side window rolled down automatically. "Tell them what happened. They'll know what to do."

The car was gone in a flash. All that remained was the card she had left behind and a blur of taillights. Seconds later, the ambulance roared to a stop and two paramedics bailed out.

On the way to the hospital, in the back of the ambulance, Lupita took the card from her pocket and found the words KATE THE LESBIAN printed in bold black letters. She put the card gently to her swollen lips and then tucked it away again into her pocket. Warm, safe feelings began working their way through her body, feelings of trust, certainty, and determination. Sleep would come much easier for her now. It seemed like months since Lupita had felt safe enough to sleep.

Chapter Two

Four weeks ago, 7:05 p.m., SBC Building, Downtown

Jane Whitley left the office and caught the elevator just before the doors eased closed. Hoping the clock in her office had been wrong, she shifted her briefcase to her other hand and glanced at her watch again. She had less than an hour to get home and take a quick shower before Miriam was due to pick her up for dinner. They hadn't been able to spend much time together lately.

The elevator finally reached the lobby and opened in front of the security guard's desk. He was on the telephone and didn't look up as Jane pushed open the door to the parking garage. The clicking of her heels echoed through the night, while a car alarm went off somewhere in the distance. She glanced at her watch once more and resigned herself to the fact that she was running late.

She had her keys ready once her car was in sight. Disengaging the alarm with a push of a button on her key ring, the car answered with what Jane liked referring to as "that cute little dolphin noise."

She set her briefcase and raincoat down, opened the door and tossed her purse on the seat. As she reached for her briefcase and raincoat, someone grabbed her from behind.

"Scream and I'll kill you," he snarled.

Jane's terror was absolutely paralyzing. She couldn't move. She couldn't speak. The huge arm around her upper body had her in a firm iron grip. Finally, she saw the knife waving like a steamy mirage in front of her face. It was the knife that brought her around and transformed her shock into the cold hard fact that she was going to die.

He yanked open the back door of her car and shoved her in the backseat. Jane tasted her own blood from a cut on her lip. She struggled to sit up and began kicking at him with her heels. She could see the sweat on his bald head. He grinned wickedly while unfastening his belt and pants with one hand. He pushed her back against the seat, seeming to not give her flinging arms and frantic kicks so much as another thought. His enormous body filled the car as he yanked her skirt up and ripped it. Jane heard the tiny buttons on the fine silk blouse bouncing all around them.

Jane was exhausted from fighting him, but driven by pure adrenaline. She never stopped struggling, pounding at his arms and shoulders, scratching his face and neck at even the slightest of opportunities. He no longer had the knife, but it was obvious to both of them that he didn't need it. His sheer strength was more than enough to do anything that he wanted to do.

She heard someone yelling just outside of the car, and the man's rough, callused hands suddenly stopped grabbing at her. He scrambled up in a fit of rage, the heaviness of him forever imprinted in her brain. She tried to sit up again and felt like the very life had been crushed out of her. Jane heard loud voices and pulled herself to the far corner of the backseat, straightening her torn, mangled clothing as she moved. She then heard a calm voice asking the man to get out of the car.

Jane could see a figure dressed in black standing near the opened car door. Who it was didn't matter to her. All that mattered at the moment was that she was no longer alone.

"He has a knife!" Jane yelled, not recognizing her own trembling voice.

"Shuddup!" the man barked as he grabbed his loose pants and tightened the belt around his waist. His hands came up in the air quickly before he began backing away. "Just a little misunderstanding," he said.

"I understand all too well," the other voice said quietly.

It was then that Jane saw the gun for the first time. It was huge in the small, black-gloved hand that held it. Jane's heart began pounding all over again as the odds suddenly shifted in her favor.

Jane had no idea who this other person was, but the sense of immediate relief she felt was almost overwhelming. She opened the door pressing against her back and stumbled out of the car. Squinting for a better look at the person wielding the gun, Jane was stunned to see that it was a woman. Tears clouded her vision as she tried to focus and get a better look at her. She had never been so happy to see a stranger!

"Get in," the woman said to him, motioning with the gun. Jane noticed the black car parked a few feet away behind them. "I said get in."

"Fuck you, bitch."

Jane watched in momentary horror and then utter delight as the woman pulled back the hammer on the gun and shot him in the hand. The sound of the gun was deafening as it echoed through the parking garage. The man screamed and bounced off Jane's car door, falling to his knees.

"You *shot* me! You fuckin' *shot* me!"

"Get up," the woman said with a tinge of boredom in her voice. When there was no immediate response from him, the gun was cocked once more and aimed steadily and confidently at his chest. "I said get up."

He muttered something and stumbled to his feet, clutching his wounded hand to his chest.

Motioning again with the gun, the woman said, "Now get in."

Jane noticed that the trunk of the black car was open.

"Get in where?" the man roared. "In *there?* I can't fit in there!"

"Either get in, or I'll shoot you again. Your choice."

He seemed to consider his options for a moment before finally shuffling to the car and gingerly crawling into the trunk. All else was quiet in the garage as the woman closed the trunk with a firm thud.

Fascinated, Jane watched her every move. She had the grace of a dancer, and something else that Jane couldn't quite put a name to. The woman was commanding and confident in everything she did, and she was much younger than Jane had first thought. The word "regal" came to mind as she continued watching her. *Regal and stately*, she thought.

The woman got something out of her car and came around to the other side where Jane was still standing. Jane waited as the woman moved closer, neither of them making a sound. The woman reached down and picked up Jane's raincoat that was on the pavement beside her briefcase. She draped the raincoat around Jane's shoulders and tugged gently on the lapel before turning away.

"Thank you," Jane said, still trembling from her ordeal.

The woman opened her car door and tossed that mane of jet-black hair away from her beautiful face. "You're safe now. The police are on the way."

"Who are you?" Jane asked. She was on the edge of panic at the thought of this woman leaving.

A rush of heavy footsteps could be heard coming toward them from the lobby entrance. Jane looked and saw the security guard reaching for his gun as he ran. Jane pulled the raincoat tighter around her and watched the black car speed away. At the far end of the row of parked cars she could see taillights just before they disappeared around the corner.

With her blouse open and ruined, she slipped her arms into the raincoat and tightened the belt. She shoved her hands into the pockets of the raincoat and began to shiver.

Jane felt the stiff white card against her palm and pulled it out of her pocket, reading the words KATE THE LESBIAN embossed in small black letters. Jane didn't remember slipping the card back into her pocket that first time, but off and on during the remainder of the evening she must have gone back to it a hundred times.

Chapter Three

Present Day, 8:10 p.m., Women's Resource Center

Bridget McBee sat in her car in the small parking lot, hoping to eventually muster up the courage to go inside. She had arrived for her appointment early, but as of yet hadn't found the urge to do too much about it. Her windows were beginning to fog up, and the chill of the November night air was starting to seep through her thin jacket. A car pulled in and parked next to her and a woman got out. Bridget knew that this was it. If she didn't go in this time, then she would probably never go in at all. Taking a deep breath, she opened the car door and decided to get it over with.

The building was warm inside, and the soft mumbling of female voices reached her from across the room. Bridget had been to the Women's Resource Center several times during the last few years, once for a fund-raiser for the Texas Gay Rights Lobby and again for a fund-raiser for the Texas Lesbian Conference, but this was the first time she had ever felt uncomfortable here. She studied the three women near the coffeepot and refreshment station and still wasn't sure whether or not she was doing the right thing. One of the women smiled and made her way over toward her.

"Number Seven?" the woman asked. She was a little older than Bridget, possibly in her early forties, and had a friendly smile.

Bridget nodded, remembering that for now numbers instead of names would be used for those being interviewed. Offers of coffee were made and politely refused. Bridget was anxious to get things underway and over with.

"I'm Dorothy Holt," the woman said. "I'm the director of the Resource Center. There's a room in the back where we can talk."

Bridget followed her down a long hallway and into an office. There was a gray metal desk near the window and a leather couch against the wall near the door. Dorothy picked up a clipboard on the desk and smiled again.

"This should do," she said, and motioned toward the couch where they both settled in comfortably. Bridget caught the sweet scent of Dorothy's perfume, which offered the only refreshing note to an otherwise long, tedious day.

"Do you have any questions before we get started?" Dorothy asked. Her thick dark hair touched her shoulders and revealed only an occasional glimpse of silver on the sides.

"Hundreds," Bridget said finally, and then laughed. "I guess I'm having a little trouble with this."

"That's perfectly understandable. It's been hard for most of the women to come forward at first." She set the clipboard down between them. "Believe me, I understand. I know you've had a traumatic experience, but you'll be with women who have been through the same thing. The Women's Task Force needs your help."

Bridget remembered the voice on the phone the other night saying the same thing to her. *That's why I'm here*, she reminded herself. *They need my help.*

Bridget closed her eyes and took a deep breath as a sense of disappointment nagged away in the back of her mind. She had almost expected to find her here. Everywhere she looked now—the halls at school, in classrooms, convenience stores, restaurants—Bridget studied women in hopes of seeing Kate the Lesbian again. She couldn't help it. She wanted to find her and thank her for saving her life.

"How many of us are there?" Bridget asked. "I mean, how many women have seen Kate?"

"Ten that we know of."

There was silence for a moment as that incredible number began to sink in. Bridget took another deep breath and said, "The person I spoke with on the phone earlier was vague about certain things. I've already cooperated with the police and answered all their questions. I'm not sure what help I can give you."

Dorothy nodded and drummed her pen against the arm of the sofa. "We've heard a few things that we don't like. Disturbing things. This Kate the Lesbian, whoever she may be, is wanted for questioning by the police for suspicion of kidnapping. It's alarmed and angered a lot of women. The police are trying to keep the media out of it for the most part, but it won't be long before this whole thing breaks wide open."

"Kidnapping?" Bridget said slowly.

"Yes, kidnapping," Dorothy repeated. "She forces these men into her car at gunpoint. None have been seen or heard from since. They, meaning the police, have chosen to focus on this—the abduction of would-be rapists and batterers. The assaults these men were about to commit seem to have little bearing on anything else at this point as far as the authorities are concerned. You realize, of course, that everything I'm telling you now is strictly confidential."

Bridget, wide-eyed and speechless, managed a slight nod.

"The police want to know where these men are and what Kate has done with them," Dorothy continued. "There have been two prominent men missing as well, so there's speculation on whether that's the reason for the sudden interest in Kate's activities."

"Prominent men?"

"One of the missing men is a local banker. Another a judge from Houston who was here for a conference. There's reason to believe these men were involved in some brutality toward women and Kate intervened."

She gave Bridget a reduced copy of a city map with numbers penciled in and highlighted at various locations. "This is you," Dorothy said as she pointed to the number seven on the map.

Bridget felt a prickling sensation dart up and down her arms the moment she realized what the ten numbers represented. As she stared at the map, she didn't feel so alone anymore. Seeing the numbers spread out across the city that way made her realize that at least nine others had experienced the same or at least similar things that she had. Bridget's hands began to tremble.

"These are the ten known reported sightings of Kate the Lesbian," Dorothy said quietly. "We're not sure how many more there have been that we don't know about."

A silence followed that gave Bridget time to compose herself and quickly sort through the information. Things were moving very fast all of a sudden.

Dorothy picked up the clipboard again. "I need to ask you a few questions. Is that OK?"

"Yes, of course." Bridget cleared her throat and sat up a little straighter on the sofa. Her earlier uneasiness gradually began to slip away as she continued thinking about Kate and how she had just appeared out of nowhere that night in the San Antonio College parking lot. Bridget never stopped thinking about how such a traumatic event could have and should have changed her life. Initially, it had made her afraid to go out again and work such late hours. But that started to ease up over time and with the help of therapy. Bridget found herself being more alert to her surroundings wherever she went now, and strangers were met with suspicion and uneasiness. For Bridget it was imperative that she find this woman and she was determined to do whatever she could to help protect her. *I owe that much to Kate*, she thought. *It's the least I can do for someone who saved my life.*

Scribbling something on the form, Dorothy said, "The description you gave to the police was exactly the same as everyone else's. Everything down to the car she drove and the card she left you. Do you remember everything Kate said to you that night?"

"Yes."

"What did she say? Her exact words."

"'You're safe now. The police are on their way.'"

Dorothy checked something else off on the form and looked up. "Do you remember hearing the sirens before she said that?"

"Before?" Bridget asked with a pensive expression. "No, not before, now that you mention it. I didn't hear them until she started to leave."

"Did she give you anything other than the card?"

"You mean besides my life?" Bridget replied soberly.

Dorothy smiled. "Yes, besides that."

"A scarf. A black scarf. The police took it."

Dorothy checked another block on the form. "Did she touch you in any way?"

Bridget unconsciously brushed a fingertip over her lip. The bruise was gone now and the cut healed already. "My mouth was full of blood. She took a scarf that had been tied around her arm and got my lip to stop bleeding. I'll never forget the way her gloves felt against my cheek. They were thin gloves. Not like gloves at all, actually. I've looked for them since then, but I haven't been able to find any."

Dorothy continued to write. "Anything else that you can remember? Was she wearing perfume? Did you hear anything when she moved? Keys, bells, change in a pocket? Anything?"

"No. She was quiet. Very quiet. Even in those boots she wore, I never heard her make a sound."

"Did she say anything else?"

"No."

The scribbling continued. "Have you seen her again, or at least thought you might have seen her somewhere else?" Dorothy asked.

"No, I haven't seen her." *But I've looked for her everywhere,* Bridget wanted to say. *Absolutely everywhere.*

Dorothy set the clipboard down between them on the sofa again. "Does it bother you that these men are missing?"

"Bother me?"

"That she might have . . . uh . . . disposed of them in some way?"

A flash of memory came to her again. An enormous hand clamped across her mouth with such force that he split her lip open. Bridget narrowed her eyes and said very slowly, "No, it doesn't bother me at all that rapists are missing." Then as an after-thought, she asked, "There have been nine other women nearly raped who have seen Kate?"

"Yes," Dorothy said.

"So are there ten missing men?"

"Yes. At least ten."

Bridget nodded. "Good. The assholes."

Dorothy chuckled. "Is there anything else you can remember?" she asked. "Anything at all that you haven't told the police?"

"No, nothing." Bridget looked over at her. All the uneasiness about this meeting she'd been harboring was nearly gone now, and it had been replaced by a renewed curiosity and a stronger determination to find this Kate the Lesbian.

"That's the formal part of the interview," Dorothy said. She got up from the sofa and put the clipboard on the desk.

"Tell me what you've heard about her," Bridget said. "Do you know who she is?"

"We have no idea who she is, but we have a few leads." Dorothy leaned against the desk with her arms crossed. "The police, how-ever, have suggested that this whole thing is a hoax. That Kate and these men are in this together somehow. It's like some sort of cruel publicity stunt or something. No one gave too much thought to the missing men until the judge and the banker disappeared. The police are working on several other theories at the moment, and none of them are favorable for our Kate."

Our Kate, Bridget thought as she shifted uneasily on the sofa. The term "our Kate" disturbed her. She liked thinking of Kate the Lesbian as *her* Kate. She didn't like the idea of sharing her with anyone.

"So what is it you want from me?" Bridget asked quietly.

"We'd like for you to join the KTL Task Force. Three out of the ten women who have been attacked have agreed to help so far."

"KTL? What's that stand for?"

"Kate the Lesbian."

"Oh." Bridget looked away from her. "I can't see where I'd be of any use to you. I've already told you everything I know."

"We hope to get several of the witnesses together and pool our resources," Dorothy explained. "Kate the Lesbian could be in serious trouble if the police find her first."

Bridget's heart began to race. "You want to find her?"

"If at all possible. Don't you?"

Bridget didn't answer.

"Can we count on you to help?"

"Yes, of course."

"Good. We'll be meeting here on Wednesday evening at seven. Hopefully, we should have more information by then. In the meantime, if you can remember anything else about that night, anything at all that you didn't mention before, write it down and bring it with you to the meeting."

Bridget nodded. She felt good all of a sudden, excited and energetic. Maybe now she would get a chance to actually do something for this marvelous woman who had saved her life!

All the way down the hall and out into the parking lot where two other women stood talking, there was a sense of accomplishment in the air. Now that the darkness no longer nurtured her fear nor held her captive with its uncertainty, Bridget felt encased in hope—as though there was a force on her side more powerful than anything she could have ever imagined. Her Kate was somewhere out there right now—possibly needing her help. Bridget vowed to do whatever she could to protect her, no matter what it took.

Chapter Four

Bridget was early for the Wednesday night meeting at the Women's Resource Center. She wanted to familiarize herself with the place a bit more and be able to see the other people as they arrived. She still couldn't help thinking that Kate the Lesbian was somewhere among them, probably working at a regular boring job during the day and prowling dark alleys and parking lots at night looking for muggers and rapists. *An ordinary woman by day*, she thought, *and a lifesaver after the sun goes down*. Bridget shook her head at her own silliness. *You must've read too many comic books as a kid*.

As she stood by a tall bookcase crammed full of lesbian literature, she nodded at Dorothy Holt when she came into the room. Dorothy held her clipboard close to her chest and started in her direction, but before she got very far, the door opened and three other women came in. Bridget didn't know any of them, but once again she found herself looking closely to see if maybe one of the women could possibly be Kate.

"Good," Dorothy said. "We're all here. Let's go to one of the offices in the back."

They slowly followed Dorothy down a wide hallway to a room off to the right. Bridget noticed that two of the women were of medium height, both with dark hair. One was Hispanic and wore a long skirt and a sweater. The other one, carrying about twenty extra pounds, had on tan scrubs and an ID badge that identified her as an employee of University Hospital. Bridget imagined they all were coming from work just like her. The third woman was taller and had shoulder-length red hair. She was dressed in a light green power suit that fit her perfectly. Bridget wondered if any of them besides herself and Dorothy were lesbians.

Once they got to the meeting room, Bridget saw a small table by the window with a coffeepot, a pitcher of lemonade and a plate of cookies on it. There was a large conference table in the middle of the room surrounded by too many chairs. A rack stuffed with flyers and pamphlets stood guard by the door. The room was clean and comfortably warm. Bridget took a seat at the far end of the table so she could see the door in case anyone else came in.

"The coffee's decaf," Dorothy announced. "Help yourselves and let's get started."

Since the other three women had arrived together, Bridget had assumed at first that they all knew each other, but she eventually noticed the lack of friendly chatter among them and nothing more than the moving of chairs and curious glances at the refreshment table. *Maybe one of them knows something about Kate that could possibly help us find her,* Bridget thought. Just that notion alone was enough to keep her focused on whatever was about to happen. Bridget went over and got a cup of coffee and selected two oatmeal cookies before returning to her seat. Slowly, one by one, the other three women got themselves some refreshments also.

"Let's sit close together, since there aren't that many of us," Dorothy suggested.

The women came back to the table and moved their purses and jackets closer to where Bridget was sitting.

"The first thing I'd like to address is whether or not we want to

19

use our names during these meetings," Dorothy announced. "Up until now, privacy has been an issue and numbers have been used to identify all of you."

No one said anything and Bridget suddenly felt sorry for Dorothy. Her job wouldn't be an easy one if none of them were willing to talk. *Isn't that why we're all here to begin with?* she thought. *To discuss Kate and try and uncover something new about her?*

The longer she was there, the more curious Bridget became about what could be accomplished. During Dorothy's initial interview, the term "task force" had been used, but Bridget wasn't exactly sure what all that entailed. As she glanced around the table, none of them looked like "task force" material to her, whatever that meant. *We're just a bunch of women who are angry about being attacked and victimized.*

"At first I felt more comfortable with the numbers," the redhead began. She was sitting across from Bridget and stirred a pink packet of artificial sweetener into a Styrofoam cup of coffee.

"So did I," the Hispanic woman agreed. Her skin was a beautiful light cinnamon color and her features were almost delicate in nature, with thick dark hair hanging in long smooth curves over her shoulders. Bridget noticed how she seemed to have a hint of tired sadness in her dark eyes.

"I did, too," the woman in scrubs said. Her hair was short and a mousy brown color. Her strong, confident voice demanded attention, but she was less intense than the redhead. "But if we're going to get anything done, I think we should be a bit more open about ourselves."

Feeling as though valuable time was being wasted, Bridget made a spontaneous decision to introduce herself. "My name's Bridget McBee. I'm number seven on the map Dorothy has." As everyone looked at her, Bridget saw Dorothy's slight smile and a flood of relief cover her face.

After a moment, the woman in scrubs said, "My name's Gwen Bordovsky. I'm number eight on the map."

Dorothy thumbed through the papers on her clipboard until she found copies of the map in question. She passed them around without fanfare. As Bridget once again saw her number and the area of town where it was written on the map, a wave of apprehension swept through her.

"My name's Jane Whitley, and I'm number two on the map," the redhead said quietly.

Bridget scanned the map for that number, all the while wishing she knew more about the earlier Kate sightings. She hadn't paid much attention to the buzz of events surrounding previous attacks until she personally had been accosted in the school parking lot. The reality of being in a room with other women who had experienced a terrifying night much like hers was comforting in its own bizarre way. These were strangers who already shared something monumental and life-changing with her.

"My name is Lupita Ochoa, and I'm number one on the map," the quiet woman with the dark, sad eyes said. "Kate the Lesbian saved my life and I want to find her and personally thank her for that. Above all else, that's why I'm here."

Silence filled the room just moments before everyone began talking at once. It was as though Lupita had read the thoughts of all those who had experienced Kate's extraordinary bravery and insight. All were in agreement that thanking this woman for saving their lives was also their number one reason for being there. With such a collective motive suddenly out in the open, it was obvious that they all had more in common than just being victims of violence. Each of them had "experienced" Kate under similar circumstances.

As everyone began to settle down again and study the map, Gwen, the woman in scrubs, said, "So how do we go about finding our Kate the Lesbian and that cool Kate-mobile she drives?"

"My thoughts exactly," Jane said with an adventurous toss of her red hair.

"Hopefully, we'll all be able to figure that out together," Dorothy said.

❧

Bridget watched as the brainstorming began. Being more of a follower than a leader, she felt comfortable just listening to them for a while. Dorothy was poised to take notes while Lupita pushed up the sleeves of her sweater as if getting ready to pitch in wherever needed. Just as eager to get down to business, Jane got another cup of coffee.

"My feet are killing me," Gwen said. "Mind if I get comfy?" she asked while propping her stockinged feet up in another chair and not waiting for an answer.

Everyone had plenty to say, and eventually, one by one, Dorothy asked them for specifics about their encounter with Kate. Lupita was the first person to have seen her, so her story was the one they started with.

"You said Kate wore black pants with a zippered pocket at the knee," Dorothy said, glancing at her notes, "and that's where she kept the card."

"Yes."

"But with Gwen," Dorothy said, "Kate had the cards in her shirt pocket, correct?"

"Right," Gwen confirmed.

"Maybe she has them all over," Lupita said. "Cards in all of her pockets . . . easy to retrieve when she needs them."

"Why does it matter where she has the cards?" Gwen asked.

"It doesn't really," Dorothy said, "but I want to document and get an idea about how she does things so we can possibly gain some . . . some . . . hmm. I don't know. It just seems important that we try and piece together her movements and the conversations she had with each of you."

"I agree with Dorothy," Lupita said. "The more we know, the better chance we have of figuring out who she is and where she is."

"OK," Jane said, "so Lupita remembers the black pants with a zipper at the knee. Did anyone else get a good look at the pants?"

"Not me."

"No, me neither."

"They were leather," Lupita said. "Not made of ordinary fabric. I remember them being a little shiny in the moonlight."

Dorothy scribbled something else down. "Leather. Good. I didn't have that. What else do you remember?"

"The car," Lupita said. "I remember that, too."

"I need for all of you to do some research on the type of car you think it was," Dorothy said.

"A Maserati Spyder," two of them said in unison.

"Black," Bridget added. "With a black interior."

"And no license plate on the back," Gwen said.

"And no dome light inside," Lupita added.

"Wow," Dorothy said, obviously impressed. "There were only vague descriptions of the car given to the police. This is the first I've heard about what *kind* of car it was!"

"I thought Mitsubishi made the Spyder," Jane said.

"Maserati makes one, too," Bridget informed her.

With a pleased expression, Jane said, "I only know about the Mitsubishi because a friend swoons over them whenever she sees one. I just feel so butch sitting here with a table full of women talking about cars."

OK, Bridget thought, *so at least three of us are lesbians. "Butch" isn't a term a straight woman would use.*

"It was a great car," Gwen said.

Bridget thought so, too. There were things she would never forget—things like the man who attacked her and the way he had begged for Kate not to shoot him, the sound of Kate's voice on a clear November night, as well as the car she had forced that coward into. "She might have had the car altered in some way so that it'll accommodate putting someone in the trunk."

"I agree," Gwen said. "That jerk that attacked me had trouble getting in, but he fit in there eventually with the help of Kate pointing that gun at him."

After a chuckle went around the room, Jane said, "Well, I'll admit I'm impressed. Kate's car wasn't something I was really interested in at the time. I was just happy to see her and know she had a gun."

"It's an expensive car," Bridget said. "Not just anybody would be driving one."

"How expensive?" Jane asked.

"Around ninety thousand," Gwen said.

"Ninety thousand?" Jane sputtered. "My goodness!"

Bridget noticed that Dorothy was again scribbling furiously. At least on paper it would look like they were making progress.

"Do the police know about the car?" Dorothy asked.

With a shrug, Gwen said, "Maybe not. At the time I was attacked, I just knew the car was black and sporty."

Bridget nodded. "Me, too. It wasn't until afterward that I did some research on it."

"Same here," Gwen said. "With the help of my son, I remembered things about it afterward that led me to settle on that model."

"So how many of these cars could there be in San Antonio?" Jane asked.

"I'd never seen one before," Bridget admitted. *But I've been looking for them ever since*, she wanted to say.

"It's like when you buy a new car," Gwen said. "You don't notice how many other people have one just like it until you actually get one yourself, but I haven't seen another Maserati Spyder anywhere out and about. This is mostly SUV and bubba-truck country."

"Well, from now on," Jane said, "if I ever see a black Maserati Spyder, I'm following it until I see who's driving. It doesn't matter where they're going or who they are. They can call me a stalker or sic the cops on me—I don't care. I'm following it."

Another chuckle went around the table as all were in agreement.

They moved on to other things that were familiar to them. During the first hour they had covered the black leather pants with the zippers, where Kate kept the KTL cards, the gun she used, the car she drove, Kate's long dark hair and her black leather boots.

"Who here was physically touched by Kate?" Dorothy asked a while later. "We know she wore soft black gloves."

"She sort of touched me," Jane said, pushing at a stray red curl that had fallen across her forehead.

All eyes were suddenly on her and there was a collective intake of air as each of them gasped at the thought of Kate's touch. Bridget became alert and uncharacteristically envious of the redhead in the power suit. Just thinking about Kate touching her now made Bridget giddy all over.

"Tell us about it," Dorothy prompted.

"Yes, indeed," Gwen said. "Tell us about it."

Jane took a deep breath before beginning. "My blouse had been ripped open and my raincoat was on the pavement by my car. Kate picked up the raincoat and put it around my shoulders."

What a gallant gesture, Bridget thought as she shifted in her chair. She felt a chill at the visual Jane had described.

"With me," Lupita said quietly, "she brushed my forehead with her gloved hand. My hair was damp from the exertion of fighting with him. I remember being so tired and just so grateful to have her there."

"She's a very compassionate woman," Gwen said. "Kate found my shoe for me and helped put it back on. I was sitting on the pavement by my car. The bastard had been kicking me when Kate showed up. I remember hearing the sirens, but she still took her time helping me with my shoe. She wasn't in a hurry even though the police and EMS were on the way."

"What was it like being touched by her?" Bridget asked suddenly. *Ohmigod! Did I actually say that out loud?!*

"It was like being touched by an angel," Lupita said simply. "That's what she is to me. She's an angel."

"What does that mean?" Gwen asked her. "Like maybe she's not real?"

Lupita shrugged. Her dark eyes had a burning, faraway look in them. "Kate knew an ambulance was coming for me before I heard the siren. She also said the police were on their way, which was also true. She knew these things before she even arrived."

"She said that about the police with me, too," Jane muttered.

"Same here," Gwen said.

Bridget nodded.

"I was alone in the middle of a huge parking lot," Gwen said. "I was late for work and it was after a shift change, so there were a lot of cars there, but no people. If that bastard had killed me, they wouldn't have found my body until morning. There's no way anyone could have seen what was happening and then called the police to get them there on time. And the security patrols . . . well . . . let's just say they are nowhere to be found when you need one, no matter what time of day or night it is."

"So what are all of you saying?" Dorothy asked. For the first time that evening, she seemed to be really listening instead of constantly writing and checking her notes.

Gwen shook her head. "I don't know what any of this means. All I know is that KTL has to be the one calling the authorities and arranging for the paramedics to be dispatched. That's being done before she gets there."

"That doesn't make any sense!" Dorothy said in frustration. "How does she *know*?!"

In the silence that followed, Bridget couldn't count the number of times she had asked herself that same question over the last few weeks. Then as if the answer were right there in front of them, Lupita Ochoa said quite simply, "She's an angel."

Chapter Five

With some confusion and skepticism, Bridget observed the silence that followed. She wasn't sure whether or not Lupita was serious about Kate being an angel, but the comment had certainly stopped the chatter.

Finally, Gwen got up to get another cup of coffee and muttered under her breath, "An angel, eh?"

With a lame attempt at humor, Jane's only comment was, "There weren't any wings on the Kate I saw."

"But I can see why the police would consider how Kate and these men were in cahoots with each other," Gwen added as she came back to the table with a full cup of coffee and more cookies. "A few women get knocked around a bit, Kate shows up to save us, stuffs the bad guy in the trunk of a car and no one sees them again until the next time it happens."

"Them?" Bridget said. "Them who? Kate and the assailant?"

"Yeah, them," Gwen said. "Kate and the guy. The same two people over and over again maybe."

"What's the purpose of that?" Bridget asked. She found herself getting irritated at where this discussion was leading. "There have been no robberies. No purse snatchings. Nothing material was taken from us. These men were rapists or possibly even murderers, all of them up to no good where women are concerned."

"Maybe," Gwen said. "These two might also be a married couple who get their rocks off doing—"

"I knew my attacker," Lupita said with an edge to her voice. "He hasn't been seen since that night, and he didn't know Kate."

All eyes were on her now, and Bridget saw that faraway look return to Lupita's face.

"Oh, really?" Jane said. "Who was your attacker?"

"My husband. We had recently separated."

"I see."

"Not to mention the fact that all the attackers have different descriptions," Dorothy noted. "There's no way some of these guys are the same people. I agree with Bridget. What's the point of staging something like that?"

"Hey, Kate *shot* the guy who attacked me," Jane said. "Nothing was staged. He was playing for keeps and he bled real blood."

"I'm just throwing this stuff out there," Gwen said. "I didn't mean to imply that I believe any of it. But the fact that the police and EMS show up right after KTL does her 'put your hands up' routine has to be one of the strangest things I've ever heard of or witnessed. If Kate isn't the person making the calls to the authorities, then how did the police and EMS know where to be?"

"Even if she's the one calling 911," Jane said, "how does she know what's happening before she gets there if she's not in on it?" She pursed her lips and nodded thoughtfully. "Yes, I can see where the police would get the idea that she's a part of all this."

"Sorry, but I still don't see where any of that would lead for them," Bridget said. "It doesn't make any sense."

"Suppose KTL is a self-defense instructor and business is bad," Gwen suggested.

As Bridget began to protest, Gwen held up a hand to stop her.

"I'm playing devil's advocate here," Gwen said. "Only for the sake of argument. If we're going to find this woman, I want us covering all bases and being aware of everything. I've already had enough surprises to last me a lifetime."

With a reluctant nod, Bridget let her continue.

"Or let's suppose she's a weapons instructor and business isn't very good now," Gwen offered. "She goes out and fakes a few attacks, scares some women into wanting to learn how to defend themselves."

"Or she could be a black leather pants designer out showing off her new outfits," Bridget added. Her sarcasm brought chuckles around the table. Even Lupita managed to smile for the first time.

"Yes, indeed," Gwen agreed with a grin. "Or a black leather pants designer! She could be a lot of things, but this theory only works if KTL is in with the men on the whole thing."

"Lupita said her husband didn't know Kate," Dorothy reminded them again. "How do you explain what happened to him?"

Her question was addressed to Gwen, but everyone slowly turned their attention to Lupita.

"How can you be so sure that your husband didn't know Kate?" Jane asked her.

"I just am," Lupita said as that distant look returned to her eyes. "He was afraid. Kate shot at him to get his attention. He screamed and let go of me then. Rudy is not a screamer. He was surprised and afraid. Neither of us had seen her before."

"But how can you be *sure* he didn't know her?" Gwen asked.

"The way he talked to her," Lupita said. She shrugged. "I would have been able to tell. Like I said, Rudy was afraid. When she made him get in the trunk of the car, I could see his legs and hands shaking."

"I think Lupita would know her husband's reaction to such things," Bridget said. She wanted so much to believe what Dorothy and Lupita said that she couldn't even contemplate the various scenarios Gwen suggested.

"And we still have the missing banker and a judge," Dorothy

said. "There's no reason to believe those two knew Kate before either."

"OK, OK," Gwen said. "So maybe the police are grasping at straws with that theory, but I'm still not ready to give her wings and a halo yet."

"No, neither am I," Jane said. She sipped her coffee and went back to studying the map.

"Let's move on," Dorothy said. "Does anyone remember anything else about Kate that you haven't already told the police? We have her being about five-ten, a hundred and thirty pounds, and long black hair. Did anyone notice any type of accent? Southern? Northern? Foreign? Midwestern? Valley girl?"

Bridget shook her head. "No. I don't remember anything unusual about her voice or an accent. She could be from anywhere."

"I was too freaked out to remember much either," Gwen said, "but her car stuck in my mind."

"Does anyone have a highlighter?" Jane asked, holding up the map in front of her.

"There's one in my office," Dorothy said.

"I see something interesting here," Jane mused. "A highlighter might help illustrate this better."

Dorothy left the room while the others pulled out their copies of the map again. When Dorothy returned, she stood by Jane's chair and watched her mark a few places on the map. After a moment, Dorothy said, "Hmm. That has to be a coincidence."

"You think so?" Jane said. "What if it isn't?"

"What is it?" Gwen and Lupita asked at the same time.

Jane held up her copy of the map with the numbers for each known attack now highlighted in bright orange and connected with a line from number to number. From where Bridget was sitting, she could plainly see the big orange letter *K* on the paper.

"Well . . . hell! Will you look at that!" Gwen said.

"It has to be a coincidence," Dorothy repeated.

"Well, that's one interesting coincidence, if you ask me!" Gwen exclaimed.

Bridget reached across the table for the highlighter and made the same annotations on her own map. It did seem like an interesting coincidence, but not one she was willing to devote too much time to just yet.

"So what do you think this means?" Lupita asked, reaching for the highlighter after Gwen was finished with it.

"I don't know," Dorothy admitted.

"If the police see this, it'll just add more credence to their conspiracy theory," Gwen said.

Jane folded her map and tucked it under her coffee cup. "I guess in our terror that night we all failed to see the huge *K* on her chest."

Gwen picked up a cookie and dusted off the crumbs. "Well, thanks, Dorothy. I came here hoping to learn something new about our Kate and now I'm starting to see where the cops could be right about her."

"It's just a coincidence!" Dorothy said in exasperation. "You also need to remember that there could possibly be several more Kate-sightings that haven't been reported yet. Those could be other places all over the map . . . places that wouldn't make the letter *K* at all."

"Or," Jane said, "the other KTL sightings might reinforce the *K* on the map."

"It's a coincidence," Dorothy said again as if dismissing the whole thing.

"I think so, too," Bridget added. "There's no way this is a publicity stunt or a way to boost someone's business."

Jane reached for her map again, unfolded it, and held it up for everyone to see.

"I hope you're both right," Gwen said.

Pointing to the map again, Jane said, "Nah. We're being had, I think."

31

"So now what?" Gwen asked. "Am I the only one more confused now than when I arrived here this evening?"

Jane shook her head. "I don't know what to think. I want her to be for real and out there kicking some ass."

"It's not a hoax," Bridget insisted. "I'll never believe that."

"What about you, Lupita?" Jane asked. She held up the map again with the orange *K* on it. "Still think Kate's an angel?"

"She saved my life," Lupita said quietly, "and she probably saved yours too. Rudy had threatened to kill me if I left him. He was there ready to do it that night. In my case, there was no hoax and no ulterior motive on Kate's part. She was there to keep him from beating me again and choking me to death." She slid the highlighter across the table toward Dorothy. "She's an angel in my eyes. Draw all the fancy letters you want. Nothing will change my mind about that."

"I don't need a support group," Lupita said. "I want to find her."

"The rest of us also want to find her."

Traffic was light as Bridget drove toward the side of town where she went to high school. Her parents still lived there even though gangs had taken over the neighborhoods in the area. There had been some minor improvements when San Antonio's young mayor and his wife moved into the neighborhood, but Bridget's father often stated that he thought the mayor was probably a gang member, too.

"Do you know Dorothy well?" Lupita asked.

"No, not well. I've seen her around at various gay and lesbian events over the years, though. Her being the director of the Women's Resource Center puts her out there in the middle of a lot of things."

"Do you trust her?"

"Trust her? Do I trust her with what?"

"The information we're providing."

"I have no reason not to trust her, but then I suppose I don't really know her either. Why?" Bridget asked, taking her eyes off the road and glancing at Lupita. "What are you thinking?"

"Dorothy has no connection with our Kate. Why do we need someone to take notes and moderate our discussions about her?"

Bridget shrugged. "Maybe she's involved because Kate is claiming to be a lesbian."

"Claiming to be?"

Bridget took a moment to think about what she had just said. Other than the cards Kate had given each of them, they had no reason to suspect that Kate *was* a lesbian.

"It never occurred to me that she wasn't," Lupita said.

"Me neither. I don't know why I said that."

"If she's not a lesbian, then her name probably isn't Kate either."

Bridget felt disappointment at that suggestion. *She might be right*, she thought. *I want so much for Kate to be what I need for her to be. Get a grip, Bridget. You need some objectivity here.*

"Do you think we'll ever find her?" Lupita asked.

"I don't know."

"If we don't, there are other ways we can thank her."

"Oh, yeah? How?"

"Run an ad in the paper. Or if nothing else, we can help other women who have experienced similar things. I know I feel lucky to be alive. Kate gave me a second chance and I intend to make the most of it."

Bridget admired Lupita's commitment to helping others, but she personally had no time for that. Her main goal as far as Kate was concerned was to someday meet her face to face again and thank her for saving her life. As things stood now, she wasn't willing to give Dorothy's group much more of her time if they didn't do more than sit around and talk about the clothes Kate wore and the things she had said. In addition, Bridget didn't like feeling so uneasy about knowing that other women had experienced more intimate contact with Kate. *She didn't touch me*, Bridget thought. *Face it, Bridget old girl. You're getting obsessed with her.*

"What did you think of the other two in the group?" Lupita asked. She kept her head turned to the right and looked out the window and into the darkness.

"Gwen seems to be somewhat analytical. That could stem from her medical background. I didn't agree with a lot of what she said, but it was interesting hearing another point of view."

"I agree. I liked her. What about the other one? The redhead. I think Jane was her name."

"Nice enough, I suppose," Bridget said. "I wasn't impressed with her orange *K* discovery on the map, though. I wouldn't be surprised if she dropped out of the group. I'm not sure she's in it for the same reasons some of us are."

As she drove toward Crossroads Mall, the silence felt comfortable to her. Bridget liked not being alone after the meeting. She glanced over at Lupita who held her purse in her lap and continued looking out the window.

Finally, Bridget asked, "Did you and your husband have any children?"

Lupita turned and Bridget could see her profile in the dim light from the dashboard. She was a beautiful woman with her dark hair now pulled back away from her face.

"No," Lupita said quietly. "No children."

"Do you miss him?"

With a slight shrug, she said, "I miss the person he used to be . . . the person I thought I married. But I've missed that person for a long time now." She turned and looked out the window again. A short while later, she said, "Make a left at the next light."

Bridget followed her directions that eventually led them to an apartment complex on Hillcrest in Balcones Heights. Bridget was familiar with the area, having gone to grammar school not far from there.

"Thanks again for the ride," Lupita said as she opened the door.

"No problem. I'll see you next Wednesday."

Friday evening when Bridget got home from work, she had a message on her answering machine. It was from Gwen Bordovsky asking Bridget if she could meet the rest of the group at a coffee shop the next morning for breakfast. Bridget was curious enough to call her back to see if maybe someone in the group had found out something new about Kate. She dialed the first of two numbers Gwen had left and caught her at work.

"That Jane person has something she wants to talk to us about," Gwen said. "I told her I'd try and get in touch with you to see if you were interested in meeting again before Wednesday."

Bridget sat down on her sofa. "Yeah, sure. What time in the morning?"

She got the specifics of the breakfast meeting and promised to be there.

The next morning as she pulled into the parking lot of Jim's Coffee Shop on San Pedro Avenue, she saw Lupita get off the bus on the corner.

"Good morning," Bridget said once Lupita had caught up with her. "It's good to see you again."

"Good morning. Any idea what this is about?"

Bridget opened the door to the restaurant and let Lupita go in first. She was glad not to have arrived alone.

"Jane supposedly has something to discuss with us."

"Will Dorothy be here?" Lupita asked.

They were both looking around the crowded restaurant to see if Gwen and Jane were there yet.

"I don't know if Jane called Dorothy or not," Bridget said. "We seem to be the first ones here. Let's get a table and wait."

Lupita found a table where they could easily see customers arriving or leaving. Bridget took off her windbreaker and hung it on the back of her chair. Before she sat down, she saw Gwen and Jane arrive and waved them over to the table.

"Is Dorothy coming?" Bridget asked as soon as Jane reached them. She glanced at Lupita and saw her smile. With her hair loosely pulled back and held in place with a scrunchie, Lupita looked younger than Bridget remembered. She wore a cream-colored pullover sweater that brought out the light cinnamon color of her skin.

"No," Jane said. "I didn't call Dorothy. I'm not sure I trust her very much."

"My thoughts exactly," Gwen said as she took off her jacket and sat down. "I need some emergency coffee before I do anything else."

"Lupita just said the same thing about Dorothy," Bridget said, amazed. "Why don't any of you like her?"

Jane sat down across from Bridget and pushed up the sleeves of her Texas Tech sweatshirt. "I think she's in this to further her own agenda."

"What agenda might that be?" Bridget asked.

"Getting publicity for the Resource Center."

Bridget wasn't going to argue with any of them. She didn't

know Dorothy well enough to express an opinion either way and certainly not well enough to defend her.

A waitress came over and took their beverage orders.

"So what's up?" Bridget asked. She reached for one of the menus on the table. "Has something happened that we should all know about?"

"Any of you ever heard of a group called the Lesbian Avengers?" Jane asked. Dressed in blue jeans and a sweatshirt, she was less formidable and more down-to-earth than she had been on Wednesday night in her corporate drag. Jane spoke with confidence and obviously felt comfortable in front of a group. Bridget wondered if perhaps she might also be a teacher.

"No," Gwen said. "Can't say as I have."

"Didn't there used to be a TV series by that name?" Lupita asked.

"*The Avengers*," Jane said with a light laugh. "Not the Lesbian Avengers."

"Emma Peel in black leather," Bridget said whimsically. "Every baby dyke's dream in the sixties, I imagine. I've seen the reruns on TV, of course."

The other three stopped what they were doing and looked at her.

"Black leather?" Lupita said.

Bridget set the menu down before she dropped it. "Yeah. Black leather."

In her mind she could see a young Diana Rigg dressed in black leather with her dark hair and fluid, graceful movements. She was all woman, but had a butch flair in the way she dressed. Bridget imagined she personally had gotten her preference for seeing feminine women in flannel or neckties from this bit of British television culture. *The Avengers* had been an English spoof on espionage in the sixties, but still had a cult following. *Could Kate also have been emulating the Emma Peel character?* Bridget wondered.

"So who are these Lesbian Avengers?" Gwen asked.

39

"Before we go there," Jane said, "how many of us here are lesbians?"

The waitress arrived with their coffee and took their orders. Once she left, Jane said, "I'm a lesbian, and I've been out for about ten years."

"I'm a lesbian, and I'm out to my family, but not at work," Bridget said. She hated these types of discussions and didn't like how she always felt compelled to defend her decision to stay in the closet where her job was concerned. She'd heard too many horror stories about teachers not getting promotions because of the type of lifestyle they led, so she never talked about her private life with coworkers. Even at the age of thirty-five, she still had self-esteem issues to deal with.

"I'm a lesbian," Gwen said, "and I don't care who knows it."

Lupita went to say something and Jane waved her off. "You've got a husband. We know about you already. Do any of you find it weird that out of the ten known KTL sightings, at least three of the victims are lesbians? If we go by national statistics, only one in ten people are gay."

"I think that only applies to men," Gwen said. "The stats for women are higher. I've heard one in forty for lesbians."

"Even *better!*" Jane said. "This is just too big of a coincidence."

"Which coincidence?" Gwen asked, confused. "That three out of the ten women who were attacked are lesbians?"

"Here we go with the coincidence thing again," Lupita said.

"So what's your point?" Bridget asked Jane.

"My point is, maybe the other six women who were attacked might also be lesbians."

"So what?" Bridget countered. "What if they are? What does that prove?"

"We don't even know for sure if our Kate is really a lesbian," Lupita said.

The other three looked at her for a moment before Jane said, "What?"

Lupita shrugged, but met Jane's piercing eyes. "Just because someone has cards printed off claiming to be something, that doesn't make it so."

"Of course she's a lesbian," Jane said. "Who would lie about something like that?"

"In the meantime," Gwen said as she stirred creamer into her coffee, "I still don't know what a Lesbian Avenger is."

Bridget watched as Jane wagged her index finger at Lupita. With a wry smile, she said, "You're poking all sorts of holes in my theory already."

"I'm just asking the questions."

"I know," Jane said. "I like that. Keep it up."

"In the *meantime*," Gwen said again, "we still don't know what a Lesbian Avenger is."

"Aren't they one of those radical political action groups?" Bridget asked. "I read somewhere that Austin had a group of them there at one time."

"Yes, Austin has a group and they want to help us," Jane announced.

Gwen set her spoon down. "Help us do what?"

"Help us find Kate."

Bridget looked at this woman and realized that she was also probably much younger than she appeared to be. Even though Jane was more casual and open than she had been at their last meeting, her intense green eyes were suddenly filled with unbridled passion.

"How can a group of strangers help us?" Bridget asked. "Strangers in Austin even?"

"We're a group of strangers," Gwen pointed out.

"And so far all we've done is drink coffee and talk," Bridget reminded them.

"What is it these Lesbian Avengers do?" Lupita asked.

"Lesbian ninjas who Xerox flyers," Bridget said dryly.

Jane's laughter made everyone else laugh, too.

41

"Yeah," Gwen agreed with an eye roll. "That'll be a big help."

"But isn't that almost what Kate was like?" Lupita asked. "A ninja?"

"A ninja with a gun?" Jane said. "Maybe the way she dressed a little. I don't really know anything about ninjas other than those cute little teenage turtle things named after classical musicians or something."

"They're named after Renaissance artists," Gwen corrected. "Not musicians."

"Sorry," Jane apologized. "I'm not up on my Saturday morning cartoons or my turtle trivia."

"So is this why we're here?" Bridget asked. "To talk about—"

"Actually," Jane said, "I missed all of you. I couldn't wait until Wednesday to see everyone again."

Chapter Seven

"Well, I'm not sure bringing in more strangers is a good idea," Bridget said. She was getting to the point where discussing Kate with a group was no longer appealing to her. She would find Kate on her own if she had to. All of this yakking was getting them nowhere and just seemed like a waste of time.

"I agree with Bridget," Lupita said. "I think we have too many people involved already."

"Oh?" Jane said with an arched brow. "Who here would you like to see gone, young lady?"

Lupita's smile caught Bridget's attention. *Damn*, she thought. *I think Jane's flirting with her! Ha! And you don't like it! What's up with that? You barely know these people.*

"No one here," Lupita said defensively, "but I think Dorothy does have other ideas about what we should be doing."

"Oh, Dorothy. OK," Jane said. "Yeah, I agree with that. I say we dump her and start meeting on our own."

"What did Dorothy ever do to us?" Gwen asked.

"She's like a bloodhound after a scent when it comes to publicity for the Women's Resource Center," Jane said. "I've seen her on TV numerous times pimping for a cause just to get her name out there and to draw more attention to the Center. I don't want our work with Kate involved with any of that."

"I think that should also include keeping this out of the hands of those ninja avengers," Gwen suggested.

"Lesbian Avengers," Jane corrected. "Kate's the ninja, remember? Not the Avengers."

"Whatever," Gwen said with a wave of her hand. "There's still too many people involved. Too many Caesars ruin the salad, as they say."

The waitress arrived with their breakfast orders and the focus momentarily shifted to food. A while later, Lupita asked, "Then are we still meeting at the Resource Center on Wednesday?"

"We can meet at my house instead," Gwen said. "My kids should be settled in with homework by then."

"Thanks, Gwen," Jane said. "I like that idea. The less we have to do with the Resource Center, the better off we'll be."

"Let's say around sevenish?"

"I'll call Dorothy and let her know we won't be meeting there," Jane offered.

"Who gets to hold the clipboard while we're at Gwen's house?" Bridget asked with a smile.

They all shared a chuckle, then Gwen said, "It's my house, so it's my clipboard."

All four of them exchanged phone numbers, addresses and e-mail information. They hung around discussing Kate and their experiences with her until it was time for Gwen to go to work.

"Wednesday at seven at my place," Gwen said as she left a tip and took her check. "And don't forget to call Dorothy."

"I'll do it today," Jane promised.

"I need to get going, too," Bridget said. She had plans to take her parents to Sam's Club that day, even though she hadn't discussed a specific time to be at their house. She stood up and put her windbreaker on. "Can I drop you off somewhere?" she asked Lupita. "I'm going on your side of town anyway."

"No, thanks," Lupita said, sipping her third cup of coffee.

"It's not a problem."

"I'm fine. Thanks anyway."

Bridget had expected them all to leave together, but Jane and Lupita weren't making any moves to leave yet. Bridget left a tip on the table and picked up her check.

"Then I'll see you two at Gwen's on Wednesday."

"I'll be there," Jane said.

"Me, too."

As Bridget went up front to pay her check, she could see Lupita and Jane talking. She had no idea why that irritated her so much.

"Where do people store all of this stuff once they buy it?" her father had asked while hefting a thirty-pack toilet paper bundle onto the Sam's Club cart.

"Some people just leave it in their cars and take it out when they need it," Bridget said.

"Hmm. Can you imagine needing a roll of toilet paper and having to shuffle off to the car to get it?" her mother mused. "No, thanks! I'll find a place for it close to the bathroom."

Bridget recalled that conversation as she parked in her driveway. She toted in two four-packs of spray starch, a six-pack of Beef-A-Roni and a package of three hundred paper plates on her second trip in from the car. She had already spent the best part of an hour helping her father unload the backseat and trunk of his Lincoln Town Car with a variety of purchases.

After bringing in the last load from the trunk, she plopped down on the sofa to listen to her phone messages. The first one was her mother's voice stating that they had way too many rolls of paper towels and that Bridget was to take more home with her the next time she came over.

The second message was from Jane Whitley. "Dorothy didn't take the news about our alternative meeting site well," she said. "And we were right about her ulterior motives. Call me if you want the details."

Bridget reached in her shirt pocket and pulled out the Sam's Club receipt, a gum wrapper and the napkin with the KTL group's information on it. She dialed Jane's number.

"Hello?"

"This is Bridget. I got your message. What's up?"

"We were right about Dorothy," Jane said. "Apparently there's a reporter friend of hers sniffing around. Ever heard of Smokey Wells?"

"No. Is he local?"

"Dorothy wouldn't say, but I went online and found a Smokey Wells who writes for a Houston paper."

"Wow. When was Dorothy going to tell us this?"

"Wednesday night when he showed up at our meeting, I guess."

"That's messed up."

"Yeah, I agree. She should've discussed it with us first."

"Any idea what this reporter is interested in?"

"Not yet," Jane said. "I say we let him get in touch with us if he wants to know anything. See you at Gwen's on Wednesday."

Bridget saw three cars in the driveway at Gwen's house Wednesday evening. She was on time, but still the last one to arrive.

"Come in. Come in," Gwen said. She was dressed comfortably in green scrubs and white socks. Her hair was pulled back loosely, and she had a blue ink smudge at the corner of her mouth. "Excuse the mess. It didn't look this way when I left for work this morning. My kids are pigs."

Bridget laughed. "Sounds like your kids are just kids."

"There's one of my piglets now," Gwen said.

"I smell food," the teenage girl said. She was a taller, thinner version of her mother, with bright yellow highlights in her otherwise gothic black hair.

"Your pizza should be here any minute," Gwen said. She put her hands on her hips and looked at the other three women. "I'm not used to such punctuality! I said seven-ish and you're all here at seven!"

"Hey, I brought enough food for everyone," Jane said. "If you like Chinese, that is."

"I'm a vegetarian," the teenager said.

Bridget chuckled at Gwen's eye roll. She saw Lupita and Jane across the room and waved to them.

"Your *cheese* pizza is on the way," Gwen said.

"There's plenty of rice and Chinese vegetables," Jane announced.

"I smell food," a young male voice said.

Bridget looked behind her to find a tall teenage boy with punky spiked hair and baggy pants where the seat hit him at the back of the knees.

"There's my other piglet now," Gwen said. "And *your* pizza is on the way, too."

"So if we ever have another meeting here," Bridget surmised, "we need to be fashionably late instead of on time."

Gwen laughed. "Nah. Not at all. I'll just have my feces more coagulated next time."

The doorbell rang and Gwen's son went to answer it.

"That should be the pizza guy," Gwen said as she reached in her pocket for some money.

"Nope," her son said after opening the door. "It's a pizza girl, but I don't see any pizzas."

"Hi," the woman said. "Is your mother here?" She was dressed in chinos, a white polo shirt and white sneakers. Carrying a briefcase, she appeared to be in her early thirties with short blond hair and enough confidence to stop a run-away train.

47

"No pizza?" the young man asked.

"Not today," the woman said with a smile.

"I'm Gwen. Can I help you?"

"I hope so," the woman said. "I'm Smokey Wells from the *Houston Chronicle*. I understand there's a meeting here tonight."

Chapter Eight

The chaos that followed that particular statement was almost a blur to Bridget. The pizza delivery guy from Papa John's arrived during the heated exchange between Jane and Smokey Wells. Jane had the presence of mind to take the discussion into the kitchen while Gwen got her kids settled with dinner and homework in their rooms. Bridget didn't want to miss anything, so she helped Lupita get the Chinese food cartons out of the bags and ready to eat.

"Did Dorothy Holt give you this address?" Jane barked.

"No," Smokey said calmly. "I have all of your names and addresses from the police reports."

"Then she must've told you we were having a meeting."

"Not really," Smokey admitted. "It's actually just a stroke of luck that I've found so many of you here together. I was going alphabetically and 'Gwen Bordovsky' was the first name on the list."

"Are reporters always this lucky?" Jane asked.

"Why are you so upset? I'm here to help you." Smokey's calm demeanor was such a huge contrast to Jane's energy-packed vocals. Bridget was glad to have Jane on their side.

"Here to help us? Sure you are."

"Will you at least hear me out?" Smokey asked.

"OK," Gwen said as she hurried into the kitchen and skidded to a stop. "What did I miss?"

"Nothing more than a bit of posturing," Bridget said. "Got any paper plates?" She thought about the mountainous stack in her pantry at home.

"With teenagers in the house?" Gwen said. "Hell, yes!" She went to a cabinet and came back with several paper plates. "So Dorothy spilled the beans about our meeting tonight?"

"Ms. Reporter here claims it's just a stroke of good luck," Lupita said. She opened kitchen drawers until she found the silverware.

"You just showing up here pisses me off!" Jane said.

"If I had called to announce my arrival," Smokey said calmly, "would you have been in a better mood?"

"This is a private meeting," Jane continued. "We don't want or need a reporter."

"I suggest you think about it some more," Smokey said. "There's another reporter from Dallas also interested in this story. He won't be as nice to deal with as I'll be."

"Well, crap," Gwen said. "Reporters are the last thing we need."

"I told you Dorothy was up to no good," Jane said.

"Don't blame any of this on Dorothy," Smokey said.

"Well, let's eat and cool off," Gwen suggested. "I'm starving. Jesus, Jane. You got enough food here?"

They ate while Smokey Wells talked. She explained her intent to write a story on the missing judge from Houston. Bridget was reluctantly impressed with her. As she spoke, Smokey was articulate and sympathetic to their cause.

"Alan Harper from the *Dallas Morning News* has also been assigned to this story," Smokey said. "He's the one that got the Dallas police chief fired for taking kickbacks and the reporter responsible for the mayor's office explaining personal expenditures a week before the election. Harper is also credited with the old mayor losing the election. He's ruthless and he's interested in this story."

"And you're not ruthless when it comes to a story?" Jane asked. She set a carton of egg rolls over in front of Smokey. "Eat something. There's enough here to feed an army."

Smokey smiled and took the paper plate Gwen handed to her. "Are you hoping I'll choke on something and die?"

"With our luck," Jane said simply, "Gwen would feel obligated to save you."

"So what you're saying is," Bridget surmised over the laughter, "this story will get investigated and told by someone, so it might as well be you, correct?"

"Yes. That's what I'm saying," Smokey confirmed with a nod.

"Why should we trust you?" Lupita asked.

"I'm also a lesbian," Smokey said, "so it's only natural that I would want to know what's going on with someone calling herself Kate the Lesbian. It's a fascinating story, and I think it deserves to be told from a lesbian's point of view."

"You're a lesbian?" Jane, Gwen and Bridget said at the same time. Everyone laughed and relaxed at that bit of information. Bridget studied Smokey Wells for a moment and decided that she liked her honesty and tenacity. *It took some spunk to show up here like this*, she thought.

"So am I in?" Smokey asked. "Can I count on your cooperation?"

"I think it's a good possibility," Gwen said. "Jane finally stopped yelling at you. That's gotta be a plus."

51

Over Chinese food and a pot of coffee, they talked until every grain of rice and every last fortune cookie was gone. Bridget was surprised at how much information Smokey already knew about each of them, as well as the small details of all ten KTL sightings.

"My boss is particularly interested in what happened to Judge Logan Harold," Smokey said. "He was identified in a small article in the San Antonio paper as attacker number ten. In Houston, he was a popular judge and a family man. They're saying there's no way he could've been involved in attacking a woman."

"Yeah," Bridget said cynically. "Just like doctors and lawyers couldn't possibly sexually abuse their own children."

"I agree with you," Smokey said. "What the public sees and what happens behind closed doors are never the same thing. Anything is possible."

Bridget wondered how this woman got the name Smokey. *Could it be her eyes?* They were a smoky-gray color and seemed to reflect a kindness that Bridget was drawn to.

"How can we ever really know anyone who's in the public eye?" Gwen agreed. "Who the real person is can be a well-kept secret and a whole different story."

"Speaking of stories," Jane said, appearing to be much more calm now, "how do you think you can help us find Kate?"

Smokey smiled. "Is that what all of you want to do? Find her?"

Jane shrugged. "Find her and maybe protect her."

"Yeah," Gwen said. "Maybe even protect her from people like you."

That was something Bridget hadn't considered before and was glad that Gwen had brought it up. If needed, Bridget would do all she could to help protect Kate.

"I also want to find her," Smokey said, not taking any offense at Gwen's comment.

"I can't offer you any help or cooperation until I know for sure what your motives are," Jane said. "I'm speaking for myself. Not for the group."

"That's what I was thinking, too," Lupita said. "I need to hear what you want out of this."

"Yeah, me too," Gwen agreed.

"Same here," Bridget said. "This could very easily turn into a witch hunt."

"I understand that." Smokey looked at each of them and took a deep breath. "I guess you'll just have to trust me. That's what it boils down to."

"We don't even *know* you," Jane said with a laugh.

"Then let's change that," Smokey suggested. "We can share information and resources. I'm sure I have some info none of you has seen or heard yet. In exchange for that, maybe some of you could help me get in touch with a few of the other women who were attacked. So far the others are not willing to cooperate. Dorothy ran into that when she tried to contact them, too."

"What info do you have that we don't know about?" Gwen asked.

Smokey pursed her lips and said, "I've got the 911 tapes from all the attacks."

Bridget's eyes popped open, and she couldn't sit still after hearing that. Apparently neither could the others.

Chapter Nine

"No shit!" Jane said. "For real?" Her slippage into crude slang made the others laugh, but her comments were exactly what Bridget had been thinking.

"Yes," Smokey said. "I have them."

"With you?" Gwen asked incredulously.

Smokey patted her briefcase. "Right here."

"Well, let's hear 'em!" Gwen said.

"Wait, wait, wait a minute," Smokey said. "Do we have a deal? We all share information and you help me get interviews with the other women?"

"I'll make some calls if you get me the information on them," Gwen said.

"So will I," Lupita agreed.

"Good enough." Smokey opened her briefcase and took out five copies of the 911 transcripts. She gave each of them a copy of the transcript and kept one for herself. Bridget scanned the two-page document and couldn't stop her hands from shaking as her eyes fell on the 911 call labeled number seven. *That one's about me,* she thought as she scanned the text.

"As you can all see," Smokey said, "Kate kept her calls brief. She tells the 911 operator basically the same thing each time, only with a different location. EMS is requested along with a need for the police to be there."

Silence followed as everyone looked over the text of each known KTL 911 call. Finally, Lupita broke the silence and asked, "Do you have the actual recordings of her calls?"

"Yes," Smokey said. She reached into her briefcase and took out a small tape recorder and then pushed the "play" button.

"Nine one one."

"There's a woman being beaten in the parking lot of a Kwik Wash Laundromat near the intersection of Hillcrest and Babcock."

"Are you there now?"

"Send the police and an ambulance."

"Who's calling?"

Bridget heard the sound of Kate hanging up and the operator saying, "Hello? Hello?"

After that there was a moment of silence before she heard the 911 operator again on the tape. It was the second call.

"Nine one one."

"Listen carefully. I don't have much time. There's a woman being held at knifepoint in the SBC Building parking garage downtown."

"Where are you located?"

"Send the police and an ambulance."

Another click and a pause followed. Bridget held her breath as the tape continued and one by one she read the transcript of the calls. By the time the tape had reached the seventh 911 call, Bridget's hands trembled so badly she could hardly hold the paper.

"Nine one one."

"Listen carefully. I don't have much time. There's a woman

being held at knifepoint in a SAC parking lot near San Pedro and Ashby. Send—"

"Where are you located?"

"Send the police and an ambulance."

"Who's calling?"

There was another sound of a click and then the 911 operator saying, "Hello? Hello?"

They sat through all ten 911 calls before Smokey turned the tape recorder off. Everyone sighed heavily into the silence. The tension in the air was almost thick enough to see.

"Where did you get these?" Jane asked finally.

"I have some local connections," Smokey said.

"Police connections?"

"Yes."

The four women seemed to be in shock and still recovering from what they had just heard. After a while, Gwen asked, "Can you tell us what the police are thinking? What direction they want to go with this?"

"Their theories are in a mass of disarray at the moment," Smokey admitted. "Up until the banker and the judge disappeared, they were going on the notion it was a series of hoaxes. Now they're looking for Kate to charge her with kidnapping."

"Kidnapping," the four women repeated at the same time.

"That's gotta be a joke."

"No joke."

"It's just not fair," Gwen said. "She saved my life. They should be looking for her to pin a medal on that lovely black leather chest!"

"I agree," Lupita said.

"Me, too."

"You've been up-front with your information," Jane said. "I apologize for my earlier outburst. Now maybe we have something for *you*." She turned to Gwen and asked, "Do you still have your copy of the map we had the other night?"

Gwen smiled and excused herself from the table. Bridget was eager to see what Smokey's reaction to the orange *K* on the map would be.

As Jane explained what the map was and how the *K* came about, all Smokey could do was stare at it.

"Dorothy and I think it's a coincidence," Bridget finally said, in hopes that Smokey would agree.

Smokey set the map down and slowly scratched her head. "That's one hell of a coincidence."

"No shit," Gwen said simply, making the others laugh.

"Lupita thinks Kate's an angel," Jane said.

Bridget glanced at Lupita and saw her smiling at Jane. *If I didn't know better,* she thought, *I'd say those two were interested in each other.*

"That would sure explain a lot of things," Smokey said.

"So how are you going to approach this article?" Gwen asked. "What's your focus right now?"

Smokey shrugged. "My readers in Houston want info on Judge Harold. His family is offering a nice chunk of money for information leading to his safe return."

"So you want the money?" Lupita asked.

"I want the story on Kate," Smokey said. "By getting that, the story on the judge will practically write itself. I need to keep my boss happy." She opened her briefcase and took out two pieces of paper. Smokey gave one to Lupita and the other to Gwen. She also passed around business cards to each of them. "My cell phone number is on there. Please let me know if anything else comes up." To Gwen she said, "You two decide who gets in touch with the other six women. I'd like to interview them as soon as possible. Especially number ten—the one who claims Judge Harold was her attacker."

"Claims?" Bridget said as the hair on the back of her neck stood at attention.

"Just a figure of speech," Smokey said.

"Yeah?" Jane said. "Well, you're starting to piss me off again."

"Look, I'm on your side. You have to believe that."

"Ha!" Jane said. "Who are you kidding? We don't have to believe anything. You want a story. You're on the side of Smokey Wells. Period. You came here uninvited, and you'll be leaving with more than you came here with."

"More what?" Smokey asked as she packed up her briefcase. "An egg roll you wanted me to choke on?"

Gwen's chuckle helped lighten up the mood a little.

"No," Jane said. "The map! We told you about the *K* on the map."

"Oh, yes. That coincidental *K* on the map."

"You'll probably be phoning in that tip to your police friend before you're even out of Gwen's driveway," Jane said accusingly.

With an indignant huff, Smokey said, "I'm not sharing any of this information with the police!"

"We'll see," Jane said. "You're probably not a lesbian either."

"What does that have to do with anything?" Smokey asked, her surprise genuine.

Bridget and the others were enjoying the exchange between them. There was a spark of sexual energy in the air at the rapid-fire dialogue pinging around the kitchen.

"It helped you weasel your way in here," Jane noted.

"You think I lied about my sexual preference to get all of you to open up to me?"

"Sure! Why not?"

Smokey shrugged. "I don't have anything tangible to show you. They don't issue us cards when we kiss our first female, you know."

"Do you have a toaster oven?" Gwen asked.

The laughter that followed eased what little tension that remained. Smokey shook her head and smiled as she finished packing up her briefcase to leave. "This is gonna be a very interesting story. I can tell that already."

❧

"That was kind of fun," Jane said once Gwen came back to the kitchen from showing Smokey out. "She threw us a few crumbs and we threw some her way, too."

"What crumbs did she give us?" Gwen asked. "Those 911 tapes? That's all probably public record. Maybe even available through the Freedom of Information Act. We could've gotten that on our own."

"I agree," Bridget said. "She needs us more than we need her."

"So do we help her with these other women?" Lupita asked, holding up the list of names Smokey had given her. "Dorothy didn't get far with them. Why should we do any better?"

"I say we get in touch with them and see if they know anything new that can help *us*," Jane said. "Forget the reporter. She's in this for herself."

"You're so cynical," Gwen said with a teasing smile. "Why is that, Ms. Whitley?"

"Not really. I'm just realistic." Jane stood up to help clean off the table. "I think we all need to keep our cards closer to our chest now. It'll be interesting to see if anything about the map shows up in the media. I'm thinking that whatever we find out in the future, we keep to ourselves until the right time comes. I'd hate to see us do more harm to Kate than good."

"Then what's next?" Bridget asked. "What if these other women don't have anything else to add to what we already know?"

"Something will come up," Gwen said. "I don't think we've heard the last of Kate."

A few days later on Friday evening when Bridget got home from having dinner with her parents, she had a message from Jane on her answering machine. She called her back and was told that one of the other six women had agreed to meet with them.

"Lupita convinced her to talk to us," Jane said excitedly. "We're meeting at the same place we met for breakfast the other day. Can you be there in an hour?"

"Sure."

"Excellent! We'll see you then."

Bridget finished unloading the four rolls of paper towels and ten rolls of toilet paper her mother had insisted she take with her. *No telling what the neighbors think*, she mused while filling her arms with the paper products and trudging into her house with them.

On her way over to the coffee shop for the meeting, she wondered which number on the map this new woman would turn out to be. *I wonder what Lupita said to convince her to meet with us*, she thought. It wasn't until Bridget arrived at the coffee shop that she realized Lupita would probably have to take the bus to get there. Bridget vowed to try and remember to offer her a ride when these spontaneous meetings were announced in the future.

She met Gwen in the parking lot and they walked in together. Bridget couldn't get over how glad she was to be seeing these women again. Granted, she didn't know any of them well, but the circumstances that had brought them together was a bond that would be hard to break.

"I'm not sure what to tell Smokey Wells about this new woman," Gwen said.

As they walked in together, Bridget saw Jane pull up and park. Lupita got out of the car with her and once again Bridget felt a nagging irritation at seeing them together.

"How many of the others on the list were called?" Bridget asked.

"I called three and Lupita called three. One of my three is still recuperating from her injuries. The other two I spoke with are just too traumatized to even talk about it much less meet with us right now."

"I can understand that."

"Yeah, me too," Gwen said. "Will you look at that?" She nodded toward Jane and Lupita walking close together on the sidewalk.

"You noticed that, too, I see."

"She's got a husband."

"A missing husband," Bridget said as she opened the door to the coffee shop.

Once they were inside, Bridget saw a woman sitting in the lobby waiting area. She had a sling on her left arm. She stood up as soon as she noticed them.

"Excuse me. Are either of you Lupita Ochoa?"

Bridget smiled. The woman was obviously nervous, but this had to be who they were there to meet. She was about Bridget's height and wore sweat pants and a light blue sweater. Her short brown hair was curly and gleamed in the lights from the restaurant lobby. She was about their age, possibly a few years younger. Even though the woman's hair was short, Bridget wasn't quick to assume she was a lesbian. She saw a flicker of apprehension in the woman's eyes that made Bridget want to protect her. The woman appeared more delicate than anything else, and Bridget admired her courage for being there.

"Lupita's right behind us," Gwen said. "You must be Number Ten."

The door behind them opened up and a laughing Jane came in first with Lupita right behind her.

Hmm, Bridget thought. *I wonder what's going on with these two?*

"Number Ten?" Jane asked.

Nervously, the woman moistened her dry lips and nodded.

"We're all here," Jane said. "Let's find a table and get to know each other better."

Just then the restaurant door opened and Smokey Wells came in. "Look what I found," she said with a hint of irritation in her voice.

"Who called this one?" Gwen asked, pointing to Smokey.

A string of "not me's" followed as everyone in the group stared at Smokey. She smiled and said, "I thought we had a deal."

"We changed our minds," Jane informed her.

"I'm going home," a trembling Number Ten said.

Lupita touched the new woman's arm to stop her. "Please. Wait. I'm Lupita. The one who spoke with you."

Number Ten's shoulders drooped and she seemed to relax a bit.

"We'll figure out what's going on here and decide what to do," Lupita promised. She turned to Jane and said, "Won't we?"

"You're damn right we will." Jane got in front of Smokey and stood uncomfortably close to her. "How'd you know we'd be here? Which one of us are you following?"

"Georgina Philips. Number Ten," Smokey said. "The last person to have seen the judge."

"And you followed her here?"

"Yes, ma'am. And who do I find here? The Four Mouseketeers sneaking around behind my back! I thought we had a deal!"

"We changed our minds," Jane said again.

Gwen leaned over to Bridget and whispered, "Let's take this somewhere else. People are starting to stare."

Bridget looked over at Lupita and found her whispering to the new woman. Tugging on Gwen's arm, Bridget led the way to where Lupita and the woman were standing.

"Gwen thinks we should go somewhere else," Bridget said.

"I was just explaining who this Smokey woman is," Lupita said. "Georgina wants to get it all over with now."

"Meaning?" Gwen asked.

"Meaning she'll tell her story to all of us now—including the reporter—if we promise to leave her alone after that."

Gwen left Bridget's side and went over to where Jane and Smokey were still arguing. "Hold your horses, you two. Number Ten wants to talk to all of us."

"All of us?" Jane repeated incredulously. "This weenie, too?" she said, pointing to Smokey.

Gwen just shook her head. "She's probably thinking we're all a pack of weenies by now, so put a lid on it before you scare her off forever."

Chapter Ten

The hostess escorted them to a table in the back. Bridget found it endearing the way Lupita stayed close to the new woman, as if protecting her from the rest of them. Bridget could also tell that Jane was still agitated by Smokey's unwanted presence. Her eyes were like summer lightning, full of pent-up energy and anger at having their plans changed. They had underestimated Smokey Wells. After this meeting Bridget was going to suggest they regroup and attempt to be smarter in their actions when dealing with her.

After they all got seated around the large table, Gwen said, "Should we introduce ourselves?"

Uneasy under their scrutiny, the new woman mumbled, "It doesn't matter to me who any of you are. I'll answer your questions this time, but after today I want to be left alone. Is that understood?"

Murmurs went around the table. On one hand, Bridget felt embarrassed to be a part of this, understanding completely what the woman was going through. But on the other hand, if there was a possibility of discovering something new about Kate, then she was willing to put almost anyone through another brief interrogation in order to get new information. Bridget could also see how much she herself had improved since her own attack had taken place. This woman was still healing mentally as well as physically from her ordeal. Bridget was relieved to at least have part of that behind her, even though she wasn't sure anyone ever fully recovers from such an experience.

"Can I ask you some questions?" Smokey said. She took out her small tape recorder and turned it on and set it in the middle of the table.

"Is that necessary?" Jane barked.

"It'll help me keep the facts straight."

"Is it OK if she records the conversation?" Lupita asked the new woman, as if her answer would make a difference in what Smokey chose to do.

"It doesn't matter to me. I just want this over with."

The waitress came over and took their drink orders. Bridget was getting even more irritated at Smokey's intrusion on their meeting as she watched her unpack her briefcase and get set up to record the interview. After the waitress brought their drinks and was told no one would be ordering from the menu, Georgina Philips, Number Ten on their KTL map, began her story.

"I work for an escort service," she said in a quiet, resigned voice, as if holding her raw emotions in check. "I received a call from my boss one afternoon stating that a Mr. James needed a dinner companion. I was to meet him in the lobby of the River Center Marriott at seven."

She works for an escort service? Bridget thought. *Whoa!* With a quick glance around the table, she saw Jane's eyebrows shoot up as well.

"This Mr. James was actually Judge Logan Harold?" Smokey asked.

"I don't know who he was," Georgina said. "That's just what I was told. He didn't refer to himself nor introduce himself to me as a judge." Taking a deep breath, she continued. "I was there on time, and we went to dinner at Ruth's Chris Steak House downtown. It's only a few blocks away from the hotel, but he drove his car and he was a gentleman on the way over. During dinner and after several glasses of wine, he began to change. Mr. James tried to put his hand up my dress under the table and once reached over and squeezed my breast." She stopped, visibly shuddering at the thought, before composing herself again and continuing in a near monotone. "I excused myself to go to the ladies room where I called my boss to tell her what was happening. She advised me to leave immediately and said she would handle it. So I went up to the front of the restaurant and had them call a cab for me. In the meantime, Mr. James must've seen me leave the ladies room. Before I knew what was happening, he took me by the arm and literally forced me out of the restaurant. I was so shocked at how quickly things had happened. We were outside and around the back of the building before I knew it. He shoved me into his car and drove toward the east side of town. There's a cemetery on Commerce Street. Even though he had only consumed a few glasses of wine, he appeared to be intoxicated. He became belligerent and called me a whore. He said he had paid for me that night and he wouldn't be denied. I told him there had been a mistake. I was terrified. I reached into my purse to get my cell phone to call my boss again. I tried to explain to him that once he talked to her, she would be able to assure him that I wasn't a prostitute, and that I actually work for a legitimate escort service."

Georgina stopped to compose herself again. Bridget could see the mental and physical exhaustion in her eyes.

"My boss is very careful about that," she said in a low voice, forcing Bridget to lean slightly closer toward her in hopes of hearing her better.

"But when Mr. James saw I had my phone out, he grabbed for it and tossed it out the window as he drove down the street. He pulled into the cemetery and stopped the car. It was dark and I was freaked out enough by what was happening without having to be in a cemetery at night. I tried to get out of the car and run, but he caught me before I got very far. I don't know what set him off, but the harder I fought him, the meaner he got. He was on top of me tearing at my dress when I heard the other car pull up."

Georgina's monotone gave more credence to the violence she described. In a subdued, fragile voice, she continued.

"It was dark and I was absolutely terrified. Someone had a gun to his head and ordered him to get off of me. Suddenly he was the one who was afraid. His pants were down . . . and he had trouble standing up. I could tell that the person with the gun was a woman. She was dressed in black, and she made him move away from me. She opened the trunk of her car and told him to get in. He kept saying it was just a misunderstanding." She looked at each of them then and shook her head. "Now *he* was the part of a misunderstanding . . . when . . . a few minutes earlier my circumstances were anything *but* a misunderstanding."

It was the first time Bridget heard any anger come from her.

"The next thing I knew, he was in the trunk of her car, and she slammed it shut. Mr. James began banging and yelling for her to open it, but she didn't seem to give him another thought. She came over to where I was lying on the ground, and she helped me sit up. My shoulder hurt and my lip was bleeding. She told me the police and EMS were on the way and that I shouldn't be afraid any longer. She gave me a card and then got into her car and left."

Everyone at the table except for Smokey was just as exhausted as Georgina was by the time she finished her story. It was obvious that hearing her relive her ordeal made each of them immediately identify with what she had been through and recall their own nightmares of being attacked. It wasn't until Smokey said something that Bridget realized how important it was that all of them stick together now. There was too much at stake here, there were too many people out for themselves. Those who had been personally touched by Kate were now a part of a special group, almost like a sisterhood. *Yes*, Bridget thought. *That's exactly what it is—a sisterhood.* Their mission had suddenly changed, and Bridget would make sure they all understood that at some point.

"Can we ask questions now?" Smokey said, interrupting Bridget's thoughts.

"Give us a minute here, you heartless twit," Jane snapped. Everyone at the table jumped at the viciousness in her voice.

"Hey, no need to get so testy," Smokey said.

Just from the expressions on their faces, Bridget could tell how affected the others were by Georgina's story. All but Smokey had been in Georgina's shoes at some point in the very recent past. Smokey's goal was to get a story no matter what the cost, whereas Bridget and the others wanted to help each other get through this ordeal without losing their sanity. Bridget felt relieved to know the others would also be there to help protect not only Kate, but every woman who had experienced this type of violence. *That's what this group is about now*, Bridget thought. *That's what we've become. That's who we are. Women like Smokey Wells and Dorothy Holt have no idea what it means to feel so helpless and terrified. In that respect, they are outsiders.*

Jane signaled the waitress to get fresh drinks and to give them a few minutes to recover from hearing about Georgina's ordeal. Bridget was tired and wasn't sure how much more of this intensity she could handle. Apparently Georgina wasn't the only fragile one among them.

"I've told you my story," Georgina said. "I don't have anything else to say."

"Hey, what about a few questions?" Smokey asked. "I thought this was an interview."

Georgina looked down at her untouched coffee cup. Bridget saw Lupita lean over and say something to her. Georgina nodded.

"She'll answer two questions from each of us," Lupita announced.

"*Two*?!" Smokey bellowed. "I've got two *pages* of questions I need to ask her!"

"You can have my two then," Lupita said. "That gives you four questions."

Gwen shook her head. "You can have my two also. That gives you six."

"I'm keeping my two," Bridget said when Smokey looked at her expectantly.

"Same here," Jane confirmed. "You're getting nothing from me."

"Then start asking," Georgina said. "I want to get home before it gets dark."

Bridget and Jane scribbled their questions on a napkin and smiled at each other across the table when they exchanged them. Their two questions were nearly identical.

"I'll ask these," Bridget said as she held up the napkin Jane had given her. "You think up two more."

"Gee thanks."

"Come on," Georgina said. "Ask me something. Let's get this over with."

"I'll go first," Bridget said. Tilting her head ever so slightly, she looked down at the end of the table at Georgina and asked, "Are you a lesbian?"

Georgina's eyebrows arched in surprise. "Why would you ask me that?"

"Because we are," Bridget said. "All except for Lupita."

Lupita's smile was disarming. Bridget couldn't help but be enchanted by it.

"Why would a lesbian work as an escort?" Smokey asked.

"Is that one of your six questions?" Gwen inquired.

"Uh . . . no. Never mind."

"Georgina didn't answer the question," Gwen noted.

"If she is, that's forty percent of us so far," Jane said. She looked down toward the end of the table at Lupita and asked with a teasing smile, "Are you sure you're straight? That's messing up one of my theories."

Everyone but Georgina laughed. Lupita met Jane's teasing look and said, "You're the one who keeps assuming that I'm straight."

There was a collective gasp from Bridget, Gwen and Jane as they all stared at her with wide eyes. Bridget tried to remember what had been said in the past to make her believe Lupita couldn't be gay. *It was the husband*, she thought. *You don't know any married lesbians, but maybe your gaydar was right!* Bridget glanced across the table and noticed the way Jane was looking at Lupita. *Ahh*, she thought. *Now there's a connection that can't be denied.*

"You have another question," Smokey reminded Bridget. "Even though she didn't answer that one." Smokey seemed anxious. Bridget attributed that to her wanting a chance to ask her own group of questions.

Bridget took a sip of lukewarm coffee before asking Georgina, "Do you remember anything about Kate, the gun, or the car she drove that might be helpful?"

"Very good," Gwen cooed. "That was actually three questions, but asked in such a way that it's really just one."

Georgina shook her head. "I was in shock. Once I saw her holding the gun on him, I thought she was there to kill us both. It wasn't until she got him in the trunk of the car and came back over to where I was on the ground that I realized she was there to help me."

"Now that's interesting," Gwen said. "Did anyone else feel threatened by Kate's presence? I remember feeling elated at seeing her there. I never once felt any danger once I realized she was a woman."

"No," Bridget said, "I didn't feel threatened by her either."

"I remember feeling relieved," Jane noted.

"So did I," Lupita said.

"Are you interested in seeing Kate again?" Bridget asked.

"That's three questions for you," Smokey said with a tinge of irritation.

"I'll make that one of my questions," Jane said. She looked down at the end of the table and asked the question once more. "Are you interested in seeing Kate again?"

With a shake of her head, Georgina said, "No. I just want this to be over with."

Chapter Eleven

The waitress came back and freshened up their drinks. Bridget noticed how Smokey kept tapping her pen on the edge of the table hard enough to get everyone's attention, even though that apparently wasn't her intention. After they glared at her long enough, the tapping eventually stopped. It was evident that the others were just as annoyed with Smokey's rude impatience when Gwen finally said, "Why don't we let the reporter go next? She's starting to really piss me off."

All eyes were on Smokey now. She set her pen down and sipped her coffee, not bothering to hide her irritation. Bridget wasn't sure what to think about her any longer, but even those previously admired smoky-gray eyes weren't as sexy as she remembered them being the last time she'd seen her. *What a fickle thing I can be sometimes,* Bridget thought with unabashed amusement.

"Ask your questions," Georgina said in a tired, stoic voice at the other end of the table.

Smokey took a deep breath. "I can't do what I need to do if I'm limited to so few questions. I need to speak with you privately, Ms. Philips."

"Then we have nothing else to talk about," Georgina said. She spoke with quiet but desperate firmness and moved her chair back so she could stand up. "I've told you and the police all I know. Now please leave me alone."

"Wait!" Smokey said.

Georgina collected her purse and turned to leave.

"Now look what you did!" Jane hissed at Smokey. Sudden anger lit her eyes, and Bridget was once again relieved to have Jane on their side. Bridget's aversion to confrontation had always been something she tried to work on, but it was nice to have someone else take on that role for the group. Jane slipped into it so easily, and Bridget admired that quality in women.

Gwen pushed her coffee cup away. "We shouldn't have bothered this woman. It's too soon for her."

Smokey snatched up her tape recorder and stuffed it in her briefcase. Georgina didn't get far before Smokey caught up with her. The others watched from the table, and Jane craned her neck to get a better look. After a moment, Gwen said, "Are those two leaving together?"

"Well, damn," Jane mumbled under her breath.

"I'd say it's more like Georgina's leaving and Smokey's tagging along after her," Bridget said, casually amused. She watched them leave the coffee shop and slowly walk by the huge windows in front of their table. It was dark outside, but the lights from the restaurant and the parking lot made it easy to see what was going on. Smokey and Georgina stopped on the sidewalk where Smokey was now doing all the talking. Georgina, however, seemed to be interested in whatever it was she had to say.

With a furrowed brow, Jane said, "They're getting into a car together. Whose car is it? Does anyone know?"

"Georgina's getting into the driver's side, so I'd say it's hers," Lupita reasoned.

"That Smokey must be a smooth talker," Jane commented. The admiration for Smokey's gift of persuasion was evident in her tone. Bridget reluctantly had to agree with her. Smokey had been able to convince them to help her get a meeting with Number Ten when Dorothy Holt hadn't been able to accomplish that. She also talked her way into Gwen's kitchen the other night with very little trouble. *Hmm*, Bridget thought. *We've grossly underestimated Smokey Wells.*

"She's getting her interview," Lupita noted. "That's all she cares about."

"None of that matters," Gwen said. "We shouldn't have bothered that woman. She wasn't ready for any of this."

"Some women will never be ready."

"Is that the difference with us?" Jane asked as she looked around the table at each of them. "We've all had time to get over the initial shock of being attacked?"

"I think it has more to do with the kind of people we are," Lupita said.

"OK, so we learned something today," Bridget said.

Jane shook her head. "Yes, we did."

"What exactly did we learn?" Gwen asked. She took a sip of her coffee and appeared to relax a little. Bridget imagined that Gwen wasn't really upset with any of them, but more annoyed at how the search for Kate was going in general, not to mention how Smokey's arrival had thrown them all off.

"We now know there's a certain degree of ruthlessness out there when it comes to Kate and her story," Jane said. "People like Smokey Wells will do whatever it takes to get what they want. I understand that better now. Your basic human decency doesn't really apply when it comes to reporters."

"Amen to that."

"Isn't that the truth," Bridget said. "Like those spots you see on the news where the house is engulfed in flames and the TV reporter has a microphone stuck in a guy's face saying, 'Tell us how it feels to lose all six of your children in a fire.' I've always wanted to drive to the TV station and just slap those people silly each time I see something like that."

"Oh, hell yes!" Gwen agreed.

"When it comes to investigative things," Jane said, "all of that's out of my league. By nature I'm not really the curious type. I work with numbers all day . . . concrete theories . . . cut and dried rules, policies and laws. All of this deviousness is foreign to me, so I was able to be suckered in by the likes of a Smokey Wells."

"We all were," Lupita said. Her gaze went to the window where it was easy to see Smokey and Georgina in the car still deep in conversation. "She's grilling someone who just wants to be left alone."

"When does 'no' really mean 'no'?" Jane asked. "Or when does 'leave me alone' really mean 'get in the car so we can talk about this some more'?" With a brief glance out the window she shook her head. "I don't get it."

"The thing I find the most interesting about all of this is how good my instincts are when it comes to people," Gwen said as she looked away from the window. "I'm learning so much about myself. There was something about Dorothy Holt I didn't like and there was something about Smokey I didn't like. I'm usually a good judge of people and I've always assumed others were, too. But when Georgina began talking about how frightened she was when Kate arrived at the cemetery, it struck me how not everyone has those types of instincts going for them." She tossed a thumb over her shoulder toward the parking lot. "Like Georgina there. She spoke of being afraid of Kate, but she's now in a car with Smokey! Go figure. It doesn't make any sense to me."

"Maybe it was because Kate had a gun," Bridget suggested.

"I don't think Smokey is dangerous," Lupita said. "Persistent and aggravating maybe, but not dangerous."

"You left out calculating and sneaky," Bridget added.

Jane said, "And none of those qualities are appealing to me."

"The four of us are all different," Lupita said quietly, "but there's something bringing us together. Do any of you feel that? It's something bigger than we are. It's something more powerful than I can even explain."

The sisterhood, Bridget thought. *So I'm not the only one who senses it.*

"I know we've mentioned trust a lot over the last few days," Gwen said. "It's strange how I feel as though I could tell the three of you anything, and I don't even know any of you well. I felt comfortable enough with all of you to invite you into my home. I have friends and coworkers I've known for years who don't know where I live, but I opened up my home to all of you without giving it a second thought. That's pretty remarkable to me."

As Bridget glanced at each of them, she could see in their eyes how much Gwen's revelation meant to them. Once again it was nice knowing she wasn't alone and had these three women in her life.

"The other evening when I called everyone together to talk about the Lesbian Avengers," Jane said, toying with the handle of her coffee cup. She looked out the window again to check on Georgina and Smokey who were still sitting in the car. "Remember when I jokingly said I'd really just gotten you all here because I missed you?"

Bridget and Gwen chuckled.

"Well, I wasn't really kidding," Jane confessed. "I *did* miss being with all of you."

Bridget stopped and looked more closely at her. She heard something different in Jane's voice and saw the sincerity in her eyes. *What a brave thing to say,* she thought. Bridget's previous impression of Jane suddenly changed and she saw her in a totally different light. It occurred to her how vulnerable each of them was and how much she personally needed to be a part of something like this. Her loneliness and fear had unexpectedly taken a backseat in her life, and she was able to function better with each passing day.

"I can't stop thinking about Kate," Jane continued, "and I can't stop thinking about how close each of us came to being brutalized." She looked up and blinked several times. Tilting her head back, she sighed and said, "Until I met all of you, there was no one else in my life who understood what I was going through. Somewhere . . . somewhere . . . the answers I need are out there. I can't find them on my own. I need help."

Bridget felt such a huge sense of relief listening to Jane describe how she felt. *And all this time you thought you were just weird, Bridget old girl, when in fact there's at least one other person who has these exact feelings.*

"It's the same for me, too," Lupita admitted. "I'm at my happiest when I know I'm going to see the rest of you." Her disarming smile was directed at Jane. "I haven't gone to the trouble of inventing reasons to call us all together yet, but that might have been only a short way down the road for me, too."

"I have a full-time job that's demanding and two kids who take up a lot of what spare time I have," Gwen said, "but I'm eagerly making time to meet with the three of you. It's like this little coven we've created is what's keeping me from going over the edge sometimes."

"Coven," Jane repeated after practically spewing coffee everywhere. "We're like a little band of witches?"

"Sure! Why not," Gwen said with a laugh. "That's my broom parked out there beside Georgina's car, by the way."

The easy laughter didn't lessen the seriousness of their confessions. No one appeared to be embarrassed. Bridget was glad to know the others also felt a connection. It made her feel more normal than she had in a long time.

"Witches," Lupita said.

"I've been called worse," Jane admitted with a laugh.

"I was just thinking," Lupita said. "Once we run out of options on what to do next about Kate, I have an idea."

"Options?" Gwen said. "It's like Bridget reminded us before. All we do is drink coffee and talk. We don't have any options and we don't have a plan."

"What's your idea?" Jane asked. "We're getting nowhere with all these meetings, other than making ourselves feel better by spending more time together."

"There's a woman I know of," Lupita said. "She's a *curandera*."

"A what?"

"A *curandera*," Lupita said again. Her pronunciation of the Spanish word made Bridget's heart skip a beat. *Whew*, she thought. *Everything she says sounds sexy. Get a grip and pay attention.*

"It's like a fortune-teller."

"Ahh," Gwen said. "I've been to one of those before. She told me I was pregnant with my son before I had even missed a period."

"Some of those people are for real," Jane said. "My grandmother's sister could look at a little kid and tell how they would turn out. 'Don't waste money on college with little Jimmy,'" Jane said in a nasal voice. "'He's gonna be a mechanic.'"

There was more quiet laughter before Jane added, "So if any of you need work done on your car, I'll give you my cousin Jimmy's phone number."

"Then you can recommend this curan-whatever?" Gwen asked Lupita.

"This one is good," Lupita confirmed. "My mother used to go to her all the time to find out what my father was up to."

Low chuckles went around the table.

"This woman would tell her things and when my father finally came home again, there would be a big fight. After that everything would be fine again until the next time." Lupita looked up and was totally unaware of the captivating picture she made when she smiled. "My father called this woman a witch, but my mother called her a friend and a secret weapon."

"So would your mother's friend be able to help us?" Bridget asked. She wasn't sure that she believed in such things, but they surely weren't getting anywhere meeting for coffee a few times a week! She was willing to go along with whatever the rest of them wanted to do.

"She works out of her home and asks for donations," Lupita explained. "I don't know if she can help us or not."

76

"I'm game," Jane said. "It sure couldn't hurt to check her out. What do we have to lose?"

"Then let's go," Gwen said. "Where does she live?"

As they left the coffee shop, they had to walk by Georgina's car where she and Smokey were still talking. Bridget was no longer concerned about anything that they might possibly be discussing. Finding the judge had never been a priority for any of them, and Smokey's story had very little to do with what they wanted to accomplish.

"For someone who didn't want to talk," Gwen noted with a nod toward Georgina's car, "she's sure chatting it up in there."

"No kidding," Jane said. "There's no telling what Smokey promised her." With a shake of her head, she tossed the red hair out of her eyes before announcing, "Lupita's going with me. You two follow us over there to the witch's house."

Lupita threw her head back and laughed. It was the most delightful sound Bridget had ever heard. She felt incredibly envious of Jane's ability to dictate who would be riding where. *Why didn't I think of asking Lupita to ride with me?*

"You can't be calling her that," Lupita said.

Jane's teasing smile was almost as appealing as Lupita's laugh had been. "I see. So it's OK if *you* call her a witch, but I can't?"

"I called her a *curandera* and a fortune-teller."

"Her father called her a witch," Bridget reminded them.

"See? I told you."

"Yeah, yeah, yeah. Whatever," Jane said while pushing the button on her key ring and automatically unlocking her car doors.

"Drive slowly and don't lose us," Gwen said.

"Are we sure this woman's open for business?" Bridget asked as she unlocked her own car door.

"Hey," Jane said, "if she's any good at this, then she should already know we're coming."

Chapter Twelve

As Bridget pulled out of the parking lot, she gave Georgina's car another close look. Smokey was still holding court and apparently getting the interview she'd been after. Bridget followed Jane's car and made sure Gwen was behind her. She no longer had the need to try to understand why she felt so close to these women. It was a relief to know the bond wasn't something she had imagined since the others felt it, too.

They drove over to the northwest side of town to an area that wasn't far from where Bridget's parents lived. It still surprised her how much the neighborhoods had declined. She heard a coworker explain the increase in gang activity in the city as a product of "the *tías* moving away to the suburbs and taking those extra eyes and loving arms away with them." Bridget remembered thinking at the time, *Oh, great. One more thing to blame women for.*

From the way the oncoming cars shone their lights into the car up ahead Bridget had the opportunity to see Jane and Lupita talking and laughing. To get her mind off that, Bridget turned on the radio and eventually got caught up in a local right-wing-Republican-tainted talk radio station. She liked listening to those types of programs, not because she agreed with anything they said or the issues the guests supported, but because it helped to keep her informed about who her enemies were. Bridget made it a point not to support their sponsors and kept a mental list of the subjects they covered. She was quick to agree that her selective form of boycotting wasn't much, but she did what felt right for her.

She glanced into her rearview mirror to make sure Gwen was still behind her. With the help of the streetlights, she could see that Gwen was on the phone. *Probably talking to one of her kids,* she thought. Bridget turned her focus back to the traffic and the car in front of her, wondering briefly if Jane had any children. With a smile she shook her head. *You're all over the place with those two up ahead,* she thought. *One minute you're swooning over how good Lupita looks in a sweater, and the next minute you're impressed beyond words at Jane's "in your face" handling of Smokey Wells. Aren't you a little old to still be having crushes on women?*

"Nah," she said out loud. "As long as I'm breathing I'll be having crushes on women."

Her cell phone rang and she checked the number on the digital display. She didn't recognize it as she pushed the button to answer the call.

"Hello."

"Hi. It's Gwen. Where the hell are they taking us?"

Bridget laughed and looked in her rearview mirror. "They seem to know where they're going," she said. "So what do you think about seeing this *curandera?*"

"I like to keep an open mind," Gwen said. "The brief experience I had with one turned out favorably. All I know is we're not likely to just bump into KTL on the street somewhere. We can use all the help we can get finding her."

Bridget thought that line of reasoning made sense. One of the things that she really liked about all three of these women was their honesty and their willingness to try new things. Their personal experiences with violence hadn't left them too jaded or broken to see the good in others. It was also nice to know they had a certain amount of adventure in them. Bridget was great at following, but her leadership skills had always been lacking. It was a refreshing change to be a part of something so unique without having to be in charge of anything.

"I have to admit I'm a little excited," Gwen said. "I've always wanted to go back to see a *curandera*, but the one I went to before moved away. Three of us from work went to see her a few times."

"Then you're about to get another chance," Bridget said as she noticed the blinker on Jane's car up ahead.

"Looks like we're turning," Gwen said. "We'll talk more when we get there."

"OK. Bye." Bridget touched the "end" button on her phone and set it in the seat beside her. Jane's car slowed down as they cruised by several streets.

A few minutes later they pulled up in front of a house that had all of its lights on inside and three cars parked in front of it. Bridget found a free space a few houses down and got out of her car. It was a quiet, older neighborhood, but the yards all were kept up. She met the others on the sidewalk near where Jane had parked.

"Are you sure this is the place?" Jane asked Lupita. "Everything looks pretty much the same."

"Yes. I'm sure. It's the only house with a palm tree."

Until Lupita mentioned it, Bridget hadn't noticed the palm tree.

"I expected to see a sign or something," Gwen said with an arched brow. "It's a business, right?"

"Yeah," Jane agreed. "One of those flashing neon signs that says 'Witch's House'."

"Shh," Lupita hissed. "Will you stop calling her that?"

"Well, are we going in or not?" Bridget asked.

"We're here," Jane said, "and we're going in." She lined up behind Lupita. "This was your idea, so you go first."

They followed Lupita up the sidewalk single file. As soon as they got to the front door, it opened up and someone came out. It was an older woman who looked away from them before hurrying off the porch and down the sidewalk. Lupita opened the door and tried to let the others go in first ahead of her.

"Oh, you think that's cute, huh?" Jane said. "*I'll* hold the door open while *you* go in first."

"I don't mind holding it," Lupita said with a nervous laugh.

"Neither do I," Gwen said. "Here. Let me have that door."

"I've got the door," Jane announced. "Everybody just get in."

OK, Bridget thought. *We're all nervous. Let's just get this over with.* To keep the confusion down to a minimum and the scene on the porch from looking too much like a Keystone Cops episode, Bridget went in first.

The front room was set up as the waiting area. There were four white plastic chairs, a worn sofa, a matching love seat and a small table surrounded by three dinette chairs. Bridget stood there looking around, trying to decide where to sit. There were two other people already waiting. A stooped old man was at one end of the sofa with his hat in his lap, and a woman in her late forties sat in one of the white plastic chairs.

"*Siéntese,*" the woman said. "*Ella nos toma en orden de llegada.*"

Bridget blinked a few times, but understood enough high school Spanish to know she had been told to sit down. The other three women in Bridget's group took seats at the table. Bridget grabbed the nearest plastic chair and joined them.

On the wall to the left were shelves that went all the way up to the ceiling where tall glass candles for every occasion were lined up. Bridget could see the words "Bingo" and "Luck" on a few of the candles, while most of the others had the name and picture of a saint on them. She also noticed a glass case where packets of herbs were for sale.

In a low voice, Gwen asked Lupita, "What are those for?" She pointed to the rows of glass candles.

"It's believed that certain patron saints are associated with specific professions, illnesses, and causes," Lupita explained. "Whenever my mother lost something she would pray to St. Anthony and soon the item would show up again. One of the candles up there is probably for him."

"So she prayed to St. Anthony whenever your father wouldn't come home?" Jane asked with an innocent smile.

"Nooo!" Lupita said, enjoying Jane's teasing manner. "She would pray to St. Anthony for things like lost car keys or an earring. Little things like that."

"Is there a saint for bingo?" Gwen asked.

Bridget glanced at the rows and rows of tall glass candles. "Looks like there's a saint for everything."

"Find a saint for lottery games, and I'll pray to that one," Jane said.

The door beside them opened and made all four of them jump. A young woman came out and then left through the front entrance. A voice just inside the door said, "Next," and the man on the sofa got up and shuffled across the room. As the door closed behind him, Bridget could hear muffled voices inside for only a moment.

"That scared the crap out of me," Gwen admitted with a nervous laugh.

"Me, too," Jane said.

"Remember that she takes donations for her time," Lupita reminded them.

"How much should we pay her?" Bridget asked.

"Maybe it depends on what kind of info she gives us," Gwen suggested.

"My mother never had much money, but she always gave her something," Lupita said. She looked at the woman waiting on the other side of the room and asked, "*A venido aquí antes?*"

"*Sí. Muy sequido.*"

"*Cuanto le paga a ella cada vez?*"

"*Diez dolares.*"

"*Grácias,*" Lupita said to the woman. She leaned closer to her friends and whispered, "She's a regular customer and gives her ten dollars each time."

"We can all go in as a group, right?" Gwen wondered.

The four of them looked at each other.

"Well, I'm not ready to go in there by myself yet," Gwen said. "We have questions as a group."

"Will you do all the talking for us?" Jane asked Lupita.

"Sure. I can do that."

"Hopefully in English," Jane added.

"I'm sure she speaks English."

A while later the door suddenly opened again, causing them all to jump once more. The old man came out of the room and put his hat on. The mysterious voice inside said, "Next," and the other woman got up and walked past them. The door closed behind her, and Bridget heard a brief exchange in Spanish and then laughter before the muffled voices moved away farther into the other room.

"We're next," Gwen said. "Why am I so nervous?"

"Witches make me nervous, too," Jane whispered with a grin.

"*Dios mío*," Lupita mumbled. "Will you stop calling her that!"

They continued their wait by walking around and looking at the various herbs in the glass case. Lupita explained what she knew about them.

"Some are love potions. I'm not sure about the others. I remember my grandmother used to burn sage in her house when she felt my dead uncle José there. It's called smudging, I think. Sometimes she was afraid of him when he played tricks on her."

"Tricks?" Gwen said. "Your dead uncle played tricks?"

Lupita didn't answer and Bridget felt uncomfortable in the silence. As she studied Lupita further she could see the heat stealing into her face.

"I have a friend who might have a similar problem," Gwen said. "She bought a home recently only to discover someone had died in it a few years ago. Swears she hears things in the middle of the night. Did burning sage help your grandmother?"

With a slight shrug, Lupita said, "It made her feel better. That's all that counts."

As Bridget stood there with her hands clasped behind her back, she continued to look at the herbs and the candles on the shelves. It was a relief to know that Lupita's revelation about her family had been met with curiosity instead of ridicule. Once again these women had pleasantly surprised her.

"How can we find out which saint is in charge of the lottery?" Jane asked.

Everyone chuckled and diverted their attention to the candles. Without warning, the door to the other room opened and the customer left.

"Holy shit, that scared me," Gwen muttered under her breath.

Bridget's heart pounded in her chest as the four of them stood there waiting. With the door now open only about six inches, the mysterious voice from inside the room said the only audible word that had been uttered from there since they had arrived.

"Next."

Still standing there frozen in front of the glass case, Jane finally gave Lupita a nudge and said, "You go first. This was your idea."

"I'll hold the door," Lupita said as she took small, shuffling steps toward the mysterious voice.

"Here we go with the door thing again," Gwen said.

Suddenly the door swung open wide and a woman in her late fifties stood there wearing red shorts, a black tank top and sandals.

"Come in," the woman said. "I've been expecting you. Slide two of those chairs in here."

Chapter Thirteen

Gwen and Bridget each got a white plastic chair and followed the others into the room. There was a large wooden desk with a security monitor on it. As Bridget glanced at the monitor, she could see the entire area they had just come out of.

Oh, great, Bridget thought. *She's been watching us poke fun at the saint candles.*

"Everyone have a seat," the woman said. "My name is Consuelo. I'm sensing some apprehension from some of you. Please relax. There's nothing to be nervous about."

Bridget felt most comfortable being the closest to the door. She got a whiff of cigar smoke and saw half of an old unlit cigar perched on an ashtray on the desk. Even though it wasn't lit at the moment, the pungent aroma still permeated the room.

So she smokes cigars, Bridget thought as she looked at Consuelo more closely. The only light in the room came from a lamp on the desk. Consuelo's wild black and gray hair made her seem appealingly foreign and interesting. Bridget smiled. She had never met a woman who smoked cigars.

"What can I help you with this evening?" Consuelo asked.

There was silence as the four of them glanced at each other out of the corners of their eyes. Finally, Jane nudged Lupita with an elbow.

"We're looking for a woman," Lupita said, the words seeming to pop out of her mouth with the help of Jane's elbow.

"The woman in the fancy car?"

Bridget heard herself gasp and felt her face flush in surprise.

"Yes," Lupita said with relief. "The woman in the fancy car."

Consuelo reached into a small wooden box and pulled out a deck of cards. From where Bridget sat, she couldn't really see the cards well, but didn't recognize them as regular playing cards.

"This woman lives alone," Consuelo said as she shuffled the cards three times and began to slowly turn them over face up in front of her on the desk. "She has much sadness in her life."

"Where is she?" Lupita asked.

Bridget imagined that her own eyes were huge and she couldn't stop staring at Consuelo's hands as she continued to turn the cards over and line them up in several rows.

"There is a man who has been taken from you," Consuelo said as she glanced up from the cards to look at Lupita. "He was taken away in the fancy car."

"Rudy?" Lupita said, raising her voice.

"He is a violent man," Consuelo said. "That's why the woman in the fancy car took him away."

"You know where Rudy is?" Jane asked.

All four of them understood the significance of this line of questioning. If they could find out where Lupita's husband had been taken, then maybe they could eventually find out where Kate was.

"He's in a barn," Consuelo said. "With the others," she added.

"The others?" Gwen repeated. "The other rapists?"

Consuelo nodded. "There are many of them. All violent men. All there for the same reason."

"Where are they?" Lupita asked.

"In a barn," Consuelo said.

With a tinge of impatience in her voice, Jane said, "Where is this barn located?"

Consuelo shook her head.

"This is Texas!" Jane said in exasperation. "There's probably ten thousand barns around this area."

"Down, girl," Gwen said as she patted Jane on the knee.

"It's out in the country," Consuelo said.

"Oh, that's a big help," Jane said, rolling her eyes. "Imagine that. A barn in the country."

"*Down*, girl," Gwen said again before asking, "Do you get a sense of any kind of fruit around them?"

Jane turned to look at her. "Fruit? Did you say *fruit*? What the hell kind of question is that?"

"You know," Gwen continued. "Strawberries maybe? Watermelons? Or some nuts, perhaps? Like pecans or peanuts?"

Consuelo stopped turning over the cards and held one out in front of her in midair. She peered at Gwen curiously and then had the beginning of a smile on her full lips.

"Peanuts," she said, obviously impressed by Gwen's question. "I see peanuts."

"OK," Gwen said. "Then I bet the barn is in Floresville. That's the peanut capital of Texas, you know."

"And strawberries are in Poteet!" Lupita said excitedly.

"Watermelons and pecans?" Jane asked with a smile.

"Stockdale and Seguin," Gwen replied. "It pays to know your Texas trivia."

"OK," Bridget said, "so the rapists are being held in a barn in Floresville. Now what? Does anyone have any idea how many barns there are out that way? It's a rural area. Every peanut farmer in the whole county probably has at least two barns." She could hear the frustration in her voice, so she folded her hands in her lap and decided to try to focus on specific questions to ask next. Negativity wasn't going to help their cause.

"Consuelo," Jane said. "I can't even begin to tell you how much we appreciate your talent and insight into all of this."

Consuelo's wry smile caught Bridget's attention.

"Do you still think I'm a witch?" Consuelo asked her pointedly.

This time the gasp came from Jane. She started to cough and eventually choke on something. Gwen gave her a few hearty pats on the back. After a moment Jane said weakly, "Damn. You made me swallow my gum."

All five of them laughed. Consuelo set the deck of cards down and lit the cigar. She blew smoke rings that drifted in the air through the light from the lamp, making her look like a seedy gambler. Bridget couldn't help but be fascinated by her. What she found even more intriguing was how everyone was taking this woman's word for everything almost without question, no matter what she said, as if there was no reason to doubt anything she told them!

"I'm sorry about the witch thing," Jane said. Her voice hadn't fully recovered from the choking episode. "It was a silly joke. I was way out of line."

"I understand," Consuelo said as she blew another smoke ring.

"What else can you tell us about the woman in the car?" Lupita asked. "Is she close to this barn? Is it on her property?"

"She's not there often," Consuelo said, "but the car is sometimes kept there."

"So the barn is just the place where she takes the men," Gwen said.

"Yes."

"Is there anything unusual about the barn that you can tell us?" Lupita asked. "Any other buildings around it? Trees? Houses? Anything?"

"It's by some water."

"A lake? A pond? A creek?" Gwen asked.

"Large and flowing. Like a river."

"The San Antonio River runs through Floresville," Gwen said to the others. "How close to the river is the barn?" she asked.

Shaking her head, Consuelo said, "I don't know." She turned over another card. "There are two buildings. The fancy car is behind one building and the men are in the other."

Bridget heard one of them let out a deep sigh. She was certain

88

the others weren't interested in locating the rapists, but if it was the only way to find Kate, then they'd have to deal with it. What little information Consuelo had been able to give them was certainly more than they would have gotten on their own, but what were they supposed to do with this information now?

"We're more interested in whatever you can tell us about the woman," Gwen said.

"Music," Consuelo said. "She's always around fast music."

"She's in a band?" Gwen asked.

Consuelo shook her head and turned over another card. "No. Not a band. There's lots of energy around her, but there's also a dark cloud of despair."

"Music and energy," Jane said. "What exactly does that mean?"

"Maybe she's a cocktail waitress," Bridget said. "Lots of energy and fast music in those places."

"Driving a car like that?" Jane said. Still trying to recover from her coughing spell, she cleared her throat. "She's making some serious money somewhere. Or else she has money already."

"Let's get back to Kate," Gwen said. Consuelo's puzzled look prompted Gwen to say, "There's reason to believe that's the woman's name."

Consuelo shook her head again. "She isn't from this country. That's not her name."

"You know what her name is?!" all four of them said at the same time.

Consuelo set the cigar in the ashtray and turned over another card. "No," she said. "I don't know her name."

Bridget felt the most intense disappointment race through her body. She thought they had been teetering on the brink of discovery, only to be slapped down again with a giant thud.

"You said she isn't from this country," Gwen said. "Do you have any idea where she might be from?"

"I got a good look at her," Jane said, "and she spoke to me. I can't really say where she might be from either."

"But you know her name isn't Kate, right?" Gwen asked Consuelo.

Consuelo shook her head. "No. That's not her name. She has a short name . . . an unusual first name."

"And you don't have any idea where she works?" Lupita asked. "Or what she does? Other than she's around fast music where there's lots of energy?"

Another card was turned over. Consuelo looked at it closely. "She works around water." Picking up the cigar again, she clenched it between her teeth. "When she's around the water, the energy is slower, but the music is still fast."

"What the hell?" Bridget heard Jane mumble. "Barns in the country. Energy, fast music and water." She put her shaggy red head in her hands and wailed comically, "I'm sooo confused!"

"Aerobics," Gwen said.

Lupita leaned over to look around Jane and her theatrics and said, "What?"

Gwen glanced at Consuelo and their eyes locked. Consuelo set the cigar down on the ashtray and leaned back in her chair.

"Aerobics," Gwen said again. "Fast music. Energy. Maybe she's an aerobics instructor."

Consuelo held up another card and smiled and nodded. "She teaches water aerobics."

"Holy shit," Jane said. "Now that's some information we can use! How many water aerobics instructors could there be in this city?"

"You might be surprised," Gwen said. "With our luck there's as many of those as there are barns in the country."

"This is major," Jane said. "It's doable now. I think we can find her with this information. I bet we can do it with a computer. Everybody ready?"

"You've been very helpful," Lupita said to Consuelo.

"Yes, you have!" Jane agreed. She stood up and reached into her pocket and took out some money. "We might be back again if we hit any more stumbling blocks." She handed Consuelo a fifty-dollar bill. "And I'm sorry about that witch thing earlier."

Consuelo smiled and stood up. "I hope you find this woman. She needs your help."

The four of them froze for a moment before slowly sitting back down again.

"What did you say?" Gwen asked.

Consuelo picked up the cigar and turned over another card from the small stack remaining in her hand. "She needs your help. There's a restlessness about her. She's a driven woman and she has a mission and a calling. I can feel her strength, but little by little she is losing it."

Bridget sat there speechless. Kate needed them. Hearing that made her want to use every available resource and every ounce of energy she had in order to find her. This was the woman who had saved her life. There was nothing she wouldn't do for her.

Chapter Fourteen

Once they were all out on the sidewalk again, they gathered in a circle to try to regroup. There was an early November nip in the night air and Bridget wished she had her jacket that was in her car.

"Was that a rush, or what," Gwen said. "I'm not usually a drinking woman, but I could use a shot of something right now."

"Lupita, you're a genius," Jane said, putting her hand on her shoulder. "Thank you for suggesting this venture. I think we learned a lot in there."

"Let's go over to my place and figure out what to do next," Gwen suggested. "I've got kids to check on, but I don't want to just quit for the night. There's too much that needs processing and we need to do it while it's all fresh. Can everybody make it? I've also got a computer we can use."

Bridget was relieved that she didn't have to go home yet. She wasn't ready for the evening to end. Too much had happened and she would never get to sleep if she wasn't able to analyze each and every aspect of the evening's events.

"On the way over to Gwen's house," Jane said, "everyone should be thinking about what our course of action will be next. Maybe we can hammer out a few things before it gets too late tonight."

Bridget got in her car, cranked up the heater, and followed the taillights ahead of her. She kept the radio off and let her mind sift through the information they had gotten from Consuelo. She still wasn't sure what they would be able to do with any of it, but at least they had some place to start. Bridget also found it interesting that she wasn't giving too much thought to the barn where the rapists were, where exactly they might be, or how they were being treated. Did she and her friends have some sort of civic duty to report the information they'd received to the authorities? If Kate was torturing them, then so be it, she decided. And if they were in a barn without food, water or heat—even better. She considered them evil and believed they deserved whatever was happening to them. There were too many other things in her life to feel guilty about, and a barn full of rapists certainly wasn't one of them.

Her cell phone rang and Bridget answered it.

"Hi. It's Gwen."

Bridget smiled, childishly thinking, *I have a new telephone friend!* "Hi there. I'd say it's been an interesting evening."

"Any ideas about what we should do next?" Gwen asked. "I'm sure Jane and Lupita are doing some brainstorming right now. We might as well do some of our own for a few minutes."

"Good idea. Hmm. I have to admit I thought your aerobics deduction was a great breakthrough. Kate was in great shape when I saw her. I also wouldn't be surprised if she didn't have some martial arts training in her background as well."

"That's true," Gwen agreed. "She wasn't afraid of the guy who was beating up on me."

"A gun can be a nice equalizer."

Gwen laughed. "That's *sooo* true."

"Tell me what your thoughts are about the men in the barn."

"It made my skin crawl when Consuelo said there were so many of them there," Gwen admitted. "All this time I'd been hoping

93

Kate had tied each one of them up and thrown them in the river or something."

"I kind of like that fish-bait idea, too."

"I say we let 'em rot wherever they are. Even that's too good for them."

Bridget smiled. She liked the way this woman thought. Before the attack she would never have considered herself a vindictive woman, but now that there was a possibility that Kate was being sought for kidnapping, Bridget's sense of what was right and wrong was overshadowing everything else. Even though Kate hadn't done things by the book, it still didn't change the fact that she saved the lives of at least ten women. *Kidnapping, my ass*, Bridget thought, then suddenly she heard Gwen talking again.

"The only thing that worries me is if we can't find Kate with the info Consuelo gave us," Gwen said. "I'm not looking forward to searching peanut patches to find some barn those jerks might be staying in just on the chance Kate will be there with them. Those men are dangerous. The guy who attacked me had every intention of killing me until Kate showed up. I'm not a bit interested in a barn hunt."

"Yeah," Bridget said as a chill scampered down her arms. "I know what you mean. My attacker would have killed me, too. I'm sure they're all dangerous. Even the judge and the banker."

Changing the subject, Gwen asked, "Any idea how to find out about aerobics instructors? Are they licensed or something? Is there like a Board of Exercise and Acute Sweating in the great state of Texas?"

"I have no idea," Bridget said with a chuckle. "If there's not, then there should be!"

They shared a moment of silly laughter.

"I know the coach at school, though," Bridget added. "She might be able to tell me something. I'm thinking the water aerobics angle is the best clue we have so far. I imagine there are fewer of those types of instructors around."

"There are still so many questions I wish I had asked Consuelo while we were there," Gwen said.

"Write them down. We can go back and see her any time we need to. That whole experience was pretty amazing!"

"I wouldn't mind going to see her just for me!" Gwen said. "Ha! And that cigar! She was indeed an interesting character. So you're thinking the best way to go from here would be to do some research on water aerobics classes in San Antonio?"

"Yes. To me that sounds like the easiest way to try to find our Kate."

"I hope Consuelo was right about all of this," Gwen said. It was the first reference Bridget had heard where Consuelo's talents were even remotely in question. "OK," Gwen said. "We're getting on the interstate now. We'll talk more when we get to my house."

About fifteen minutes later Bridget parked on the street in front of Gwen's house and got out of her car. She joined Lupita and Jane on the sidewalk. All three had their jackets on now as the temperature continued to drop into the fifties.

"You two have it all figured out yet?" Bridget asked.

"Hardly," Jane said with a laugh, "but we have some ideas. I think this meeting is a good idea. We need to get on it while things are still fresh in our minds."

The porch light came on and Gwen opened the front door. "Come in. Come in. I already have my son on the computer looking for information on water aerobics classes in the local area."

"Resourceful teenagers," Bridget said. "You must be doing something right."

"Baseball and computers," Gwen said as she held the door open for them. "He loves them both. If the grades go down—no more computer and he can't play baseball. So he and I have an understanding."

"What about your daughter?" Lupita asked. "What does she like?"

"Shopping."

Jane laughed. "Now that's my kind of kid."

"Actually, she likes long skirts and combat boots," Gwen said with a smile. "She's a bit more complicated, but her grades are always good. Right now we're at odds over what color her hair will be next."

"Any body piercings yet?" Jane asked.

Gwen laughed. "Both of my kids faint at the sight of a needle, so I don't have to worry about that. But it's kind of embarrassing too, since I'm a nurse. I feel like I've failed them in that area."

"So they won't be following you into the medical field?" Bridget asked with a smile.

"Nope. Not those two." She closed the front door and locked it. "Let's go into the kitchen and find something to drink. They might've even left us something to munch on."

Once they were all gathered around the kitchen table with an assortment of soft drinks, a bag of chips and a can of bean dip, Gwen's son came in and handed his mother a small stack of papers.

"It's a short list for this area," he said, "but there were several hits for water aerobics. What else do you need?"

"This is good for now," Gwen said as she shuffled through the papers. "Holy cow! Will you look at this? Three local certified water aerobics instructors are listed!"

"By name?" Jane asked as she got up and hurried around the table so she could see better.

Bridget was already behind Gwen's chair, leaning closer and reading the information on the first page.

"Look at this," Lupita said. "Consuelo mentioned a short first name. Remember?"

On the page where Gwen pointed was the name of a water aerobics instructor. *Ola Cordician,* Bridget thought. *Ohmigod! Lupita's right! Consuelo said the woman we're looking for would have a short first name!*

"This says she has classes in aquajam, deep water exercise, water healing, water rehab, water walking, senior aerobics, therapeutic exercise, aqua plus, and aqua boxing," Gwen said. "What the hell is aqua boxing?"

"Maybe that's what you do when you can't take your gun to the pool," Jane said quietly. Her voice had a strange hollowness to it. Bridget looked over at her as she stood on the other side of Gwen's chair. Jane had her right hand on her chest rubbing it slowly as if she were in pain.

"Are you OK?" Bridget whispered.

"I don't know." She reached out with her other hand and touched Bridget's arm. "I think we've found her."

"Here," Bridget said as she grabbed her chair and moved it closer to Jane. "Sit down. You're scarin' me."

Jane sat down with a thud and reached for Gwen's arm to steady herself even more. "That's her, isn't it? Ola Cordician. It has to be her."

"We won't really know until we see her," Gwen said. "But we have a list of places where she teaches."

"Anything listed there for a Saturday night?" Lupita asked, glancing at her watch.

"Nah," Gwen said. "It's too late. We can't do anything until Monday. Her first class is Deep Water Exercise at the University of the Incarnate Word at ten." She passed around the first page and glanced at the other papers in her hand.

"Can anyone make it there Monday morning?" Lupita asked. "I have to be at work that day."

"I can," Gwen and Bridget said at the same time. Bridget couldn't keep the excitement from bubbling up inside of her. *Finally*, she thought. *I might finally see the woman who saved my life!*

Chapter Fifteen

The other papers Gwen held in front of her dealt with water aerobics and various certifications that could be earned. Apparently there were several organizations that these three instructors belonged to. In addition to Ola Cordician, there was a Jessica Gomez who taught classes at a rehab facility and the downtown YMCA, and someone by the name of Hilary Carter who had several classes at one of the universities and two of the military bases in the area. Bridget disregarded the two water aerobics instructors listed who had the longer first names since Consuelo's suggestions about the name was weighing heavily on her mind.

Bridget sat back down at the table now that the initial shock of finding Ola Cordician's name was beginning to wear off. They were all quietly perusing the papers Gwen's son had given her and occasionally one of them would read something out loud. Suddenly, Gwen got up from the table and left the kitchen. She came back a few minutes later with a San Antonio telephone book.

"Now that we think we have a name," she said, "let's see what else we can find out about her."

As she thumbed through the thick telephone book, Bridget got up to come around the table again and stand behind Gwen's chair.

"There's only one Cordician listed," Gwen said, "and the first initial is O."

"I don't think we should call the number," Bridget said. "We might scare her off."

Jane nodded. "I agree. I want to see her first and make sure it's her."

"The address isn't too far from here," Gwen noted.

"Then let's go check it out," Jane said excitedly.

"It's probably an apartment complex," Gwen said, "and gated. Plus, it doesn't give an apartment number."

"I don't care," Jane said. "I have to see where that address is."

"I'll drive," Gwen said. "I know the area better. Help me remember this address. It's 5900 Broadway."

"Got it," Jane said. "Let's go."

They were up in a flash and ready to leave before Bridget even had time to push her chair in. As Gwen went through the living room, she pulled on a jacket and went down a hallway to another part of the house.

"I'm going out again, but I have my cell phone," Bridget heard Gwen say to her kids. "Don't let anyone in and keep the doors locked. Did you find anything yet?"

Bridget heard the boy say something, but she couldn't understand what he said.

"Really?" Gwen said in surprise. "That's great! Print it all off for me. I won't be gone long."

Bridget, Jane and Lupita had their jackets on and were patiently waiting by the front door. She loved all these spontaneous fact-finding excursions—meeting at the coffee shop, going to see a *curandera* together, staking out a stranger's apartment. Being with these women was adding something to Bridget's life that had always been missing. As of yet she didn't have a firm grasp of what exactly that "something" was, but she adored each minute spent with her new friends.

"Getting him that computer was the best investment I've ever made," Gwen said as she came back into the living room. "He's checking for info on this Ola Cordician. He'll have it for us when we get back."

"Do you have any binoculars?" Jane asked.

"Yeah, why? It's dark out there. We won't be able to see anything."

"I'd feel better having them anyway. You just never know."

Bridget was in the front seat with Gwen while Jane and Lupita were in the back. Bridget felt a mischievous giddiness as Gwen backed out of the driveway.

"So do you think this is really her?" Jane asked. "It just seems too good to be true. You know what I mean? It feels like I've waited forever to find this woman."

"Things are falling into place," Lupita said.

"What things?" Jane asked. "Tell me. Please. I need to hear it all again. It makes everything seem more real to me when someone else is talking about it."

Bridget's eyes widened at the tone of Jane's voice. She sounded so much like a child needing reassurance. *Where's the "in your face" Jane we're all used to?* Bridget wondered. She cut her eyes to the left in Gwen's direction only to see Gwen looking back at her with the same puzzled expression.

"Consuelo said something about energy, music and water," Lupita recounted. "Then she mentioned a first name that was short. Now we know there's a water aerobics instructor by the name of Ola, and even though that's all very coincidental information, it seems to me that all those clues are slowly materializing and falling into place."

"What if this Ola Cordician isn't our Kate?" Jane asked.

"Then we go kick Consuelo's ass," Gwen said simply.

100

Laughter filled the car and helped ease some of the tension. Bridget was happy. She couldn't imagine being anywhere else at that moment.

"OK," Gwen said. "Here we are at fifty-nine hundred Broadway at the Starlight Condominiums. I'm sure these cost a nice chunk of money. This is a pricey neighborhood."

"And it's gated, too," Bridget said. "With a security guard."

"Let's go around the block and see if there's another way in," Jane suggested.

Gwen drove slowly around several adjoining streets. There was a seven-foot wall surrounding the facility, like a fortress protecting its inhabitants from anything menacing, and there was no other way in. Driving around to the front entrance again, Gwen parked across the street from the security guard and gate area in a King Wa Chinese Food restaurant parking lot.

"Hand me those binoculars, please," Jane said.

Bridget passed them to her over the seat.

"Guess what," Gwen said.

"What?" the other three said in unison.

"I have to pee."

Over the laughter, Bridget heard Gwen mumble, "It never fails."

"Well, hell," Jane said. "Thanks for mentioning it. Now I do, too."

"So we think we know about where Ola Cordician lives," Lupita said. "Maybe that's all we need to do tonight."

"You mean no one wants to try and scale the Starlight wall and attempt to find the Kate-mobile in there?" Jane asked.

"Scale the wall?" Bridget repeated incredulously.

"With a full bladder?" Gwen added. "I'm not scaling anything. Besides, they'd call the cops on us for trespassing." Under her breath again she mumbled, "As if any of us could scale a wall to begin with."

"So what do we do now?" Jane asked, leaning between the front seats with the binoculars.

"We go back to my place and use the bathroom," Gwen said. She started up the car and pulled out of the restaurant parking lot. Jane sat back in her seat again.

"I feel like we're so close," Jane said. "I'm having a hard time containing all this energy I feel. If I have to wait until Monday to know something about this Ola woman, I'll explode."

"There will be no exploding in my car," Gwen said. "I'm very particular about that sort of thing."

"Yeah, yeah, yeah," Jane said. "I hear you. I'm the same way with my car, too."

They got back to Gwen's house and all took a turn in the bathroom. Gwen's son had another small stack of papers waiting for his mother when they arrived.

"Looks like she's a published author," Gwen said as she scanned the documents a while later. "She's also certified in all kinds of things and belongs to a number of organizations. The Aquatic Exercise Association, Aerobics and Fitness Association of America, Aquatic Alliance International, American Council on Exercise. She's a Water Safety Instructor and belongs to the United States Water Fitness Association."

"All of that's tax deductible, you know," Jane said, which made the other three chuckle.

"Do we have a plan?" Lupita asked. "We have a name, we have her schedule, and we think we know where she lives. Now what do we do?"

"According to the schedule we have, thanks to your son," Bridget said to Gwen. "By the way, what are your children's names? I've only heard you refer to them as 'my kids.'"

"Logan is my son and Emory is my daughter."

"Emory," Jane said. "What a great name for a girl!"

"Thank you," Gwen said. "She hates it. All her little friends are either Jessicas, Ambers, or Heathers."

"She'll appreciate it more when she's older," Jane promised. "People will take her more seriously than they will a Tiffany or a Jennifer."

"Anyway, as I was saying," Bridget continued, "we know this woman's schedule. Her first class is at ten on Monday morning. I can be in that Chinese restaurant's parking lot at seven a.m. and check out each car as it leaves the Starlight Condo compound."

Jane shook her head. "Compound is right. I'm surprised they don't have a moat around the place."

"If I see the Kate-mobile leave," Bridget said, "I'll follow it and give each of you a call."

"I can go with you on Monday morning," Gwen said. "The kids find their own way to school, and I'm off on Monday."

"Excellent!"

"Tomorrow's Sunday," Jane said with a little pout. "I won't see any of you until Monday?" There was a whine in her voice that Bridget remembered hearing before.

"I'm teaching a class on Monday evening," Bridget said, "so I'll be out of the loop after five." Then as if the words tumbled out of her mouth all on their own accord, she said, "Why don't all of you come over to my place tomorrow afternoon? We can throw something on the grill and we'll do more brainstorming." To Gwen she smiled and said, "Bring Logan and Emory, too. We'll make a day of it."

The smiles and mutual looks of relief made her feel good about the suggestion. It was nice knowing the others also liked the idea of being together again so soon.

Chapter Sixteen

Sunday morning Bridget rolled over in bed and peeked at the clock. She had slept well and was excited about having her friends over later that day. Making a mental list of the things she needed to do before everyone arrived, she stretched and fluffed up her pillow. The house could use some dusting and overall sprucing, but she had time to do that if she got started soon.

Throwing the covers off and swinging her bare legs over the side of the bed, Bridget got up and stretched again. Before she could get dressed, the telephone rang.

"Hi. It's Jane. You're up and moving around already, right?"

"Just barely," Bridget admitted.

"Lupita got a call this morning from a guy named Alan Harper. He was asking her questions about Georgina Philips—Number Ten. The judge's escort."

"Alan Harper. Who is he?"

"The reporter from Dallas that Smokey told us about."

"Oh," Bridget said as she sat down on the edge of the bed. "So what did he want?"

"Info on Georgina and that judge who attacked her. He's working on a story."

"Jeez. Isn't everybody? How did he get Lupita's number?"

"According to Smokey, information on all of us is easy to get, so I'm not sure. I don't like it, though. The more people out there lurking around, the better chance there is that things will just get all stirred up. You know how it is with copycat crimes, not to mention there's probably a lot of guys who would love to get an opportunity to pop Kate a good one. Publicity isn't in anyone's best interest right now."

Bridget lay down on the bed again. "It's weird that the reporters are so focused on this judge. Why isn't the real story about Kate the Lesbian and all the things she's done to help women?"

"A lesbian protecting women isn't newsworthy," Jane said dryly. "At least not as newsy as a kidnapped judge, apparently. Hey, I don't really get it either. Anyway, I'm just letting you and Gwen know that there could be someone new sniffing around. This Harper guy might only be interested in Lupita because of her contact with Georgina. He might not care about anything the rest of us have to say."

"Well, thanks for the info. I'll keep an eye out for him."

"Oh, by the way, I'm bringing a spice cake and a three-bean dip. They're both specialties of mine. I'm looking forward to seeing everyone again."

Bridget smiled. "I know what you mean."

"See ya later."

Bridget lay there on the bed looking up at the ceiling. *I wonder how much time Jane and Lupita spend together on the phone each day?* She was still confused about how she felt about them. Jane's smile and quick wit were appealing to her, but Lupita's shyness and that raw undercurrent of sexuality she had was also something that continued to catch Bridget's attention, too. The thought of Jane and Lupita as a couple stirred mixed emotions within her, but Bridget didn't like dwelling on it too much. *Once women start to pair off, they no longer have time for their friends,* she thought. *All they make time for then is each other.*

The first to arrive that afternoon was Gwen and her two teenagers. Logan brought in a small ice chest and a shopping bag full of chips, while Emory's attention was focused on the cell phone she had pressed to her ear.

"You didn't have to bring anything," Bridget said as she showed them into the kitchen.

"The way these two eat?" Gwen said. "We always travel with a few staples. How are you today?"

Gwen was dressed in denim slacks with a flare-cut at the bottom and what appeared to be new white Nike Airs. She had on a white shirt with the sleeves rolled halfway to her elbow and she smelled dreamily of Obsession perfume. Bridget liked the way Gwen and her children made themselves at home so quickly.

"I have a computer in my study down the hall," Bridget said to Logan. "You're welcome to use it."

His smile made her feel as though she had said the magic words. He set the ice chest down and pulled a can out of it and was off in the direction she had indicated.

"We won't see him for hours," Gwen said.

"You play chess?" Emory asked Bridget. She was off the phone and helping her mother get some chips into bowls.

"I do," Bridget said. *She must've seen the chessboard set up in the living room,* she thought. "My father and I play whenever my parents come over."

"Can we play?"

"You and your brother?" Bridget asked as she got two containers of dip out of the refrigerator. "Sure. I've got some movies and CDs that might be interesting, too. I doubt that we share the same taste in music, though, but feel free to check things out."

"No," Emory said. "I meant you. Can you and I play a game of chess?"

Bridget stood up a little straighter and looked at her. She also noticed the smile Gwen was trying to hide.

"I'd say 'no' if I were you," Gwen whispered to Bridget out of the side of her mouth.

Looking at Gwen with a raised eyebrow, Bridget asked, "Why is that?"

"Mom!" Emory said.

Gwen pantomimed zipping her lips closed, but continued to smile. "Sure," Bridget said to the teenager. "I'm up for a game, but I have things to do here, so it'll have to be a quick one."

Emory laughed and tossed her dyed jet-black hair away from her face. "Oh, it'll be a quick one all right."

"I warned you," Gwen said to Bridget.

"I must've missed you unzipping those nice lips," Bridget said to her with a wink. *Oh, goodness,* she thought. *Did I just call her lips nice?!*

Feeling somewhat relieved that Gwen hadn't responded to that small bout of flirting that had so innocently rolled off her tongue, Bridget followed Emory into the living room looking forward to the chess game. The doorbell rang and Bridget went to answer it, letting Jane and Lupita in. She helped them with the various bags they were carrying.

"Looks like we'll be eating for days," Bridget said.

Jane set the cake down on the counter near the sink. "Then I say we keep meeting at Bridget's house until all the food's gone!"

Jane volunteered to do the grilling, which was fine with Bridget. It gave her more time to devote to the chess game she had promised Emory. Bridget liked the way her friends seemed to feel so comfortable there. Gwen and Lupita piddled around in the kitchen and got things set up in the dining room while Jane familiarized herself with the grill outside on the patio. It was a mild November day, but a bit too cool to do much outside. Once Jane got the chicken, sausage and ribs going on the grill, she came in from the patio and went to the video cabinet to check out Bridget's movie collection.

"You have a nice assortment of Godzilla flicks," Jane said with a laugh. "I used to love watching those as a kid."

"I did, too," Bridget admitted. "Now I stick one in when I need to clean the house. They seem to make me clean faster."

"I can imagine," Jane said. "Can we watch one?"

Bridget laughed. "Sure. You can do anything you like while you're here." She glanced down at the chessboard and watched as Emory contemplated her next move. They had only been playing about ten minutes and already Bridget had three of Emory's pawns, a knight and a bishop.

"So what did that Dallas reporter want to know?" Gwen asked Lupita as they sat down in the living room. Gwen was next to Bridget on the sofa, while Lupita was in the love seat across from them. Emory and Jane were sitting on the floor—Emory on the other side of the coffee table scrutinizing the chessboard, while Jane was already engrossed in the Godzilla movie.

"He'd gotten my name from Georgina," Lupita said. "She probably gave it to him so he'd leave her alone."

"What did he want to know?" Gwen asked.

"I think he's leaning toward the kidnapping angle in his article. Supposedly that judge was on an important case coming up in Houston," Lupita said. "Alan Harper had questions about our Kate, but nothing that he couldn't get from the police reports or other stories that have already been printed. He was nice enough, but still kind of pushy like Smokey was. I didn't much care for him."

"When Jane called me this morning and told me about Harper," Gwen said, "I couldn't help but remember how Consuelo had said Kate needed us. It's like we'll have an opportunity to do something for her, but what if we never know what that 'something' is? Or when this will all unfold? How will we know anything? I can't stop thinking about it."

"We'll know more soon," Lupita said. "I'm envious of you two being off tomorrow and possibly getting to see her. If Ola Cordician is our Kate the Lesbian, you two will get to see her first."

Bridget felt a chill race down her arms at the thought of seeing Kate again. *Those kind dark eyes and that unwavering cool confidence that radiated from her,* she thought. Bridget wanted nothing more than to be in her presence again, to experience that feeling of complete safety and overwhelming gratitude.

Having momentarily forgotten where she was, Bridget saw Emory make her next chess move and then lean back on her arms. Emory's smile was one of satisfaction, as if all her mental processing and intricate maneuvers were about to pay off.

Almost without thinking, Bridget slid her queen across the board and said, "Check."

Emory leaned forward and peered closely at the chessboard. "What?" She looked up at Bridget with surprise etched in her eyes. That Wednesday Addams look Emory usually strived for had suddenly been replaced with the shock of an ordinary teenager who was about to unexpectedly lose at something. "No way," she said and then studied the board again.

Bridget looked over at the big-screen TV in the corner as Jane pushed a button on the remote and rewound Godzilla's latest move.

"What the hell?" Gwen said, studying the chessboard.

"I've gotta see that again," Jane said. "I *love* these movies!"

"Who's minding the grill?" Lupita asked.

Bridget glanced down at the chessboard again and watched Emory slowly make her next move. *Time to go in for the kill,* Bridget thought as she reached over and slid one of her bishops across the board.

"Checkmate," she said. "Good game, Emory."

"Ack! Ohmigod! Mom! Did you see that?!"

Gwen threw her head back and laughed.

"Logan!" Emory yelled as she scrambled up from the floor. Even in combat boots and a long skirt, she was uncommonly graceful. "Logan! Come here. You have to play her next!"

❧

Once the meat on the grill was done, they all gathered around the table in the dining room. Bridget had promptly taken care of Logan in a chess game that had left both teenagers speechless. While scooping out a portion of three-bean dip on her plate, Bridget leaned closer to hear Gwen's question.

"You're very good. Who taught you to play chess?"

"My father," Bridget said. "We still play whenever we have the time. Who taught your kids to play?"

"My ex," Gwen said. "She was pretty good and got them interested in it. Now both of them are in the Chess Club at school and are undefeated as long as they don't play each other."

"I think all kids should learn the game." Bridget speared a beef rib and a chicken leg from the meat platter. Everything smelled good. "How long has the ex been an ex, if you don't mind me asking?"

"It's been about two years now," Gwen said. "She's a nurse in the Air Force and got transferred to England. The kids didn't want to leave their friends, so things sort of fizzled after about six months of promises to visit."

"I'm sorry to hear that," Bridget said sincerely.

"Yeah, me, too. But sometimes things work out for the best. She's in another relationship now and seems to be happy. The kids and I keep in touch with her through e-mail. She spent some time in Uzbekistan supporting the war. We're still good friends. The kids might go and spend a few days with her over the Christmas holidays."

Bridget nodded. She understood the dynamics of how lesbians and their exes usually went on to form deep and lasting friendships. Bridget had one ex whom she kept in touch with on a weekly basis, another that she heard from only about twice a year, and another one that she hoped to never see or hear from ever again.

"I want a rematch," Logan said to Bridget as he sat down at the dining room table next to his mother.

Bridget smiled and nodded. It was refreshing to see teenagers who were interested in things other than loud music, drugs and hanging out at the mall. The classes Bridget taught at one of the local junior colleges were filled with high school graduates who barely had a fifth-grade reading level and no interest in applying themselves to anything other than locating the next party. Gwen's kids were smart and articulate. Bridget could tell she had done a good job raising them.

The beads of sweat continued to pop up on Logan's peach-fuzz-covered top lip. Bridget had him in "check" three times already, and it was only a matter of time before she beat him again. Emory was sitting beside her brother watching the game. Occasionally she would look up at Bridget and smile, seeming to take pleasure in her brother's undoing.

"He hates to lose," Emory said as she leaned back and propped herself up with her arms.

"It's safe to say we all do," Gwen said.

Bridget noticed the Frankenstein movie on the TV now. Lupita sat on the love seat with Jane curled up on the floor at her feet. The possibility of those two pairing off was disappointing, but there wasn't anything she could do about it. *Fickle, fickle, fickle,* she thought. Even though it was nice having people other than her parents over for a change, she wished Lupita wasn't sitting quite so close to Jane. Bridget hosted two events a year in her home—one in December and the other at the end of May when the semesters were over. Spending time with straight colleagues was different than sharing a lazy Sunday afternoon with friends. Bridget's house was practically glowing with good vibes despite the fact that Logan was experiencing some uncommon distress at the hands of a better chess player. Bridget wanted more of these types of gatherings in her home, and made a promise to herself to make it happen.

"You've got me," he said as he nudged his king back a space. "I'm hosed."

Bridget moved her rook and said, "Check."

He graciously made the only move he could and then took a deep breath before Bridget captured his king with a knight.

"Checkmate," she said. "Good game, Logan."

"I want another rematch," he said.

His mother laughed. "Maybe later."

"There's still plenty of food left," Bridget announced. "Is anyone hungry again?"

"I'm too full to move," Jane said as she stretched her legs out on the floor and leaned back against Lupita who was still sitting on the love seat. "Oh, watch this part! Check out Frankenstein's square head. He's supposed to be made out of old body parts, but who has a head like that anyway? And can you imagine what that guy smells like? Yuck!"

"So you're a horror movie buff?" Gwen asked Bridget.

"Just the old ones. All these new movies where the hacker-slicer-stuff takes place, no thanks. I'll take the *Creature from the Black Lagoon* over *Halloween* and *Freddie* any day."

"Wow. The *Creature from the Black Lagoon*," Logan said as he set the chessboard up again. "What's that about?"

"It's about a creature," Gwen said, teasing him.

"And I bet he lives in a black lagoon," Emory added.

"Stick around," Jane announced. "We're watching that one next!"

By seven that evening everyone was slow to collect their things. It made Bridget feel like the perfect hostess when it became obvious that no one really wanted to leave.

"Come on, kids," Gwen said. "It's a school night. We need to get going."

Bridget made sure to send everyone home with enough leftovers to get them through a few more meals.

"And thanks for the veggie tray," Gwen said to Bridget. "My little vegetarian and I really appreciate it."

"They're good for all of us," Bridget said.

"So I'll see you in the morning?" Gwen said. "We're staking out the Starlight Condominiums, right?"

"Yes, we are. How about I pick you up at around six forty-five?"

"Perfect."

"We wanna go, too," Jane said in that little whiny voice she occasionally resorted to.

"You'll both get a full report as soon as we know something," Gwen promised.

"It's not the same," Lupita said.

"I know," Gwen agreed. "I'm sorry you two have to work."

They all gathered up the containers they had arrived with in addition to all the rest of the food Bridget was giving away. She turned on the porch light and held the door open for them.

"Watch your coffee intake in the morning, Gwen," Jane said once they were out on the sidewalk going to their cars. "You'll get all still in Bridget's car and then have to pee."

"Oh, you be quiet!" Gwen said with a laugh. "But thanks for the suggestion."

Chapter Seventeen

Monday morning Bridget was up early and was conscious of Jane's warning about not consuming too many liquids before leaving the house to pick up Gwen. But she decided that she needed at least *some* coffee to get her body jump-started at such an early hour. She took a quick shower to wake up and dried her hair while her Pop-Tarts cooled. Bridget never got up this early during the week since she taught afternoon and evening classes.

Cagney and Lacey on a stakeout, she thought with a smile as she carefully selected her clothes for the day. Bridget turned on the television to catch the weather. Dressing in layers seemed like a good idea from what she was hearing. Bridget settled on something and finally got dressed.

She left the house at six-thirty with a jacket, a small travel mug of coffee and one Pop-Tart wrapped in a paper towel. Her thoughts drifted back to the previous evening and the number of chess games she had won. It had been obvious that Logan and

Emory were not accustomed to losing. In addition, it had been awhile since Bridget had played against someone other than her father. It was nice to finally have a chance to win a few games! As she continued to contemplate the previous evening's events, she had also liked the way Gwen had been so open about her relationship with her ex-lover and their amicable breakup. She was looking forward to spending more time with her. She liked Gwen's humor and the relationship she had with her children. Bridget admired people who had the patience to raise kids. Having known from an early age that she wasn't interested in motherhood, she had had times during her life when she wondered who would be around to take care of her when she got old. Her nieces and nephews lived too far away to burden them with that sort of guilt. *You'll be on your own*, she thought after a moment. *Drooling with the other old dykes in the lesbian home.*

Even as early as her college days Bridget had thought the responsibility of bringing another person into the world was just too overwhelming. Back then she had been amazed that some people actually chose to have children on *purpose*. But she had mellowed a bit with age and learned to respect the choices others made. Gwen seemed to be doing a good job with her two kids, and she admired that. Bridget was happy being a doting aunt when she had the chance.

Once Bridget got on her way she realized that she was early enough to beat the majority of the morning traffic. She pulled into Gwen's driveway and was relieved to see the lights on inside the house. Bridget got out of her car and knocked on the front door. Logan answered it while tucking in an orange T-shirt with a flying skateboard on the front of it.

"Good morning," Bridget said.

"Hi. Come in." He held the door open for her. "Mom!" he called. "It's the chess hustler!"

That made Bridget laugh. *He doesn't remember my name*, she thought, but it didn't matter.

"The chest what?" Gwen asked as she came out of a room down the hallway brushing her hair.

"Chess," Logan said. "Not *chest*. We know where *your* mind is today."

"Oh, you be quiet," Gwen said with a noticeable glow on her cheeks. "Hi, Bridget. Let me get a sweater and a snack and I'll be ready."

"I get a rematch sometime, right?" Logan said to Bridget.

"I need lunch money," Emory called from the kitchen.

"It's on the table for you," Gwen said.

A car honked in front of the house, causing a sudden flurry of activity. Logan snatched up a stack of books and bent over to kiss his mother on the cheek and was gone before Bridget could turn around and tell him good-bye. Emory came out of the kitchen with half a bagel between her teeth as she scooped up the money on the table. "I've got rehearsal after school," she said after removing the bagel. She also kissed her mother on the cheek and grabbed some books by the door. "Bye, Bridget."

Bridget smiled and waved. *At least one of them remembers my name*, she thought.

Gwen stood on the porch and watched both kids get into the car. Once satisfied they were safely on their way, she closed and locked the front door.

Bridget glanced at her watch and was eager to get going. Today was the day she might see Kate the Lesbian again. The butterflies in her stomach made her even more conscious of how important this was to all of them.

It was too dark to do much of anything other than watch the gate at the Starlight Condominiums and hope that the cars leaving would go slow enough for them to get a good look inside. Each woman had a pair of binoculars and was scrunched down in the front seat of Bridget's car. All Starlight Condominiums residents had to drive under several powerfully bright streetlights on their way through the gate, which gave Bridget and Gwen a perfect angle to check out each vehicle as it left.

"Well, crap," Gwen said. "Do you see what I see?"

"What?" Bridget peered through her binoculars again, scanning the area past the gate and then deeper into the compound before cutting back to the guard station. About a dozen cars had left there since they had arrived twenty minutes earlier, but they hadn't seen anything resembling the Kate-mobile yet.

"What?" Bridget said again. "I don't see anything."

"We're fogging up the windows."

Bridget took her binoculars down and noticed that the windshield had indeed started to fog up from the bottom. Since she was taller, Bridget had been able to see through her binoculars.

"This won't do," she said, and started the car. She switched on the defroster and the windshield immediately cleared up.

"Much better," Gwen said. "It's been years since I've fogged up a car with a woman."

Bridget laughed and went back to watching the guard station. "Well, that was a first for me."

"Really? How long have you been out?"

"About fifteen years."

"Fifteen years and never fogged up a car window? How many exes do you have?"

"Three serious ones," Bridget said.

"What do you consider serious?"

"Moving in together then shopping around for pets."

"Yeah, the moving in together thing is a serious step," Gwen said. "The older my kids get, the more selective I've become. I'm not as willing to put them through all that again now."

"Do their friends at school know their mother is gay?"

"Some do. They even have a few gay kids that they hang out with. Our house can be a cornucopia of diversity on any given day."

Bridget smiled. "Your kids seem well adjusted."

"They've grown up around lesbians all their lives," Gwen said.

"It's as natural to them as anything else they've been exposed to." She sat up a little. "Do you see that?"

"I sure do," Bridget said as she focused in on the black sports car driving up to the security guard's station. Her heart was pounding so hard she wasn't sure she would be able to sit still any longer.

"Well, crap," Gwen said. "There's an old man driving it."

"For real?"

"Yup. He's turning right. We'll be able to see him better."

Bridget couldn't believe the disappointment she felt when she saw the old man's gray hair and beard come into focus.

"Crap," Gwen said again. "I thought for sure that was her."

"It's still kind of early. Her first class today isn't until ten."

"What if this is all a wild goose chase?" Gwen asked with a tinge of gloom in her voice.

"Then we do what you suggested the other night."

"What's that?"

Bridget laughed. "We go kick Consuelo's ass."

Once daylight arrived, they felt a bit more uneasy sitting across the street with binoculars zoomed in on the gate and the guard station. The cover of darkness had given them a sense of security that was seriously missing now. By eight-thirty the traffic going in and out of the gate had dribbled down to nothing, but they kept a continuous lookout for the Kate-mobile.

"Where did you go to school?" Gwen asked.

They had shared their breakfast of half a Pop-Tart and a slice each of spice cake.

"UT in Austin," Bridget said. "Then my master's at Our Lady of the Lake."

"Logan really likes UT's baseball program. He hopes to get a scholarship there." Gwen set her binoculars down and took off her sweater. Under it she had on a blue sweatshirt with a row of rainbow puppies across the front. "What's the longest relationship you've been in?"

"I've had two that lasted three years," Bridget said. "The first one was in college. We were roommates. After we graduated she decided she wasn't a lesbian after all and married the first guy who showed her any attention."

"Ouch. That must've hurt."

"Yeah, it did." Bridget scanned the far edge of the wall surrounding the condos before saying, "She'll leave him for a woman someday. She's a lesbian in denial if I ever saw one."

"Do you still keep in touch with her?"

"I get one of those Christmas cards with the 'this is what we've been doing all year' letters in it, along with a picture of the family. She's actually in touch with my parents more than me. We used to spend a lot of time here in San Antonio during long weekends and spring break. My parents adored her."

"So after graduation it was—"

"*Adios*," Bridget finished for her. "Have a nice life."

Gwen took her binoculars down and glanced over at her with a dumbfounded expression. "Just like that?"

"Just like that."

Bridget had long ago gotten over the devastation of that kind of rejection. She was happy to be at a place in her life where she could talk about it now and see things the way they were.

"What was your relationship like with her?" Gwen asked. "Roommates who occasionally slept together?"

"We were a couple. A hot and heavy lesbian couple. We had to tear ourselves away from each other to get our studying done. I'm not sure you can love another woman that way without being a lesbian."

"Wow. Well, I'm sorry that happened to you." Gwen took a sip of her bottled water. "So do you have any siblings?"

"I have two older brothers," Bridget said. "One is gay and lives in New York, and the other one is a computer programmer and lives in Dallas. He's happily married and has five kids." Bridget turned her head a little and focused in on the guard station again. No one had left through the gate for quite a while now. "What about you?" Bridget asked her. "Where did you go to school?"

119

"Here in San Antonio," Gwen said. "I went to nursing school at Incarnate Word."

"Is your family here, too?"

"I was raised in a children's home in South Texas for the first five years. I was in foster care after that."

Bridget didn't know what to say.

"I got married, had two kids, then admitted to myself that I liked women a lot more than I ever thought possible." Gwen laughed and took another sip of water. "I finally confessed to my husband and he wasn't surprised at all, which really shocked me. We lived together for a few more years after that for the sake of the kids. Then he met someone else."

"So the parting was a civilized one?"

"Oh, yes. He's a great guy and a good father. His wife teaches at the high school my kids attend. She's the one who picks them up every morning."

"You're lucky things have worked out so well."

"I know I am," Gwen agreed. "When I was attacked and was having so much trouble being alone in the house those first few weeks, Dan and Karen stayed over with us and helped me through it. I wouldn't be where I am right now if it weren't for them."

Bridget smiled. "You mean stuck in a Chinese restaurant parking lot spying on a stranger?"

"No! Hey, you know what I mean!"

By ten o'clock that morning they were both tired of sitting and disappointed at not having seen the Kate-mobile leave the condo grounds.

"Well, I've put it off as long as I can," Gwen said as she set her binoculars down. "I have to pee."

Bridget glanced at her watch and was depressed to see how late it was. "Three hours we've been here." She rubbed her stiff neck and moved her shoulders to try and loosen up a little. "There's a McDonald's down the street. Let's go to the bathroom there and maybe get something to drink."

As Gwen put her seat belt on, she said, "You know what I'm remembering?"

"What?"

"Something Consuelo said. I remember her saying that the fancy car was kept out at the barn sometimes. We've been sitting here looking for the Kate-mobile when she's probably driving something else."

Bridget nodded as she pulled out of the King Wa parking lot and headed toward a McDonald's about three blocks away. "That's right. I remember that too now."

"I say we take care of our bladders and then drive over to where this Ola Cordician's first class of the day is being held."

"Excellent idea."

Gwen reached inside her sweatshirt and pulled out her cell phone. "We need to call Jane and Lupita and let them know what's going on."

"I wish we had more news to tell them."

Bridget and Gwen knew Ola Cordician's Monday schedule by heart and didn't need to consult the information they had received online. It was a quarter after ten by the time they left McDonald's. Ola's first class was at Gwen's alma mater that just happened to be less than two miles away from where they had spent the morning.

"I've never been over here on this campus," Bridget said as she maneuvered her car through the narrow streets surrounding the University of the Incarnate Word.

"I see that parking still sucks here," Gwen noted. She pointed in the direction of the gymnasium and the indoor pool. "I suggest we park anywhere that's available for now. They couldn't get a tow truck back here if they tried."

Bridget found an illegal parking place with a sign warning her about it being in a tow-away zone, but she didn't care about that at the moment. They only had about thirty minutes to find the water aerobics class to see if Ola Cordician was teaching today.

"I'm glad you know where the pool is," Bridget said.

"Well, I used to. This place has built up a lot since I went here." Gwen unfastened her seat belt. "Now that I'm thinking about it, maybe just one of us should go looking for her. I remember they used to put those metal boot things on illegally parked cars. I'd hate for us to find her and then be stuck here dealing with some bubba campus police officer."

Bridget felt as though the air had been let out of her. Two disappointments in a row—the first being the lack of a Kate-mobile sighting at the condos and now being stuck in the car when Kate the Lesbian could be in one of the buildings in front of her.

"I'll find the class, go in, check out this Ola Cordician person and then come back, OK?" Gwen said.

"Yeah, sure."

Gwen unfastened her seat belt. "Oh, please don't sound that way." She put her hand on Bridget's knee, which sent a nice electrical charge shooting through her body.

Wow, Bridget thought. *What was that? How long has it been since a woman touched me that way?!*

"I'll be back as soon as I can," Gwen said. "Wish me luck."

It was all Bridget could do to keep her voice as normal as possible. "Good luck," she said hoarsely. She watched Gwen get out of the car and disappear around the corner of the building.

Chapter Eighteen

Bridget jumped when someone tapped on her window, causing her heart to almost leap out of her chest. She saw the blue uniform of a campus police officer and rolled down the window.

"You can't park here, ma'am," he said. He was tall and heavy with a black bristly moustache that had been trimmed too short. His voice was a bit high-pitched for a man's and didn't seem to match the rest of him.

"I'm sorry," she said. "I'm new here."

He pointed to the No Parking sign in front of her car. "That means the same thing no matter where you go or where you're from in these United States."

"Thank you, Officer." Bridget pushed the button to roll the window back up and put her car in reverse before he had a chance to write her a ticket. *Jerk*, she thought. Now she'd just have to drive around until Gwen came back.

The narrow streets on campus reminded her of trying to get

somewhere in a tiny European village. One-way traffic was the norm here mainly because there wasn't any room for more than one car traveling at a time. There was a vehicle parked at every conceivable place that could even remotely be considered legal. She wondered if there had ever been any potential students who chose to go to another local school solely because they couldn't find a place to park at this one during registration.

Bridget drove slowly and decided she'd somehow maneuver and circle around the campus and hopefully find Gwen waiting for her where she had dropped her off. When she finally made it back to where the campus police officer had originally spotted her, she found Gwen waiting by the No Parking sign.

Bridget pulled up and pushed a button to unlock the door for her. "Well?"

Gwen quietly slid into the seat, looking straight ahead with a blank expression on her face.

Well, hell, Bridget thought. *Ola Cordician isn't our Kate the Lesbian. Now we're back to square one.*

"I'm sorry I wasn't here," Bridget said. "The police ran me off."

It wasn't until Gwen leaned her head back against the seat that Bridget glanced over at her and saw a tear rolling down her cheek.

"Hey, are you OK?" Bridget asked with alarm.

"We need to find a place to park," Gwen said quietly.

"Ohmigod! It's her, isn't it? You found her!"

"Yes," Gwen whispered. "It's her."

Bridget's hands began to tremble as she gripped the steering wheel. *We found her,* she thought. *Finally, you'll get to thank this woman and get on with your life.*

"There's a Denny's across the street on Broadway," Gwen said. "Let's park there and walk back over here to the gym if we don't find anything else. I want you to see her too in case I'm just freaking out about it really being her."

As if a Parking Goddess somewhere had heard their silent pleas for assistance, Bridget spotted back-up taillights up ahead and was lucky enough to be the first in line for a legal parking place. She pulled in and shut the car off, feeling too nervous and excited to do anything else. Gwen reached over and took Bridget's hand and entwined their fingers together. Her steel grip told Bridget more than words could have.

"There's no Kate-mobile parked around here, right?" Gwen asked in a quiet voice a while later. She let go of Bridget's hand and folded her arms across her chest.

"No," Bridget said. "I would have seen it by now."

"Are you ready to go find her?"

Bridget took a deep breath. "Yes. I'm ready."

They got out of the car and both reached for their cell phones as they walked toward the gym. It had warmed up into the low sixties and the sun felt good against Bridget's face.

"Jane," Gwen said into her cell phone. "This is Gwen. It's her. I've seen her. Bridget and I are going back to the gym now to see if we can catch her after class."

Bridget pushed a button on her cell phone and called up Lupita's work number. She answered the phone right away.

"Lupita, it's Bridget. Gwen says Ola Cordician is our Kate. She got a good look at her a few minutes ago. We're on our way to the gym to see her now."

"We've found her already?" Lupita said quietly. "I hate being stuck here! I want to be there with both of you!"

"I know. We just wanted to let you two know what's going on. Gwen's talking to Jane right now."

"OK. Thank you for calling, and please let us know every detail. Please!"

"We will. Talk to you later." She ended the call and slipped the phone into her pocket. Gwen had also wrapped up her call to Jane.

"It's really chappin' Jane's butt not to be here with us," Gwen said.

"Lupita's pretty down about it, too." Bridget was so nervous that her stomach felt queasy. "Tell me what happened after you left the car earlier."

"I went into the gym and saw the women's basketball team

practicing. Then off to the side in the pool area I could hear the thumping bass of some old disco music. I went in there and saw about forty or so people in the deep end of the pool and . . ."

Bridget looked over at her as they continued walking toward the gym. Gwen seemed to be lost in thought for a moment.

"Are you certain it was Kate?"

"Wait until you see her," Gwen said with emotion in her voice. "We thought she looked good in black leather. Ohmigod, ohmigod. Just wait until you see what she does to black spandex."

Another unexpected chill raced up and down Bridget's arms. *Get a grip!* she thought.

"The gym's just around the corner and up the sidewalk."

"I heard you tell Jane we were going to try and catch Ola after class. Do you think that's a good idea right now?"

"What do you mean?"

"She might not like the idea of us knowing so much about her. I'd hate for her to bolt before Jane and Lupita get a chance to at least get a glimpse of her again."

"You have a suggestion?" Gwen asked, glancing down at her watch. "We need to have some sort of plan soon. Her class is over in about five minutes."

"I'd like to know what she's driving now," Bridget said. "We missed her leaving this morning because we were looking for the Kate-mobile."

"Good point."

"So I'm thinking we just sort of hang out by the gym and see where she goes after class."

"They have a name for this, you know," Gwen said with a slight grin. "Never in my wildest dreams would I ever have thought of myself as a stalker."

The gymnasium seemed small on the outside, but the doors faced a courtyard where shade trees with quaint benches around them momentarily took her mind off their mission. Bridget sat down on a bench the farthest away from the doors, while Gwen went to the other side of the courtyard and sat on one of the benches there. Gwen called Bridget's cell phone—they would relay information to each other that way.

"If short wet people start to come out, those are the swimmers," Gwen said. "The tall dry ones will be the basketball players."

Bridget smiled and kept her eyes focused on the gym doors. "I'll remember that."

"I've been thinking about what you said earlier and you're right," Gwen said. "We should be collecting as much information as we can about her for now. You, me, Lupita and Jane have been through all of this together. When we meet Ola Cordician for the first time, we should do it as a group."

"And if that doesn't scare the bejesus out of her, nothing will."

Gwen's laughter was nice to hear.

"I wish I had a book or something," Gwen said. "Do I look like a stalker?"

Bridget took her eyes away from the gym doors and glanced over at Gwen sitting on the bench across the courtyard. She was young and vibrant with the phone stuck to her ear.

"No."

"OK," Gwen said into the phone. "They're starting to come out now. The swimmers should be getting out of bathing suits and into dry clothes, while the jocks might stay sweaty and just be looking for lunch."

Four young women came out, each carrying a gym bag.

"Tall and dry," Gwen asked into the phone, "or short and wet?"

Bridget laughed. "You just said the swimmers would be changing into dry clothes."

"Yeah, I know, but they won't be drying their hair . . . oh-migod!" she hissed into the phone. "That's her! See her? Do you see her?"

Bridget squinted in order to get a better look at the woman in the spandex. She was tall and had long black hair. She wore a black jacket and carried a small backpack. Even though Bridget knew it would have been impossible to use them now, she still wished she had brought her binoculars from the car.

"It's her, right?" Gwen whispered into the phone, desperately wanting confirmation.

"I can't really tell from where I'm at," Bridget said into her phone.

"Ha! Well, she's walking toward you. Her car must be parked over there by you."

Bridget repositioned herself so it wouldn't look so much like she was watching someone. Ola Cordician had the grace of a dancer and the confidence of a woman who felt comfortable with her body. She held her head up high and walked with determination. The closer she got to Bridget, the more she began to look like the woman who had saved her life.

"It's her," Bridget breathed into the phone as her hands began to tremble again.

"I know," Gwen whispered back. "When she walks past you, I'll get up and follow her. I'll make my way over to your bench, then you follow her from there."

The sidewalk was only about fifteen feet from where Bridget was sitting under the tree. She got a better look at Ola when she walked by. *Ohmigod!* Bridget thought. *It's really her!*

Once Gwen got close to the bench where Bridget was sitting, Bridget got up and kept a reasonable distance behind Ola. More people were now leaving the gym and stirring about as other classes began to let out. Bridget didn't have to go far before Ola got her keys out of her backpack. She stopped next to a black Lexus and unlocked the doors with a remote on her key ring. Bridget glanced down at the license plate and attempted to memorize it. She walked across the street and headed back toward the gym, meeting Gwen on the sidewalk.

"She's in a black Lexus."

"There must've been five or six of those leaving the compound this morning," Gwen said. "Let's get back to your car and call the other two."

128

Once they were in her car again, Bridget found a pen and a piece of paper to write down Ola's license plate number.

"How about you call Jane this time?" Gwen suggested. "She's a bit too intense for me. We should have to share that duty."

"Yeah, OK." Bridget got her cell phone out of her pocket and called up Jane's work number. Once she got her on the phone, Bridget said, "It's her. Gwen and I both recognized her."

"Good job, you two!"

"She's driving a Lexus. It's a nice car, but not as sporty as the Kate-mobile was."

"So you guys just followed her around? You didn't try to talk to her?"

"We did a little stalking and found out what we needed for now."

"It's probably a good thing I've been stuck here at work all day," Jane said. "I would've been all gaga over her if I'd been there."

"That's not exactly the word I would use."

"Now what?" Jane asked. "Are you two going to follow her to her next class?"

"I don't think so. Our work here is done." Bridget glanced over at Gwen and smiled. "Besides, Gwen probably has to pee again already."

Gwen heard her and playfully smacked her on the arm.

"Well, Lupita and I are going to check her out this afternoon at Ola's last class. We want to see her, too."

"Don't spook her."

"We won't. Just a quick peek."

Bridget and Gwen ended their calls and put their phones away.

"How fast can you make it back to that McDonald's down the street?" Gwen asked. "You're right, smarty pants. I really do have to pee again."

Chapter Nineteen

They unloaded their individual trays and sat down at a corner table in the Alamo Heights McDonald's. Bridget felt such a keen sense of relief at knowing so much more about Kate the Lesbian now. She wasn't a cartoon character and she wasn't a figment of anyone's imagination. Too many of Bridget's dreams had Kate out-running speeding cars and flying like Superman when the bad guys tried to get away. *You need to stop thinking of her as Kate the Lesbian the crime fighter,* she reminded herself. *She's got a real name and she's a real person.*

"I can't remember the last time I had a meal from McDonald's," Gwen said.

They had been in separate lines to get their food, but ended up ordering the same thing.

"As bad as they are for me," Bridget said, "McDonald's still has the best fries."

"Oh, I agree. I just think of them as thin golden vegetables," Gwen said while unwrapping her Quarter Pounder. "Like squash sticks or something. And vegetables are good for you. A person's relationship with their food can be a beautiful thing." Her laughter made Bridget smile.

"You must eat a lot of vegetables at your house with Emory's fondness for them."

"I sort of tricked my kids into eating better when they were little." She cocked an eyebrow at the mound of foil packets next to Bridget's Diet Coke. "Got enough ketchup there, kiddo?"

With anyone else, the question might have embarrassed her, but instead, Bridget said, "It's not a burger without the proper amount of ketchup. So how did you trick your kids into eating better?"

"I would never let them have candy, but I would allude to the notion that all dried fruit and nuts were candy." Gwen chuckled as though the memory was a good one. "I'd leave little bags of trail mix in places where it sort of looked like I was hiding it from them. Then I'd pretend I was reluctant to let them have much of it. Now they love the stuff and prefer trail mix to cookies and candy bars."

Bridget finished doctoring her Quarter Pounder with three packets of ketchup on each side of her burger. "I wish I had better eating habits," she admitted. "My parents didn't let us have much candy either, but that didn't help me once I got out on my own."

She took a big bite out of her Quarter Pounder and within seconds a huge dollop of ketchup fell on her shirt. Bridget set her burger down in horror as she looked down at the mess on her chest. *Why didn't I see that coming?* she asked herself as she grabbed for some napkins. Her eyes opened wide with surprise when Gwen reached over with a French fry and dabbed it in the ketchup on Bridget's chest.

"No sense in wasting it."

Bridget looked down at her shirt again and laughed when the second fry gently plunged into the bright red glob on her chest. Her irritation and embarrassment slowly turned into light amusement as they both sat there dipping crispy fries into the concoction prominently displayed on the right side of her shirt.

After a while, Bridget gave up trying to hide the ketchup stain and decided to just keep her jacket on until she got home. Gwen's attempts to convince her that the stain looked like an unusual pendant weren't working, but Bridget did notice that her personal discomfort over her stained shirt wasn't nearly as unsettling with this woman as it would have been with someone else. At one point Gwen suggested they draw some legs on the stain so people would think she had an exotic red bug perched there.

"No, that's OK," Bridget said as she pulled her jacket on.

"I have a question," Gwen said. "Do you think Ola Cordician is really a lesbian?"

"Truthfully? No. She's not radiating any lesbian vibes my way at all."

"Me neither," Gwen said with a disappointed edge to her voice. "Then why would she pass out cards stating that she was?"

"I don't know. Women shouldn't need to use that sort of thing as an excuse to be strong and kick some ass when it's needed."

"Not all lesbians are strong."

"Don't I know it." Bridget dunked her last French fry into a fresh pile of ketchup on her burger wrapper. "But isn't that how the general public sees us—strong and independent? Like Amazons who for various reasons can't get a man?"

"Is that how they see us? I'm lucky to work in a profession where being gay is normal."

Bridget shrugged. "Maybe we're wrong about her. Maybe she is a lesbian and our gaydar is just whacked on this one."

"Maybe," Gwen said reluctantly, "but I don't think so. I think there's something else going on with her and all this lesbian stuff."

"Like what?"

"Like I don't know yet, but I do know this much. I'm not just in this now to meet her and thank her for saving my life. I want to know why she went to so much trouble to have us think she's a lesbian."

"We don't know for sure that she's *not* a lesbian," Bridget reminded her.

"She's not. I feel it in my bones." Gwen's certainty was reflected in her animated eyes. "And you know what else? I want to know how she knew where to be when each of us needed her. That's been messing with my head ever since I found out there were other women that she'd helped. That's just too weird, Bridget. Something's up with that."

"I'm thinking I know enough already. And maybe I even know too *much* already."

"Ha! Not me. I want to sit this woman down and have a looong chat with her. I've had time to think about it, and I need some questions answered."

"Maybe we should talk things over with the other two and see what they have to say."

"It doesn't matter to me what Jane and Lupita have to say. If no one else feels this way, that's fine. But I want some answers. I'll approach this woman alone if I have to."

Bridget sighed heavily and shook her head. "Well, at least wait until Lupita and Jane get a chance to see her first. After that the three of you can do whatever you want. But if you scare her off before those two see her again, that's not going to sit well with them."

Gwen folded up her burger wrapper and placed it neatly on the tray. "I'll wait awhile before I do anything. So you're telling me you're not the least bit curious about how Ola's made all of this happen?"

"Sure I'm curious, but not curious enough to confront her about it. What do you plan to do, walk up to her in a parking lot and start asking her questions? The woman carries a gun, for crissakes."

"Hmm. The gun. I forgot about that."

Bridget grinned. "Let's not give Kate the Lesbian a reason to want to do away with us, too. She's a kidnapper, remember? I'd hate to see the three of you tied up in some barn with those other dregs of society."

133

"She couldn't get all three of us in the trunk of her car," Gwen said with a laugh.

"Once she starts waving that gun around, she can do anything she wants to."

Gwen picked up her Diet Coke and took a sip. Her devious grin caught Bridget's attention.

"What are you thinking about?"

Gwen chuckled. "Can you imagine how cool it would be getting stuffed in a trunk with Jane and Lupita?"

"Cool?" Bridget squeaked. "Are you nuts? I think my claustrophobia just kicked in." She rubbed her throat to keep herself calm.

"Let me rethink this a bit further then." Gwen shook her head. "You're right. She carries a gun and she's a kidnapper. Have you always been so logical and conservative?"

"I think maybe 'chickenshit' is the word you're looking for. That would best describe me in most situations."

Gwen tilted her head back and laughed. "Not at all. Besides, is 'chickenshit' one word or two?"

"According to Merriam Webster, it's one," Bridget said. Gwen's laughter became even more outrageous as they cleaned up the table and got ready to leave.

Bridget drove back to Gwen's house. They both needed to spend some time winding down and getting ready for work. She parked in the driveway and Gwen opened the car door.

"Can you come in for a few minutes?"

Bridget checked her watch and saw that it was after one already. "I need to get going."

"Well, it was fun today. We were good little spies."

"I've waited a long time to see her again. In a way, I'm feeling this sense of disappointment that the search is over."

Even though the door on the passenger's side was open, Gwen wasn't making any effort to get out of the car yet.

"Will I see you again?" Gwen asked quietly.

Shocked by the question, Bridget said, "Of course you will. Why wouldn't you?"

"I was just wondering. I plan to call Lupita and Jane so we can make plans to meet with Ola. You've made it clear that you're not interested in doing that."

"And now I'm out? No more brainstorming?"

"What happened today seems to be enough for you," Gwen said. "I can see you leaving a Hallmark thank you card under her windshield wiper while she's off somewhere teaching a water aerobics class. That'll be enough for you." Gwen shook her head. "But it's not enough for me, and I'm betting it won't be enough for Jane and Lupita either."

"So that's it?" Bridget asked. She could feel the heat rising in her face. "I don't get to hang out with any of you now if I don't agree with everything you decide to do?"

"That's not what I said. Hey, don't get your knickers in a wad."

"Leave my knickers out of this." Bridget was already into a full-fledged pout. "It's been nice knowing you."

"Oh, get over yourself. This isn't about you. This is about truth and curiosity. You're willing to wave at a distance while the rest of us want to shake this woman's hand and grill her for answers."

"Yeah, whatever." Bridget felt tears on the way and she wanted desperately to be alone.

"Yeah, whatever," Gwen repeated and got out of the car.

Bridget barely waited until Gwen was in her house before she left. Her drive home was done through the blur of tears.

Chapter Twenty

Bridget hated the fact that she spent the rest of the afternoon either crying or too angry to rationalize what had happened. It never occurred to her that she could lose her new friends over something as simple as her need to avoid confrontation. What kind of friends were they if that could happen? She called her therapist, but couldn't get an appointment until later in the week. She felt lonely and emotionally out of control.

"Great," she mumbled as she looked in the mirror at her puffy eyes and glowing red nose. There was no way she could ever hide the fact that she was upset. Her face always gave her away like a blinking neon sign advertising her distress.

She took a shower and stayed under the hot spray until the numbness she felt inside slowly began to wash away. After her shower, Bridget put on more makeup than usual in hopes of hiding her red nose.

"No more crying," she told herself as she looked in the mirror.

"So what if the three of them are off on a new adventure without you?"

Wrong thing to say, she thought as another tear rolled down her cheek. *Get a grip*, she reminded herself. *You have to be in front of thirty students in over an hour.*

Bridget woke up late the next morning and felt groggy from too much sleep. The covers on the bed were as scrambled as her hair. It had been a fitful night of tossing, turning and wild dreams of abandonment and confusion. She was too tired to do anything, and too depressed to even want to pull herself out of this funk she now found herself in. A shower sounded like a good idea and would hopefully make her feel better. She had to teach a five o'clock class that afternoon and still had some papers to grade. She wasn't in a mental place where she could concentrate well enough to do her students justice at the moment, but she anticipated being there after a strong cup of coffee.

After her shower, the phone rang. Bridget glanced at the caller ID in hopes of seeing Gwen's phone number there, but it was her mother instead.

"Bridget, dear," Mrs. McBee said, "your father and I are going to Los Patios today for lunch and we're wondering if you'd like to meet us there."

"Actually, I haven't been up long and I'm just about to have my first cup of coffee."

"It's almost ten! You're just now getting up?"

"Long night," Bridget said, in no mood to try and explain herself to her mother.

"We'd love to see you for lunch," Mrs. McBee said. "Let us know if you change your mind."

Maybe getting out would do you some good, Bridget thought, but then just as quickly she decided against it. Staying at home sulking all day in her jammies sounded like a better idea to her.

"Maybe another time," Bridget said, "but thanks for asking."

"Then we'll see you later this week."

Once Bridget got off the phone with her mother, she went to fix another cup of coffee. A few minutes later Jane called.

"Lupita and I saw Kate or Ola What's-Her-Name yesterday afternoon," Jane said excitedly. "Gwen told us where her last class of the day was, so after work we went on our own little stakeout in the Morningside Manor parking lot."

Bridget could easily picture them in the front seat of Jane's car, much like she and Gwen had done the previous morning. Now it seemed more like weeks ago instead of just yesterday that they'd been together.

"How did you feel when you saw her?"

"Intense relief," Jane admitted. "I also felt proud of all of us for our resourcefulness and determination. We did some amazing things, Bridget. We kept an open mind and followed our instincts. We should all be proud of that."

Bridget smiled. "I am and you're right. We should be."

"We know more about all of this than the police and those reporters do. I'm just happy we stayed vigilant in our pursuit."

"Hmm," Bridget said, wondering if that had been a little zing at her decision to leave Ola Cordician alone. Bridget didn't really know Jane well enough to tell whether or not she was being critical.

"After we did our stakeout," Jane continued, "Lupita and I went to dinner and talked for about two hours. We were so excited we couldn't shut up. Then Gwen called me on my cell phone and we went over to the hospital to see her."

Already they're doing things without me, Bridget thought sadly. She plopped down on the sofa with the phone pressed to her ear.

"What time did you two get to the hospital?"

"It was about eight-thirty," Jane said. "We planned our next strategy. That was fun. We had a lot of good laughs."

Bridget felt a sinking sensation in the pit of her stomach. *At eight-thirty I was still in class,* she thought. *They've moved along so easily without me.*

"Aren't you going to ask me what our next bit of strategy is going to be?"

Bridget sighed heavily and realized hearing all of this hurt much more than she ever imagined it would.

"Not really," she said with another sigh.

"Well, I'm going to tell you anyway. We came up with two different plans. The first involves Ola what's-her-name."

"Cordician."

"Yeah, whatever. Anyway, we want to leave a note on her car to see if she'll meet with us. It needs to be something brief and anonymous. Maybe leave a cell phone number or an e-mail address."

"Why should she trust us?" Bridget asked. "She's committed some serious crimes, according to the police. Any contact we make might spook her."

"Hmm," Jane said. "Good point. We need your sense of logic, Bridget. That was missing last night during our brainstorming session."

"Sure it was," Bridget said with a cynical smirk.

"Hey, it *was!* I'm the one who still wants to scale the wall at her condo compound, remember? Look, Bridget. We're all in this together and we each bring something different to the table. Some of us are better at certain things than others. Gwen and I would have no problem now walking up to Ola and letting her know who we are and what we want, so it's important for the two of us to have you and Lupita around to reel us in when we get that way. You're part of the balance. You and Lupita are the glue that holds this team together!"

Bridget smiled. *How pathetic is that?* she wondered. *Someone refers to you as "glue" and you're all happy about it. Yes, Bridget old girl! You need to call your therapist again and see if you can get an earlier appointment!*

"So will you help Lupita with all this glue business?" Jane asked. "She missed you a lot last night once Gwen and I started talking about various ways we wanted to get Ola's attention."

"I appreciate you doing this," Bridget said. The lump in her throat was a clear indication what Jane's phone call meant to her.

"So you're back on the A Team?"

"Think of me as a glue stick at your service."

Jane's hearty laughter made Bridget laugh, too. She couldn't believe how much better she felt over this silly glue conversation.

"We're meeting at Gwen's house after work tonight. Can you make it?"

"I'm teaching a class this afternoon. I can't be there until after seven."

"Excellent. I'll let them know. Thanks for . . . for . . ."

"No," Bridget said. "Thank *you* for calling. I feel a lot better about things now."

"Tonight will be important. We need to figure out what to do next, so give it some thought before you get to Gwen's house."

Chapter Twenty-one

Bridget spent the majority of the afternoon trying to figure out what exactly it was that she wanted. *Maybe a few answers would be nice,* she thought. *So if I do happen to want more information about Ola Cordician, what would I be willing to do to get it?*

She didn't like not being a part of the group, so making that clear to the other three women was first on her agenda. *Then after that,* she thought, *what would be the best way to approach Ola with what they all wanted?*

A note under the windshield wiper on her car, she thought. *First of all, if something like that was on my car, I'd be irritated knowing someone had been close enough to touch my vehicle in such a way. Secondly, I probably wouldn't give it more than a five-second glance, so the message or subject line needs to grab her attention right away. If we don't get her attention immediately, there's a good chance the note, letter or card will end up on the floorboard of her car and won't be given another look.*

All the way over to the San Antonio College campus that afternoon, Bridget thought about the various scenarios they could use to contact her. *A card wouldn't be tossed aside,* she thought. *A sealed card would probably be the best way to get her attention. But then maybe sending her an e-mail would be better,* Bridget thought. *Was her e-mail address on the résumé Logan downloaded for us?* she wondered. *If we don't have it yet, that'll be easy enough for one of us to get. That's how most instructors communicate with their students these days, but we'd need to make sure she didn't delete the e-mail. It would be pretty easy to think of it as spam.*

Bridget found a good parking place at work and collected her briefcase and a jacket from the front seat. She checked her surroundings and saw several students leaving and some just arriving. She was early enough to get something to eat before her class started.

This e-mail idea, she mused while paying for a ham and cheese sandwich and a bag of chips. *To keep Ola from deleting it, we could have the subject line say "Kate The Lesbian." Ha! She would open it then! OK, OK, OK,* Bridget thought as she took a seat in the corner of the break area near a row of vending machines. *So we get her attention and she opens the e-mail. Then what?* she wondered. *What do we say to her in the e-mail?*

"Hello, Ms. McBee," a young voice beside her said.

Bridget looked up to see one of her students from her Monday night class carrying a tray and sitting down at the table next to hers.

"Hello," she said with a smile. "What class do you have this evening?"

"American History," he said, pulling out a chair. "My dad says it'll help make me a better citizen."

"Something this fine country of ours could use a lot more of," she said. Glancing at her watch, she picked up the unopened bag of chips and put it in her briefcase for later. She had ten minutes to get to her class.

❧

Bridget spent a few minutes after class answering questions from her students. After that she found a security guard to walk with her to her car.

"Thanks, Roscoe," she said as she found her keys in her purse. There was a chill in the air and promises from the weatherman for rain to arrive later that evening.

"Not a problem, Ms. McBee," he said.

Once Bridget was safely in her car and out of the SAC parking lot, she was able to give more thought to the e-mail idea. *What should we say in the e-mail?* she wondered. *Keeping it simple would be the best way to handle things. We need to tell her who we are without giving our names,* Bridget thought. *Should we ask to meet her, or do everything through e-mail?*

She pulled onto the expressway and shook her head. *Maybe having Jane and Gwen approach her in the Morningside Manor parking lot is a better idea,* she thought. *We'd get it over with and not have to wonder if she was deleting our e-mail.* With a shake of her head she thought, *As long as Ola didn't use her gun on them, we'd be fine.*

Bridget saw Jane's car parked behind Gwen's in the driveway and felt a twinge of irritation that the other three women were in there talking without her. *For crissakes get a grip,* she reminded herself. *One hour a week with a therapist might not even put a dent in all the things you need to cover these days.*

She parked in the street in front of the house and rang the doorbell. Logan answered and smiled as soon as he saw her.

"Back for a rematch?" he asked.

"Maybe if we have time later. Is your mother here?"

"In the kitchen with the others."

Bridget made her way to the kitchen, where she could hear the laughter and chatter long before getting there. Jane saw her first, and her beaming smile and expressive eyes made Bridget feel better. She loved being with these women and felt such a huge sense of relief at their delight in seeing her again.

"Sorry I'm late."

"We've been waiting for you," Lupita said. "Sit here. We saved some pizza."

"The glue has arrived!" Jane said.

Bridget sat down across from Jane and had Gwen on her left and Lupita on her right. A paper plate with a slice of mushroom pizza appeared in front of her along with an ice-cold Diet Coke in a can.

It's a good thing I'm thirsty and a little hungry, she thought.

"I hope you can come up with better ideas than what these two have," Lupita said. "They're starting to scare me."

"So what's been going on?" Bridget asked. "What do we have so far?" She took a bite of cold pizza and loved it.

"These two want to join one of her water aerobics classes and get to know her that way," Lupita informed her.

"Hmm," Bridget said with a slight shrug. "That's better than the 'scaling the compound wall' idea I've been hearing."

"Yeah, but I'm not too happy with the idea of having to get in a bathing suit," Gwen said. "I'd need to go on a diet first. Hell, just thinking about dieting made me hungry. Pass me another slice of pizza."

The sound of their laughter was just what Bridget needed. *Instead of paying my therapist seventy-five bucks a visit,* she thought, *maybe I should just pay these three women twenty-five dollars apiece since they seem to be all the therapy I need.*

"What are your thoughts on what our next step should be?" Lupita asked her.

"I'm thinking we should put a note on her car or perhaps send her an e-mail," Bridget said.

"Do we have her e-mail address?" Jane asked.

"We had her résumé, but I don't know where it is right now," Gwen said. "She's probably got it listed there. Let's see if Logan can find something for us."

"If it's not on her résumé," Bridget said, "I'm sure her students have it or can get it for us. I know I have a special e-mail address at school that I only give out to my students. I get faculty announcements on it, too. She probably has the same setup there at Incarnate Word."

Gwen left the kitchen and came back a few minutes later. Bridget also told them about her flyer-on-the-windshield idea.

"But that's less likely to get her immediate attention than an e-mail with a 'Kate the Lesbian' subject line will."

"No shit," Jane said.

"OK," Lupita said. "So let's say we send her an e-mail, we have her attention, and she opens it up. Then what? Any ideas what it should say?"

"It's like Bridget mentioned earlier when we discussed this briefly," Jane said. "We don't want to spook her."

"Yeah," Gwen agreed. "She's got a gun and some of us have seen her use it."

"I'm not interested in pissing her off," Jane said with both palms up and out in front of her. "I personally like this side of the dirt myself."

Chuckles went around the table.

"Somehow we need to let her know that we're on her side, and we just want a few answers to some questions," Bridget said. "The most non-threatening way to do that would probably be through e-mail, if she'll cooperate with that."

"I agree," Gwen said. "We've all seen her now and we know she's real. I could live with e-mail answers to my questions. How about the rest of you?"

Jane bobbed her red head from side to side. "Maybe. It depends on how detailed her answers are."

"What if this e-mail idea doesn't work?" Lupita asked. "Then what do we do?"

"I say we scale that compound wall and go knock on her door!" Jane said.

A short while later Logan came into the kitchen and handed his mother several sheets of paper. Apparently Ola Cordician had two

145

different résumés posted online and each one had the same two e-mail addresses listed.

"All faculty at Incarnate Word have an e-mail address associated with the University, just like Bridget said," Gwen announced as she perused the papers.

"That's probably the e-mail address she gives her students," Bridget said.

"I'm also thinking that's not the one we should use," Lupita said. "If our subject line on the e-mail will be 'Kate the Lesbian,' that's not something we want out there on the University's server."

"Good point," Jane said. "I think we should go with the other e-mail address she has listed."

Gwen left the table and came back with a legal pad and a pen, which she handed to Bridget. "You're the English professor. You write the e-mail."

Bridget suddenly felt nervous. Were they really about to do this?

"I say we keep it short and sweet," Lupita said. "Less is more sometimes."

"Not if you're talking about sex, it isn't," Jane said.

All three of them looked at her and burst out laughing.

Chapter Twenty-two

Bridget picked up the pen and tried to concentrate, but she couldn't stop thinking about how important this e-mail would be. She was certain they would get Ola to open it with the subject line they had decided on, but the tricky part was knowing what exactly should go in the message itself. As she began to write, her three friends gathered around her chair and looked over her shoulder. One of the women had their hand on Bridget's back, and she wasn't surprised to see that it was Gwen touching her. With pen in hand, Bridget began to write. When she finished, she read over the first draft, crossed out a few words here and there, and added several more. Once she was satisfied with it, she held up the tablet for the others to see more clearly. The paragraph said:

> *We are four lesbians who were saved from rape and certain death by someone calling herself Kate the Lesbian. We believe you are that person and we have*

*gone to great lengths to find you and thank you for
saving our lives. In addition, we have some questions for
you that we need answers to. We will leave it up to you
how to best make this happen. Thank you for your
courage, strength and time. We are forever in your
debt.*

Four Grateful Lesbians

"It's perfect," Lupita said. "It's like an invitation for her to open up some dialogue with us."

"And I love how you signed it," Gwen said with a little rub on Bridget's back. "Four Grateful Lesbians, indeed. That's exactly who we are!"

"Whose computer should we use?" Jane asked. "We don't want to give ourselves away too quickly."

"I've got CINBAD on the computer here," Gwen said. "We can make up a screen name and send it tonight. She won't be able to tell anything about us from that."

"Wow!" Jane said. "Can you believe we're really doing this?"

"It sure as hell beats that wall-scaling thing you keep talking about," Gwen noted. "Logan," she called. "Come here. We need you!"

Logan made the screen name they told him they wanted. Their new e-mail address was 4Gr8fulLesbians@CINBAD.com. After the preliminaries, Logan turned the computer over to Bridget, who typed up the e-mail with a subject line that simply stated "Kate the Lesbian." She made everyone read it over several times before holding up a shaking hand for all to see.

"Why am I so nervous?" she asked with a laugh.

"Hey, I'm just standing here watching and it's making me nervous, too," Jane admitted.

Bridget clicked the mouse and officially sent the letter on its way.

"How often do you check your e-mail?" Lupita asked Gwen.

"Usually once a day," Gwen said. "Friends and coworkers send me jokes and things. But now I'll be checking it about every two hours or so!"

"Well, if you hear back from her," Jane announced, "I wanna know!"

"Me, too," Bridget and Lupita chimed in at the same time.

"I don't care what time it is or where I am," Jane clarified. "Call me. I want to know what she says. Wow. I'm almost as jazzed right now as I was when we saw her in the parking lot yesterday."

"Mail's here," the computer said.

All four of them froze right where they were. The flag on the little mailbox was up and a little yellow envelope was sticking out of the box.

"Holy shit," Jane breathed. "Did she read it already? Ohmigod! Is that her?"

"Chill, mama," Gwen said calmly. "We probably just got spammed or something."

With Gwen being more familiar at checking e-mail on this server, Bridget got up from the chair and let her sit down.

"It could even be someone wanting to increase my penis size or something," Gwen said. "Or maybe it's CINBAD welcoming us under a new screen name." She held up her hand to show the others how badly hers were shaking, too.

"Well, open it up already, for crissakes," Jane said. "It might be Ola What's-Her-Name wanting to check *our* penis sizes!"

Gwen placed the arrow on the mailbox on the screen and clicked. A menu for a list of incoming mail popped up and there sat a response from "Cordician" and an e-mail with the subject line that read: RE: Kate the Lesbian.

"Holy shit," Jane said. "It's *her!* She answered us already! Open it! Open it!"

"Mission Control," Gwen mumbled, "we have contact." She double clicked on the e-mail and opened it up.

There on the screen in large red, bold letters was: I DON'T KNOW WHAT YOU'RE TALKING ABOUT!

"What?!" Jane bellowed. "She's denying us? She's going that route?"

"It's OK," Lupita said calmly. "That's a normal reaction under the circumstances. At least we know she received it and read it."

"Well, now what?" Jane barked.

"We send another e-mail," Bridget said simply.

Gwen clicked on the Reply button and got up out of the chair and made Bridget sit down again.

"Start composing," Gwen said. "We've got her attention. Like Lupita said. Let's open up the dialogue. Damn the torpedoes and full speed ahead, mates."

Bridget began to type.

We know who you are and what you've done for each of us. We are convinced that Ola Cordician and Kate the Lesbian are the same person. We mean you no harm. All we want are some answers to a few of our questions.

"How's that look?" Bridget asked as she read over her message one more time.

"Perfect," Lupita said.

"'We mean you no harm,'" Jane repeated. "Sounds like we're communicating with aliens on a space ship or something. Send it . . . and hurry up before she signs off."

Bridget clicked on the Send button, hurling their new message out into cyberspace.

"She's not going anywhere," Gwen said with a new degree of confidence. "She's glued to her computer and shaking in her boots right now."

Jane held up a trembling hand for all to see. "You mean like this?"

"Yeah, like this," Gwen said as she held up a shaking hand of her own. "She's probably more nervous than we are."

"You think so?" Bridget asked. She turned her head toward the left and Gwen was right there, leaning closer to get a better look at the computer screen. Gwen put her hand on Bridget's back and gently rubbed.

"Mail's here," the computer said, making all four of them jump.

The arriving mail announcement made the tingling warmth of the back rub fade from Bridget's body.

"Holy shit," Jane said once more. "That's her again!"

Bridget clicked on the little yellow envelope sticking out of the mailbox, which brought up the e-mail screen. There it was: another response from Ola Cordician. Bridget double-clicked and opened it up. In bold red letters on the screen were the words: LEAVE ME ALONE!

"Well, crapola," Jane said. "Now what do we do?"

"We could threaten her with Smokey," Gwen suggested.

"And the Bandit?" Jane added. "You think that would work?"

Once again their laughter brought them through what could have been and should have been an intense, difficult moment.

"No!" Gwen said over the laughter. "Smokey the reporter. Sheesh. Smokey and the Bandit," she mumbled. "You're showing your age, Jane. Maybe we should let Ola know that if she doesn't tell us what we want to know, then perhaps we'll be letting a reporter in on all we've discovered so far."

"Our goal is to help protect her and thank her for what she's done for us," Lupita reminded them. "Not threaten her."

Bridget stared at the three words on the screen with a vague sense of uneasiness. She cleared her throat and said, "I think there's something we're all overlooking here."

"What's that?" Lupita asked.

"What are the chances that she already knows where the ten of us live?"

"If Smokey found us, I'm sure Ola could, too," Gwen replied with a nod.

"And that Harper guy," Jane added. "He called Lupita on her cell phone, so our information is known by a lot of people. Why? What are you thinking?"

Standing up straighter by the chair Bridget was sitting in, Gwen asked, "Do you think Ola would try and hurt us?"

"We know nothing personal about this woman," Bridget said, "especially in terms of how stable she is." Mentally kicking herself for not thinking all of this through better, she added, "If she's nuts, she could be on her way to one of our houses right now looking for us."

"Holy shit!" Jane said. "You really think so?"

"Send her another e-mail!" Lupita said.

There was a renewed sense of energy in the room as they all stared at the screen again. If Ola Cordician didn't have a firm grip on reality, then it was possible that none of them were safe now.

"OK, OK, OK," Bridget said as her hands began to tremble again. "Lupita's right. We need to send another e-mail. As long as we keep her talking here, she can't be prowling around town looking for us."

She clicked on the Reply button and began to type.

Answer our questions, and you'll never hear from us again.

"How's that?" Bridget asked.

"Send it," Lupita said.

"That's all you're going to say?" Jane asked. She had her arm around Lupita's shoulder and gave her a hug.

"That's all we need to say," Lupita commented.

"Send it," Jane agreed.

Bridget clicked the Send button and sighed heavily. She felt exhausted and her back was tight with tension. Then as if Gwen were somehow able to read her mind, Bridget felt hands massaging her neck and shoulders. A slow moan escaped from her throat as she relaxed and moved her head to get the full effect of what was happening to her.

With her eyes closed, Bridget dreamily whispered, "You have no idea how good that feels."

"We're all a little tense," Jane said.

Logan came into the room for a book and Gwen sent him to the kitchen to bring back more chairs. She never stopped what she was doing.

"It's great having kids once you get them out of diapers and into school," Gwen said as she continued to rub Bridget's neck and shoulders. "I enjoy all that 'bring Mom this' and 'bring Mom that' stuff."

"I remember those days when I was the one doing all the 'bringing,'" Bridget said as she moved her neck around. Gwen's fingers slipped up into her hair and behind her ears in a gentle, sensual dance. The door to the room opened and Logan, Jane and Lupita each came in with a kitchen chair. Bridget was so into the massage that she hadn't realized the other two had left.

"You know what I was thinking?" Jane said as she placed her chair beside Bridget's. "We should have some questions ready in case Ola lets us ask her something."

Gwen's laughter made the others laugh, too.

"You're right," Lupita said. She reached for some paper and a pen on the computer desk and was immediately poised to write. "So what's our first question?"

"I want to know how she knew where to be each time," Jane said without preamble.

"Yeah, me too," Gwen said. Her fingers were back to slowly rubbing Bridget's neck again.

"OK," Lupita said while writing. "Question number two?"

"How about—"

"Mail's here," the computer said.

"Holy shit," Jane barked with a flinch. "That thing gets me every time!"

"Open it up!" Lupita said.

Bridget clicked on the mailbox and brought up the list of e-mails received. She double-clicked on the latest "Cordician," opening the e-mail. It read: WHAT QUESTIONS DO YOU HAVE?

"Ha," Gwen said gleefully. "We're in!"

Chapter Twenty-three

"Type up this question," Lupita said, handing over the piece of paper she had been writing on.

Bridget typed: *How did you know where to be each time a woman was about to be assaulted?*

"How's that look?" Bridget asked after her English-professor eyes had scanned the question for typos and verb agreement.

"Perfect," Lupita said. "Send it."

"Now for question number two," Jane said.

Bridget clicked on the Send button and began to relax again with Gwen's fingers slowly moving up into her hair.

"Anyone have an idea what question number two should be?" Jane asked. "We need to be prepared here."

"I'd like to know what she plans to do with the men she took away," Lupita said in a low, steady voice. "Rudy's mother has been inconsolable since he disappeared. Ola's answer might also give us some insight into her own state of mind."

"Good idea," Gwen said. "Write that question down." She

lifted part of Bridget's hair off the back of her neck and began to massage more tense muscles.

"Did anyone notice what happened with Ola's last e-mail?" Jane said. "By asking us about our questions, she's no longer denying who she is. I think that's a major breakthrough. At least on her part."

Lupita finished writing question number two and set the pen down on the computer desk. "This would be so much easier if we could talk to her in person or at least on the phone."

"She probably wouldn't go for that," Jane said. "I doubt if any of us would be comfortable with it either."

"Mail's here," the computer said.

All four of them stared at the screen. Bridget reached for the mouse and clicked on the yellow envelope sticking out of the little mailbox in the corner. She opened the e-mail that said: IT'S TOO COMPLICATED TO EXPLAIN.

"Hmm," Bridget said as she clicked on the Reply button and typed a one-word answer.

Try.

Over the next forty-five minutes, the following e-mail exchange took place:

Cordician: I HAVE DREAMS.

4Gr8fulLesbians: *Dreams? What do you mean?*

Cordician: I SEE THESE UNFORTUNATE EVENTS IN MY DREAMS.

4Gr8fulLesbians: *The dreams tell you where to be?*

Cordician: YES.

4Gr8fulLesbians: *So you're psychic?*

Cordician: NO. SOMEONE IS SENDING THE INFORMATION TO ME FROM BEYOND.

4Gr8fulLesbians: *You've had ten dreams about women being assaulted and because of those dreams you've been able to help them. Is that what you're saying?*

Cordician: YES. BUT THERE HAVE BEEN MORE THAN 10 DREAMS. THERE HAVE BEEN 12 DREAMS. TWO OTHER NEAR-ASSAULTS WERE NOT REPORTED.

4Gr8fulLesbians: *What happened to those other two women?*

Cordician: THEY RAN AWAY RIGHT AFTER I LEFT THEM AND BEFORE THE POLICE ARRIVED.

4Gr8fulLesbians: *You said someone was sending you the information through your dreams. Who is that person?*

Cordican: WHAT OTHER QUESTIONS DO YOU HAVE?

4Gr8fulLesbians: *What will you do with the men who assaulted us?*

Cordician: WHAT OTHER QUESTIONS DO YOU HAVE?

Bridget sat back in the chair and could feel the tension returning to her neck and shoulders. The other three were also sitting beside her now staring at the computer monitor.

"Looks like Ola doesn't want to tell us anything else," Jane said. "Maybe it's time to turn it up a notch. Type this, Bridget. Type, 'We know the men are being kept in a barn in Wilson County. What will you do with them?'"

Bridget smiled, typed the e-mail, and sent it on its way.

"There," Jane said. "If she's going to launch on us then that should do it."

"I guess I'm missing something here," Lupita said. "Why do we want her to launch? To me, intentionally provoking an unstable person doesn't sound like a good idea."

"She's getting complacent now," Jane said. "Ola isn't shaking in her boots anymore. We've been playing it safe and we're non-threatening. We need to get her adrenaline pumping again in order to keep her interest and to keep her talking."

"Mail's here," the computer announced. Bridget clicked on the yellow envelope sticking out of the mailbox.

Cordician: HOW DO YOU KNOW WHERE THEY ARE??!!

"Aha!" Jane said. "See? We have her attention again. Type this, Bridget. Type, 'We had a dream.' See what she says then."

Gwen laughed. "Oh, you're bad, Jane. But I love it when you're bad."

Bridget typed the response and sent it off. She moved her head around to try and loosen up the muscles again. She wasn't used to dealing with so much intensity. It wasn't long before the computer announced, "Mail's here."

Cordician: TELL ME HOW YOU KNOW ABOUT THOSE FILTHY BASTARDS IN THE BARN!!

"OK," Jane said. "The Cordician adrenaline is off and spurting now! Type this, Bridget. 'We'll tell you what you want to know if you tell us who the person is that's sending you the dreams.'"

Bridget typed as Jane spoke. The four of them read the response over carefully before agreeing to send it off.

After the new message was on its way, Lupita asked, "How much information do we want out of her?"

"Hmm," Jane said. "I don't know. Probably all we can get."

"Are we really ready to have her answer our questions and then just leave her alone?" Lupita asked.

"Sure," Jane said. "Why not?"

"I think I'd miss Ola and all this Kate the Lesbian drama that's going on," Lupita admitted. "Right now we've got this . . . this . . . this Ola thing to focus on. We're united because of our experiences with her. Once all of that gets resolved, what will we do with our spare time?"

"I know what you mean," Gwen said. "I wake up every morning wondering what adventure or mischief the four of us will come up with next. The meetings, the stakeouts, the *curandera*, the sniffing reporters—"

"Scaling the wall," Jane added.

"Yeah!" Gwen said with a laugh. "Scaling the wall. I've never had so much fun in my life. I'm not sure I want to end our relationship with Ola either."

"But we told her we'd leave her alone if she'd answer our questions," Bridget reminded them.

"So we lied," Gwen and Jane said at the same time.

"Mail's here," the computer finally announced. It had been nearly twenty minutes since their last communication. Three of them had spent the time getting fresh drinks, while Gwen checked on her kids and their homework.

"Wow," Jane said. "She's back."

Bridget returned to the computer and opened the e-mail. It was a long one, which made her feel better.

Cordician: TWO YEARS AGO MY YOUNGER SISTER WAS KILLED BY A STALKER. HER KILLER WAS FOUND, BUT ESCAPED WHILE IN POLICE CUSTODY. RECENTLY MY SISTER HAS BEEN COMING TO ME IN MY DREAMS. SHE TELLS ME IN DETAIL HOW OTHER WOMEN WILL BE ATTACKED. THE DREAMS ARE SO VIVID THAT IT'S BEEN EASY FOR ME TO SEE WHERE THE EVENTS WILL BE TAKING PLACE AS WELL AS THE TIME OF NIGHT THEY ARE GOING TO HAPPEN. SOMETIMES I'M WAITING CLOSE BY WHERE I CAN SEE WHAT'S GOING ON AS THINGS BEGIN TO UNFOLD. IT'S FRIGHTENING HOW REALISTIC THE DREAMS ARE. THERE HAVE BEEN TIMES WHEN I DON'T WANT TO GO TO SLEEP FOR FEAR OF WHAT I MIGHT SEE NEXT. IN THE BEGINNING . . . AFTER I HAD ONE OF THE DREAMS AND WAS ABLE TO STOP AN ASSAULT, I THOUGHT PERHAPS THE MAN I HAD FORCED INTO MY CAR MIGHT POSSIBLY BE THE ONE WHO HAD KILLED MY SISTER. BUT THAT WASN'T THE CASE BECAUSE MORE DREAMS KEPT COMING AND THE NUMBER OF EVIL MEN KEPT INCREASING. I FINALLY REALIZED THAT MY SISTER WAS USING ME TO HELP OTHERS FROM WHEREVER IT IS SHE'S AT NOW. THAT'S THE PURPOSE OF THE DREAMS. IT'S THE ONLY WAY I CAN EXPLAIN WHAT'S HAPPENING. THAT'S ALL I KNOW. IT'S WHAT I BELIEVE. I'VE ANSWERED YOUR QUESTION. NOW YOU NEED TO ANSWER MINE. HOW DO YOU KNOW ABOUT THE MEN IN THE BARN?

"Whew," Gwen said with a huge sigh. "How awful. Can you imagine having dreams like that?"

"It must be horrible," Lupita said. "Dreams vivid enough to tell her what and where things will happen."

"Now what do we do?" Jane asked.

Bridget took a deep breath and felt unsettled by Ola's explanation. "We have to tell her about Consuelo, without giving out any names or too much information about her."

"Will she believe us?" Lupita asked.

"We're pretending to believe *her* story," Jane said. "It's only fair that she pretends to believe ours."

"Let's work on our answer," Gwen said. "How terrible it must be to have dreams like that. When I'm sleeping, I want pleasant thoughts and peace and quiet."

"OK, Bridget," Jane said. "Type this."

They spent a good ten minutes composing their response.

4Gr8fulLesbians: *We are saddened by your sister's passing and we all know personally how horrifying such violence can be. We have you and your sister to thank for saving our lives. To answer your question, we consulted with a curandera to help guide us to you. This person had general information that was quite accurate, very much like the information your sister has been sending to you. The clues we received from the curandera helped us eventually find you. Our original purpose was to discover who you are and to personally thank you for saving our lives. We and our families owe you a tremendous amount of gratitude. Now we only have three more questions to ask you, then we'll leave you alone. Our first of the three questions is—What will you do with the men in the barn? Please answer as best you can.*

"How does that look?" Bridget asked.

"It looks good to me," Lupita said.

"Me, too," Jane confirmed. "Send it."

Bridget clicked on the Send button and took a deep breath. She wondered if they would really be able to leave Ola Cordician alone if she answered all of their questions. And would the four of them remain this close to each other without this diversion in their lives?

159

Chapter Twenty-four

They waited another ten minutes or so for Ola's answer. When her e-mailfinally arrived, all four women were disappointed in what she had to say.

Cordician: I DON'T KNOW.

"What the hell?" Gwen said. "She's got a dozen perverts in a barn and she doesn't know what to do with them?"

"Does she think she can just leave them there?" Lupita asked.

"Well, what would *you* do with them?" Jane wondered out loud. "She can't let them go."

"Hmm," Gwen said with pursed lips. "I know what I'd *like* to do with them, but I'd never have the guts to do it."

"We need to say something here," Bridget reminded them, pointing to the monitor. She clicked on the Reply button and waited for some guidance from the others. Over the next twenty minutes, the following electronic conversation took place:

4Gr8fulLesbians: *You can't just leave them there in the barn.*

Cordician: I CAN'T LET THEM GO. THEY CAN IDEN-TIFY ME.

4Gr8fulLesbians: *How often do you check on them?*

Cordician: OFTEN ENOUGH. THEY HAVE ALL THEY NEED. WHAT OTHER QUESTIONS DO YOU HAVE?

4Gr8fulLesbians: *Are you a lesbian?*

Cordician: NO.

4Gr8fulLesbians: *Why did you lead everyone to believe you are?*

Cordician: IF YOU'RE REFERRING TO THE CARDS I LEFT FOR EACH OF THE WOMEN, THOSE CARDS WERE NOT FROM ME.

4Gr8fulLesbians: *What? Explain. Who were they from? You gave one to each of us.*

Cordician: THE CARDS ARE FROM MY SISTER. I JUST DELIVERED THEM.

4Gr8fulLesbians: *What was your sister's name? Was she a lesbian?*

Cordician: HER NAME WAS KATRINA. SHE WAS CALLED KATE ALL HER LIFE . . . AND SHE REFERRED TO HERSELF AS KATE THE LESBIAN WHENEVER SHE DISCUSSED HER SEXUALITY.

4Gr8fulLesbians: *Did she tell you to give each of us a card?*

Cordician: NO. I MADE AND DISTRIBUTED THE CARDS IN HER HONOR. SHE IS THE ONE WHO MADE IT POSSIBLE FOR EACH OF YOU TO BE UNHARMED. I HAD VERY LITTLE TO DO WITH IT.

4Gr8fulLesbians: *I'm sure we can speak for all twelve women when we say how grateful we are to both of you.*

Cordician: WHAT OTHER QUESTIONS DO YOU HAVE?

"OK," Bridget said as she clicked on the Reply button again. "What other questions do we have?"

"I don't know," Jane said. "She's answered them all, but how much of what she says can we believe? Or do we want to believe?"

"Yeah, this is all kind of far-fetched," Gwen admitted, "but so was our explanation about how we found her in the first place, and all of that was true."

"We need another question here," Bridget reminded them again.

"Ask her if there's any way we can help her," Lupita said.

"By doing what?" Gwen asked. "Holding her gun while she stuffs the next guy in the trunk?"

"I don't know," Lupita said with a shrug. "Maybe there's a way we can help her get out of this kidnapping thing. And what if one of those scumbags dies while she has them locked up? She'll be held responsible for that, too."

With fingers poised on the keyboard ready to type, Bridget said, "So what's our next question?"

Lupita leaned forward. "Type, 'Is there anything we can do to help you?'"

Bridget typed the message and sent it on its way. A few minutes later they received an answer back.

Cordician: NO. THERE'S NOTHING ANYONE CAN DO. WHAT OTHER QUESTIONS DO YOU HAVE?

"OK," Bridget said. "Now what?"

"This is it, peeps," Gwen announced. "We either get real chatty with her again, or we have to cut her loose."

"Well, crapola," Jane said. "It's getting late, I'm tired, and I can't think of anything else to ask her, but I'm not ready to cut her loose yet."

"Me neither," Gwen agreed.

"But we promised her we would after our three questions," Bridget reminded them again.

"We lied," the other three replied.

"So give me something to type here!"

There was a sufficient amount of "hmms" and "uhhs" going on around her, but Bridget didn't hear anything helpful until Lupita finally said, "Ask her if she's tried to contact her sister in any way other than through her dreams."

"What?" Jane and Gwen said at the same time.

"There's no hotline to heaven, baby," Jane murmured.

"I think the hotline goes in the other direction," Gwen said.

"Her sister is obviously not at peace wherever she is," Lupita said, ignoring them. "Forgive me. I'm a recovering Catholic. I'm finding myself sympathizing with her restless dead sister. She could still be waiting in purgatory or something."

"Whoa, babe," Jane said as she put her arm around Lupita and pulled her closer. "We need to work on that. You're having a little Catholic relapse there."

They weren't too tired to chuckle. Gwen poked Bridget in the arm.

"Remember what Consuelo said to us? She told us that the woman in the fancy car would need our help, so maybe Lupita's got something there."

"I'm not holding any gun while Ola stuffs a sweaty fat guy in her trunk," Jane said, making the others laugh.

"That's not the kind of help she needs," Gwen said. "I see her as having two problems. Bridget, start typing. I'm having a brainfart here. Let's get it all down before we lose her."

4Gr8fulLesbians: *We see two problems. (1) You are being sought by the police for kidnapping. (2) You have a restless sister who is using you to help other women. We think we can assist you with both of these things.*

Cordician: HOW?

4Gr8fulLesbians: *Who owns the barn where the men are being kept?*

Cordician: WHAT OTHER QUESTIONS DO YOU HAVE?

"She always sends that message back when she doesn't want to answer the question," Bridget noted. "Has anyone else noticed that?"

"Ask her if she has any great fondness for this country," Jane suggested. Bridget typed and sent the question.

Cordician: WHY DO YOU ASK THAT?

4Gr8fulLesbians: *We can arrange to have the perverts released from the barn, but you would need to be out of the country when it happens.*

Cordician: OUT OF THE COUNTRY FOR HOW LONG?

4Gr8fulLesbians: *Possibly forever.*

Cordician: THAT IDEA DOES NOT APPEAL TO ME.

4Gr8fulLesbians: *How does the thought of twelve counts of kidnapping appeal to you?*

Cordician: THAT DOES NOT APPEAL TO ME EITHER.

"Hey, will you look at that?" Jane said. "Our Ola might have a tiny sense of humor."

"Now what?" Bridget asked.

"OK, OK," Gwen said excitedly. "Type this, Bridget. I'm having another brainfart."

4Gr8fulLesbians: *We suggest you get your affairs in order, get a passport if you don't have one already, and plan to go to Mexico, Canada or somewhere in Europe.*

Cordician: FOR HOW LONG?

4Gr8fulLesbians: *You may never be able to return here if they discover who you are. You have no choice. You can't stay here in this country and be safe.*

Cordician: THIS IDEA DOES NOT APPEAL TO ME.

"What the hell?" Gwen said after reading Ola's last comment. "I had hopes that she was smarter than the slugs she's been kidnapping. Type this, Bridget."

4Gr8fulLesbians: *Right now if you were to be caught, you would be facing twelve counts of kidnapping. That is a long prison sentence. If one of those perverts happens to die while you have them in the barn that becomes a murder charge. Right now you are in more trouble for kidnapping them than they would be for attempted rape or assault on the women. Eventually the perverts will be found. The curandera told us that you keep the Maserati Spyder there near the barn. The police will eventually be able to trace that car to you.*

There was a lengthy wait after Bridget sent the e-mail. She glanced at her watch and saw that it was after ten already.

"So that's our plan?" Lupita asked. "We get her out of the country? Then what?"

Bridget moved her neck and shoulders around to try and relieve some of the tension. Gwen was behind her and began massaging her neck and shoulders again. "We tip off the police or one of those reporters on where the judge or the banker are being held," Bridget said. *Jesus that feels good,* she thought. "No one really cares about the others, but the police will do what they can to at least find the judge."

"If Ola leaves the country," Jane said, "I get dibs on the Maserati Spyder!"

"Ha!" Gwen said. "Like hell you do!"

Their laughter helped pass the time as they waited for Ola's answer.

"Do you think she'll go for this leaving the country idea?" Lupita asked.

"If not, it'll only be a matter of time before she gets caught," Gwen said. "Nobody said life was fair."

"Mail's here," the computer announced. Bridget clicked on the little yellow envelope.

Cordician: LET ME THINK ABOUT IT.

4Gr8fulLesbians: *Don't think too long. If you decide to leave, it needs to happen quickly.*

Cordician: WHERE WOULD I GO? I HAVE A SUCCESS-FUL CAREER HERE.

4Gr8fulLesbians: *You can probably do what you do practically any-where in the world.*

Cordician: THIS DOES NOT APPEAL TO ME.

4Gr8fulLesbians: *We see prison and ugly uniforms in your future.*

Cordician: THAT DOES NOT APPEAL TO ME EITHER.

"We're getting nowhere with this line of thinking," Gwen said after reading what Ola had sent.

"Let's get back to the sister," Lupita suggested with a yawn. "I think Consuelo could help us with that."

"The witch?" Jane said. "How so?"

"I don't know exactly."

"This purgatory thing has you wrapped up pretty tight, babe."

"We need another question here," Bridget said, pointing to the monitor.

Pulling away from Jane's attempt to hug her, Lupita said, "Tell her we want to meet with her to discuss her sister."

"What?!" the other three said.

"I think all of us, including Ola, should go see Consuelo and see what she has to say."

"First off," Jane said, "I'm not at all interested in meeting Ola face to face. She might decide to whack us all and stick us in the barn, too."

"I'll meet with her myself," Lupita said defiantly.

"I need a question here," Bridget reminded them. "Ola won't stay glued to her computer much longer if the questions don't keep flowing."

"You're not meeting this woman alone," Jane said adamantly.

"No," Gwen agreed. "We're all in this together."

"Type this," Lupita said as she stood up and started to pace.

4Gr8fulLesbians: *Your sister's inability to be at peace now is of concern to us, as we're sure it is to you. While you're thinking about our suggestion that you relocate, it might be helpful if we try and explore the issues that continue to plague your sister now. Do you agree?*

Cordician: WHAT DO YOU MEAN?

4Gr8fulLesbians: *You can't continue communicating with her this way. The violence will eventually get someone killed.*

Cordician: HOW CAN I NOT HELP THESE WOMEN?

4Gr8fulLesbians: *Maybe instead of doing all of this yourself, you can tell the police about it and they can be the ones to stop the attacks instead of you.*

Cordician: I TRIED THAT AFTER THE FIRST DREAM. THE POLICE WOULD NOT TAKE ME SERIOUSLY.

4Gr8fulLesbians: *Maybe they will now that the dreams have been right twelve times in a row.*

Cordician: PERHAPS, BUT I'M NOT WILLING TO TAKE A CHANCE ON TRUSTING THEM.

4Gr8fulLesbians: *Would you be interested in seeing the curandera with us to see what we can find out about your sister?*

Cordician: NO. I CAN'T TAKE THE CHANCE OF

LOSING CONTACT WITH KATE. THAT IS IMPORTANT
TO ME.

4Gr8fulLesbians: *You can't continue on this way. How much sleep
do you get a night?*

Cordician: I HAVEN'T SLEPT IN TWO NIGHTS. I'M
AFRAID TO SLEEP.

4Gr8fulLesbians: *Can't you see how this is affecting you? We also
believe that as long as you have good memories of Kate, she will always be
with you.*

Cordician: SHE NEEDS ME TO AVENGE HER DEATH,
OR PERHAPS FIND THE ONE WHO KILLED HER. THAT
IS MY SOLE PURPOSE NOW. I WANT TO FIND HIM.

4Gr8fulLesbians: *So if you were to find the stalker who killed Kate,
do you think she could finally rest?*

Cordician: MAYBE.

"That's it," Lupita said. "That's how we do it. We get Ola to
Consuelo's place, and I bet we can find out where Kate's killer is
with Consuelo's help."

"You think so?" Jane asked with an arched brow. "*Then* what do
we do?"

"Take the info to the police," Lupita said. "The case is still open
and unsolved. Ola said the guy escaped. He's out there somewhere."

"So we find him and then what?" Jane asked.

Lupita shrugged. "We can phone in a tip. They'll be all over it."

"This is getting way out of hand," Gwen said. "We went from
wanting to meet someone we thought was Kate the Lesbian to
tracking down a murderer. When did that happen?"

Someone tapped Bridget on the shoulder. She looked up to see
Lupita standing behind her.

"Get up, please," Lupita said with an edge to her usually calm
voice.

Bridget got up from her chair and moved out of the way. Lupita
sat down and began typing.

4Gr8fulLesbians: *We've given you some good suggestions and advice. The next step is up to you. We want to help you. Call this number to make arrangements to meet when you're ready . . . 555-4312. Good night.*

"What?!" Gwen yelped as Lupita clicked on the Send button. "You sent her your phone number?! Are you nuts?"

"I don't believe you did that," Jane said. "We weren't finished talking to her!"

"There was nothing else left to say," Lupita said.

Bridget stretched and was personally glad the e-mail exchange had been brought to a close. *Lupita is right*, she thought. *We weren't getting anything else accomplished.*

"Can you take me home?" Lupita asked Bridget quietly.

Surprised, Bridget nodded. They collected their things and within only a matter of seconds, Lupita was at Gwen's front door ready to go.

"I'll take you home," Jane told her.

"That's OK," Lupita said. "I have a ride. Are you ready, Bridget?"

"Yes. Sure. Good night, you two."

On the way out Gwen's front door and on down the sidewalk to her car, Bridget felt the tension in the air. She wasn't quite sure what had just taken place, but it had looked and sounded very much like a lover's quarrel.

Chapter Twenty-five

Bridget didn't notice the drizzle until she had to switch on her windshield wipers. It was getting colder outside and her jacket felt good against the evening chill.

"That woman infuriates me sometimes," Lupita said as she fastened her seat belt. "Making fun of someone's religious beliefs is so uncouth."

"I think it's Jane's nature to make light of things she doesn't understand."

"It gets old fast."

They rode a while in silence with nothing more than the occasional swish of the wipers in the background. Finally, Lupita said, "Would you be up to going to see Consuelo tonight?"

Bridget's eyes widened at just the thought of doing something so spontaneous, not to mention the fact that they would be venturing out on their own without the other two.

"If you're not interested, I'll find someone else to go with me."

"Of course I'm interested," Bridget said, nudging her surprise and uneasiness to the side. "I find that woman fascinating. Are you sure she's open this late? It's almost eleven."

"I'm not sure about anything anymore."

Bridget drove over toward the side of town she remembered them being in before. A while later they were stopped at a railroad crossing with a few other cars. The drizzle picked up its pace, reminding them once again that winter was on the way.

"What are we going to ask her?" Bridget wondered out loud as they sat there waiting for the train to pass.

"It just seems like things wouldn't have gotten so complicated if the police were involved in this Ola and Kate situation," Lupita said. "Are there any police departments that use paranormal tools to solve cases?"

"Maybe on TV," Bridget said, "and then certainly not to prevent a crime. Only to solve one after the fact."

"There needs to be some sort of task force that'll work with Ola on this. She's in such a unique position to help people."

"She's a criminal herself now," Bridget reminded her. "There's not much we can do about that."

"Maybe Consuelo can help us see another angle with this problem."

"Just our luck," Bridget said as she watched the train slowly come to a complete stop on the tracks. Even though it was late, she didn't mind being stuck there with Lupita. It reminded her of the first night they had met at the Resource Center. That night seemed like such a long time ago now.

"I love weather like this," Lupita said. "Fall is my favorite time of the year."

"Mine, too. A light rain is so nurturing and relaxing to me." Bridget glanced in her side mirror and could see several cars behind them backing up to find an alternate route, while the two cars in front of her turned off their engines to wait.

"You've never been married?" Lupita asked.

"No. That's one mistake I saved myself from making."

"I wish I had done the same. You're lucky to have come out in time to prevent that. I spent a long time in denial. That's why I got involved with someone like Rudy in the first place." Lupita leaned her head back against the headrest. "By the time I figured out who I was and what I really wanted, I was in a bad marriage and dreading each and every new day."

"That's no way to live."

"I agree. In a lot of ways, I'm lucky. At least there weren't any children involved." Lupita smiled. "I have a gay sister. She hates Rudy with a passion. Whenever they were together at a family function she was in his face about his macho attitude."

"How long have you been out?" Bridget asked. She felt as though she were taking a gamble asking the question since she remembered how Lupita had been tap dancing around that information several times already.

"Officially?" Lupita asked.

Bridget laughed. "What constitutes an 'official' lesbian?"

"For me? Admitting it to myself. That happened about six months ago. I left my husband and was trying to get my life together. We were in debt with nothing to show for it. Rudy couldn't hold a job and my salary couldn't support both of us along with his drinking and gambling habits. Ever since then it's been a struggle for me having to deal with his family day after day. With Rudy missing, his family hasn't let up about me filing for a divorce."

"Can you get a divorce with him missing?"

"Everything's been put on hold because of that," Lupita admitted with a sigh. "I haven't told his family, though. In my head, just knowing the paperwork is out there and will be moving forward again someday brings me peace of mind. I'm also able to sleep at night knowing Rudy's not around to cause more trouble."

"His family might leave you alone if they knew the divorce can't go through without finding him first."

The train started to move again and took its time inching and chugging along. As soon as the last train car was in sight, the vehicles in front of them started their engines.

"Do you know where we are?" Lupita asked once they were on their way again. "I think you turn left up there at the corner."

They drove on for a few more blocks before Bridget saw the

171

palm tree in the yard. She parked in front of Consuelo's house. It was dark inside and there was only one car in the driveway.

As if losing confidence in this being such a good idea, Lupita said, "I expected there to be more people here."

"What would you like to do now?"

With a sharp pang of disappointment, Bridget grimaced when she heard Lupita say, "Let's see if she answers the door."

With the drizzle beginning to turn into a light rain, they got out of the car and slowly made their way up the sidewalk. A dog next door began to bark, setting off several others in the neighborhood. For Bridget, the feeling in the air as they got closer to the porch was so strikingly different this time without Jane and Gwen by their side that it made this bit of spontaneous insanity even that much more bizarre. *It's that safety-in-numbers thing*, Bridget thought. *You do better with a crowd.*

The porch light came on just seconds before Lupita reached for the doorbell. The clicking of metal locks being opened from the inside made Bridget's skin tingle with momentary fear and anxiety.

"Come in," the voice said through the crack in the door. "I've been expecting you."

Bridget sighed with relief and was eventually able to smile. *What a great line for someone in her profession.*

They went inside and Consuelo switched on a light in the waiting area. The wall full of glass candles and the display cases filled with various herbs and potions came into focus.

"We weren't sure you were open," Lupita said quietly.

"If I'm home, I'm open," Consuelo said as she held the door to her office for them. "You found the woman with the fast car."

"We did," Lupita confirmed.

"What can I do for you now?"

They sat down in front of the huge wooden desk while Consuelo switched on the lamp and lit the cigar that was in the full ashtray. After blowing three perfect smoke rings, Consuelo took her seat behind the desk and looked at them.

172

"You need my services?"

Bridget was relieved to know that Lupita was once again ready and willing to take control of things.

"We found the woman we were looking for, thanks to you," Lupita said. "We've also discovered that she has a lot of problems."

"We all have problems."

Bridget couldn't agree more with that statement.

"Hers seem to be more complicated than most."

"Bring her to see me."

"I'm not sure that's possible," Lupita said.

"Then she doesn't want my help."

"But *we* want your help."

Consuelo took another puff of the cigar and set it down in the ashtray again.

"There's a man who thinks about you," Consuelo said as she looked directly at Lupita. "He has difficulty expressing himself."

"That has to be Rudy."

Consuelo gave her a half nod and half a shrug. "Violence against women is all he knows. He learned that from his father."

"I don't want him in my life now."

"You'll only have to deal with that for a short time where he is concerned."

"He needs to stay wherever he is now. I hope to be rid of him soon."

Consuelo smiled and gave her another half nod. Picking up the cigar again, she said, "Excuse me. I'll be right back. We have company."

Bridget and Lupita looked at each other curiously just moments before hearing a car drive up outside and some car doors close. Consuelo got up and left the room to let the new arrivals in.

"If she's home, she's open," Bridget said. Lupita's smile and its sweet sincerity made Bridget feel good about her decision to go with her to visit Consuelo, but nothing had prepared either of them for the arrival of Gwen, Jane and Ola Cordician.

⁂

"Well, look at this," Jane said as the three of them came into Consuelo's office. "What are you two doing here?"

"We're probably here for the same reason you are," Lupita said with a snippy edge to her voice.

Gwen helped Consuelo bring more plastic chairs into the room, while Ola stood back out of the way looking as if she were about to bolt. Dressed in black pants, a black shirt and a black jacket, she was everything Bridget remembered her being the first night they had met in that dark San Antonio College parking lot.

"How did you get her here?" Bridget whispered to Jane.

Jane leaned closer to her and whispered back, "We first convinced her to meet with us and Gwen suggested we see if Consuelo was available for a consultation. We tried to make her sister the issue. We figured that would be the only way to get her here."

"Everyone take a seat," Consuelo said as she closed her office door. "You're the woman with the fast car," she said to Ola. "We have a lot to talk about."

Bridget leaned over toward Lupita and quietly relayed the information Jane had just given her.

"Everyone sit down," Consuelo said.

Bridget found it hard to believe that all of them were there together. How could Jane and Gwen have convinced Ola to reveal herself this way in such a short period of time? Bridget tried stealing a glance down the row toward Ola, but couldn't really see anything without being obvious. *Does she have her gun on her?* she wondered. *Everyone in this room knows who she is and what she's done. What the hell were those two thinking bringing her here?!*

"What can I do for you?" Consuelo said to the group.

There was a certain amount of leaning and chair-creaking as a few of them tried to get comfortable in their plastic seats.

"We were wondering," Jane started, "uh . . . how discreet are these consultations?"

Consuelo gave a slight nod and reached into the wooden box to retrieve the deck of cards.

"I'll go to my grave knowing many secrets," she said simply.

"What happens in this room stays in this room as far as I'm concerned."

More creaking began as someone else molded her body into an uncomfortable plastic chair.

"My initial impressions were that a group interaction would be best," Consuelo said, "but perhaps separate consultations would be more appropriate."

There was an uneasy silence followed by more chair-shifting. Bridget now wished she and Lupita were sitting closer to the door. Consuelo shuffled the cards as if it were second nature to her. She looked at Ola and squinted in an attempt to see her better. With the cigar smoke in the air all around her, Consuelo once again reminded Bridget of a seedy gambler as she began to slowly turn the cards over one at a time.

"You have questions," she said to Ola.

"These women have been quite persuasive," Ola said.

Jane leaned to her right toward Bridget and whispered, "She means us. Me and Gwen. We were the persuasive ones."

Consuelo reached for the cigar and took another puff before setting it back in the ashtray.

"You want to believe in all that they've told you." Consuelo turned over another card. "There's no way to assign logic to what I do. I've been blessed with a gift that can't be explained. I think I can help you, but you must be patient and keep an open mind."

"I can do that," Ola said.

Bridget strained to hear her, feeling as though she might be able to tell from the sound of Ola's voice whether or not she was a stable person. Bridget wished a hundred times over that she had just taken Lupita home.

"You have a weapon," Consuelo said as she turned over another card.

Bridget heard a slight gasp come from Jane and an unfamiliar chuckle down at the far end of the row.

"That's very good," Ola said. "I don't leave home without it. Please continue. I'm listening."

Consuelo turned over another card. "I feel the presence of someone close to you. She's reaching out to you from the other side."

"The other side of what?" Jane asked.

"Be quiet!" Lupita hissed.

Bridget was surprised by the exchange, but glad someone had made an attempt to keep everyone but Ola and Consuelo talking. *This isn't about us any longer,* Bridget thought. *This is about Ola.*

"I see the number twelve," Consuelo said. "She's emphasizing that number."

"Twelve?" Ola said. "Why twelve?"

"That number is significant to her."

"Any idea why?"

Consuelo reached for the cigar again and took a puff, squinting in Ola's direction. "There might be a way to find out."

"How?" Ola asked.

"We can try to make contact with her," Consuelo said. "I've done this before at the request of other clients. I'm a medium."

"A medium, eh?" Jane said. "You look more like an extra large to me."

Chapter Twenty-six

After the chuckling settled down, Consuelo squinted through the cigar smoke and gave Jane a long, piercing look.

"Always the funny one," she said. "If there's someone in the room who is not a believer, then I suggest they leave. If we're able to reach the other side, it will be easier to maintain contact if everyone cooperates."

"You mean you're going to try and reach Ola's dead sister?" Gwen asked.

Consuelo took another puff on the cigar. "All I know is there's a deceased young woman who has something to say. She can't rest until that's accomplished."

"How will we know who it is?" Gwen asked.

"She'll be speaking through me," Consuelo said. "I assume someone here will know her and understand what she'll be trying to say."

"Like Whoopi Goldberg in *Ghost*," Gwen said. "Wasn't she a medium in that movie?"

"Nah," Jane said. "She was more like an extra large, too."

"Oh, puhleeze," Lupita groaned. She leaned over toward Bridget and whispered, "That woman irritates the hell out of me."

"I strongly suggest the funny one go in the other room," Consuelo said.

"No! Wait!" Jane said. "I'll be quiet. I promise!"

"You're a disruption," Consuelo said firmly.

"No, really," Jane pleaded. "I promise. You won't hear another peep out of me."

Consuelo looked at her. Jane was directly across the desk from her. "You either leave or the session is over. I could be in bed right now."

There was more noisy shifting in the plastic chairs. Bridget understood completely where Consuelo was coming from. If they were about to attempt to connect with the other side, there had to be cooperation from everyone. There were times when Jane's approach to things she didn't understand bordered on the obnoxious. Bridget imagined that Consuelo had zeroed in on that a lot quicker than the rest of them had. Banishing her from the room now would save Consuelo from having to do it later after things were underway. Jane had already gotten on Consuelo's bad side and there wasn't anything she could do to change that.

"Off to the other room with you," Gwen said finally. "I'll fill you in later."

"This sucks," Jane said.

She got up and left the room, closing the door behind her. Bridget had a mental picture of Jane on the other side of the door with an ear pressed against it.

"What now?" Ola asked.

Consuelo picked up the cards and put them in the wooden box. She took another puff on the cigar and moved the ashtray to a small table behind her.

"Let's try it this way first. Move in closer," she instructed. "Hold hands with the woman nearest you."

They scooted their chairs toward Consuelo's desk. Bridget's

knees touched the front of it, but she noticed that Lupita wasn't able to reach Consuelo's outstretched hand that well.

"On second thought, it'll be better and more intimate if we put our chairs in a circle," Consuelo said. She came out from behind the desk and took Jane's empty seat. As they all moved their chairs around, it was obvious how much easier it would be to hold hands this way.

Consuelo sat between Lupita and Ola, while Bridget was across from Ola and had Gwen on her left and Lupita on her right. *I wonder where she has her gun?* Bridget mused as she looked at Ola's regal and impeccable posture. *There aren't any bulges on her anywhere.*

"I can practically smell the fear," Consuelo said. "Everyone just relax. This is a painless exercise. At least painless in a physical sense."

There was more wiggling and plastic chair creaking as they all sat down to get comfortable again. Bridget was convinced that the fear Consuelo was sensing had to be coming from her. She found herself wishing over and over again that she hadn't agreed to do this.

"Please be patient," Consuelo said. "These things take time to develop. There's also the possibility that nothing will happen. Everyone hold hands with the woman nearest you."

Gwen reached for Bridget's hand and she noticed right away that Gwen's palm was sweaty. *At least now I know I'm not the only nervous one,* she thought. Lupita's hand, however, was soft and warm. Bridget liked the way it felt in hers, as if the simple act of touching this way had an intimacy all its own.

The room was quiet and Bridget was suddenly glad to be a part of whatever was about to happen. Something as simple as holding Lupita's hand was enough to make her no longer regret being there. *What a fickle thing you are,* she thought with a little eye roll.

Consuelo said in a low voice, "Open your mind and free yourself from whatever troubles you."

As if Consuelo had been speaking directly to her, Bridget began to relax as she closed her eyes. *Everything will be fine*, she thought. *You're with friends and we're here to help Ola.* She could feel Gwen's hand trembling in hers, but then eventually she also seemed to relax. The room was so quiet Bridget could hear the rain on the windows . . . so peaceful and soothing she could probably go to sleep sitting there.

Then as if a herd of buffalo were stampeding through the room, the door burst open, and Jane popped her head inside the office.

"Can I get anyone anything?"

"Holy shit!" Gwen barked and yanked her hand away. "You scared the crap outta me! Get the hell out of here and close the door!"

"OK, OK. Sorry."

The door closed again and there were several deep, heavy sighs around the circle. Bridget's heart was pounding and she was certain her butt must've cleared the plastic chair a good six inches when the door first opened.

"That was so not funny," Gwen said in a low, angry voice. Bridget agreed with her, but didn't say so out loud.

"Excuse me for a moment," Consuelo said as she got up and left the room.

Bridget could hear some mumbling in the waiting area. She looked around and noticed the others were showing signs of stress. Ola's dark eyes were squinty and piercing, while Gwen on the other hand continued to take several deep breaths to try to calm down. A few minutes later Consuelo came back in and locked the office door.

"Let's try this again," she said. "I'm still sensing a high level of fear and anxiety going on in here. Please try and relax."

"After *that* little episode?" Gwen squeaked. "Relax? Are you kidding me?"

Consuelo sat back down and everyone was ready to begin holding hands once more. To the left Bridget could again feel Gwen's hand trembling in hers, and on the right she had Lupita's soft, firm grip. Bridget wasn't afraid of whatever was about to happen, but she had some apprehension about Jane being in the other room plotting to scare them again. After a while the quiet in the room, gently accompanied by the soothing rain on the windows, lulled them back to a place Bridget felt comfortable in. It seemed to help having Ola there to alleviate some of the anxiety Bridget might ordinarily have experienced at such an event. *You still see her as a protector,* Bridget thought. *Ola is the person who saved you from a fate worse than death and she's here now. Everything will be fine.*

"The twelfth rapist," Consuelo said.

Bridget looked over at her and saw that Consuelo's eyes were closed and her head was slumped to the side in what looked like an uncomfortable position. Bridget had missed seeing that happen but was alert and aware of what was going on around them now.

"The last one you caught," Consuelo said, "number twelve . . . he's the one who hurt me."

All the tiny hairs on the back of Bridget's neck stood up at attention. *Ohmigod! That has to be Kate talking!* She felt Lupita and Gwen both tighten the grip they had on Bridget's hands as the three of them had to have realized the same thing at the same time.

"My search is over," Consuelo continued. "Make sure he never hurts another woman ever again. You've done all I've asked of you, my Ola. I thank you for your bravery and determination. I can rest now."

Bridget noticed right away that the temperature in the room dropped about twenty degrees. A few seconds later there was a slight draft that gently blew through her hair. She saw Consuelo's head roll to the center before she opened her eyes and sat up straight. Everyone in the room was watching her . . . watching and waiting.

Finally, Consuelo blinked several times and said, "She was here." Consuelo let go of Lupita's hand so she could rub the back of her neck. "What did she say?"

"You don't remember?" Gwen asked in a small, tentative voice. "Holy smokes it's cold in here."

Bridget looked up to see Ola across from her. There were tears in Ola's eyes and seeing them made Bridget sad. "That must've been difficult for you," Bridget said. She couldn't even imagine what all was going on in Ola's mind right then.

Ola looked at her and closed her eyes for a moment, causing tears to fall on her cheeks.

"I have my sister's killer," she said after a moment.

Bridget had been so focused on her surroundings while Kate/Consuelo had been talking, that the impact of what Kate had revealed to them hadn't had time to truly sink in yet. *We have Kate's killer! Ohmigod! How could I not have understood what that means?*

Ola turned to look at Consuelo. "How can I thank you?" She looked at each of them with tears in her eyes and added, "All of you."

Consuelo smiled and nodded. "Sessions with the other side are thirty dollars. That's how you can thank me."

"We have Kate's killer," Lupita said as if she too had just realized what had been relayed to them.

"And as far as thanking the rest of us," Gwen said, rubbing her arms against the chill of the room, "well . . . let's just say we owe you more than you could ever owe us."

"We aren't finished here," Lupita reminded them. "We've only started what we came here for. We need help figuring out what to do with the men in the barn now."

"Can we let Jane back in?" Gwen asked. "She's good at all this brainstorming stuff."

"Now what can I help you with?" Consuelo asked as everyone returned to their original places in front of her desk. She took the bills Ola had given her and put them in her middle desk drawer.

Bridget noticed a more reserved quality about Jane as she took her seat. Apparently having been scolded like a child and sent out of the room didn't sit well with her.

"We've discussed several options on how to best get these men into police custody without giving away Ola's role in any of this," Lupita said. She went on to outline what their suggestions had been earlier in the evening and how Ola didn't care for any of their ideas.

"Do you blame her?" Consuelo asked. "Leaving my home and my country wouldn't be an option I would want to consider either."

"Then do you have any suggestions?" Gwen asked her.

"The place they are being held," Consuelo started. She reached behind her and retrieved the ashtray with the cigar in it. "What purpose does it serve for you?" she asked Ola.

"It's an old barn that belonged to my sister. There's a small house next to it where she lived."

"I see," Consuelo said. "If the men were found there, the police would eventually connect you to the property."

"Yes. Eventually."

"It makes sense to me that the men need to be moved to another location. Preferably somewhere that has no relevance to you, your sister or anyone else that you know."

"You mean transport twelve dangerous men?" Gwen asked. Her voice had risen significantly with the question.

"That's a great idea," Jane said. "We can help Ola get them all to another location, one at a time if we have to, and then call in a tip to the police about where they are."

"What if the police let them go?" Gwen asked. "Or what if we screw something up and they get away?"

"Five of us could do it," Jane said. "Five of us and Ola's big gun."

Do I want any part of this? Bridget asked herself. *Being around a barn full of rapists? I'm not so certain this is a good idea at all! It sounds like a disaster waiting to happen.*

"We would have to make sure the police kept them in custody once they found them," Lupita said. "These are dangerous men."

"Well, we can't leave them in the barn," Gwen said. "If something happens to any of them now, Ola's gonna be hosed."

"Who's to say that if these perverts get into police custody they won't be posting bond and be back out on the streets again?" Jane asked.

"Maybe when we tip off the police, we can also tip off some reporters," Lupita suggested. "We tell Smokey what's happening and see if she can put some pressure on the authorities to keep them locked up."

"Our timing would have to be really good," Gwen said. "Smokey's probably back in Houston by now."

"But she'd love this story," Bridget said. "We could probably even get her to down-play the Kate the Lesbian angle."

"The reporters were all after info on the judge," Gwen reminded them. "They didn't really care about the women who had been attacked or the Kate the Lesbian thing."

"But the idea of getting those men out of where they are now and relocating them to another place is excellent," Jane said. "That would keep Ola out of the limelight, which is what we want to do, right?"

"I don't think we're in any position to relocate twelve rapists," Bridget said, finally vocalizing her fear and apprehension about this whole idea. "And even if we all decided to help with this plan, we'd need more than one gun."

"She's right," Jane said. "We'd need a gun to get them in the car to transport them, and then someone with a gun at the new site to make sure they stayed there."

"This is nuts," Bridget said. "I'm not a gun person!"

"You can be a driver," Jane said. "I think this is a great idea. It's the only way we can help Ola and keep the police from eventually connecting her to these jerks."

"And a DNA sample from the last rapist should land him in jail for Kate's murder," Gwen said. "But the others may not stay in jail long once they're in police custody."

"I'm not sure this plan is acceptable to me," Ola said. It was the first time she had spoken since this whole discussion began. "We can't just turn them over to the police without some sort of guarantee that they'll be punished."

"I would certainly press charges against the asshole who attacked me," Jane said. "Bridget? What about you?"

"Yes, I would, too."

"So would I," Gwen said.

"But what about the rest of them?" Ola asked.

"We could help the other women with their decisions," Jane said. She turned in her chair. "Ola, I know this is hard for you, but you have to see that keeping those men in that barn is not the answer. If anything happens to one of them, the kidnapping charges will be the least of your worries."

"They have what they need in the barn," Ola said. "Nothing's going to happen to them there."

"The judge is old," Bridget said. "He could have a heart attack or something."

"I say we go for it," Gwen said. "I'm willing to do what I can to help get them to another location."

"Me, too," Jane said.

"Me, too," Lupita mumbled with a sigh.

"Oh, what the hell," Bridget said against her better judgment. "Me, too."

Chapter Twenty-seven

Before they left Consuelo's house, the women attempted to make plans to find a place to relocate the rapists. Bridget could feel their urgency in getting this done as soon as possible, but she was reluctant to offer her services. One of those men in the barn was her attacker. Seeing him again and helping to arrange his turnover into police custody wasn't a priority for her. Just knowing he was off the streets was enough at the moment. *He can stay in that barn forever as far as I'm concerned,* she thought. *He has a better chance of being released once the police have him anyway!*

"We need a rural area in another county," Jane said on her way to her car. The rain fell steadily now and helped reinforce the chilly November air. "It just needs to be a place where we can line up their dirty-rat-bastard asses so the police can eventually find them."

"The county line probably isn't that far from where they are now," Gwen said. "It may not be that hard to find a new place to move them." Everyone scattered to their cars as if raindrops would cause them to melt. "Ola!" Gwen called after her. "Where are they? We need to start scouting out a place—"

"I'll call in sick tomorrow to help you," Jane said in a rush of excitement as she unlocked her car.

Bridget noticed that Ola had her own vehicle parked in front of the house next door. She had assumed the three of them had arrived at Consuelo's place together.

"Ola!" Gwen said again, trying to get her attention.

"I have all the information I need," Ola said. "I appreciate your assistance. I'll take care of things from here." She opened her car door and got in.

"Wait!" Gwen yelled, but before there was any further exchange, Ola sped away.

"What the hell?" Bridget heard Jane say. "Where is she going? We still have things to do. Get in the car!"

Bridget used the remote on her key ring to open her doors. As Jane's car pulled out around her, Gwen rolled down the window on the passenger's side and hollered, "Follow us!"

"Will this night ever end?" Lupita said as they got into Bridget's car.

"Any idea what we're all doing now?" Bridget asked. Another adrenaline rush spurred her on as she followed the taillights several blocks ahead of her.

"Ola's probably on her way to the barn now," Lupita surmised with the hint of boredom in her voice, "and we're attempting to follow her. Does any of this seem like a good idea to you?"

"No," Bridget said with a tired laugh.

A cell phone rang, and Bridget was relieved to see that it wasn't hers. She glanced down at the clock on the dashboard and noticed that it was after midnight already.

"Hello," Lupita said, answering her phone. A few seconds later she handed the phone over to Bridget. "It's Gwen. She wants to talk to you."

Bridget took the phone while attempting to keep Jane's car in sight up ahead of her. These women were beginning to grate on her very last nerve.

"Yes?"

"Is everyone as tired as I am?" Gwen asked.

"Some sleep would do us all a world of good."

"Not only that," Gwen said, "but guess who has to pee now? Wait a minute. Jane wants to talk with you."

Bridget squinted ahead through the swish of the windshield wipers and made up her mind that she wasn't going to follow them to the barn in order to deal with twelve dangerous men—at least not at this hour and not under these conditions.

"Bridget," Jane said into the phone. "Help me get her to pull over. I want to talk to her."

"The woman has a gun."

"She won't shoot us," Jane said. "We're the only friends she has."

"I'm not so sure the Ola elevator goes all the way to the top, Jane, if you get my drift," Bridget commented.

Lupita chuckled beside her.

"She's just sailing without a rudder right now," Jane said. "Ola's running on emotion. It's up to us to get her back on track. There's a few fast-food places up ahead. Help me try and box her into one of those parking lots."

"Box her in," Bridget muttered while shaking her head. "You've been watching those *Charlie's Angels* reruns again, haven't you?"

"Help me get her pulled over. I'll do all the talking. Hurry up and get closer. If she gets on the interstate, we've lost our chance to reason with her."

"Reason with her?" Bridget repeated incredulously. "Are you kidding me? She carries a gun! Rapists fear this woman! I'm not sure pissing her off right now is a good idea!"

"Quit your whining! Just do it! Here's Gwen."

"Bridget," Gwen said into the phone.

"Here's Lupita," Bridget grumbled as she handed Lupita back

her cell phone. "Apparently the Jane elevator doesn't go all the way to the top either."

"What are we doing now?" Lupita asked into the cell phone.

Bridget drove faster and finally caught up with Jane's car. They were on one of the main arteries on the west side of town. Bridget watched Jane pull alongside Ola's car and get so close to her that Ola whipped into a 24-hour Whataburger parking lot. Gwen jumped out and ran inside.

"Where is Gwen going?" Bridget asked no one in particular.

Lupita closed her cell phone. "She has to pee."

Bridget's car was parked at an angle behind Ola's, while Jane's car was in front of it. Ola wasn't able to go anywhere without hitting one of them. *How did I get mixed up in this?* Bridget kept wondering over and over again.

Gwen hurried out of the Whataburger and got back into Jane's car. Ola and Jane were talking with their car windows down. After a few minutes, the Whataburger manager came out to see what the problem was. Bridget and Lupita sat there with the motor running, the wipers going, their windows up and the car doors locked.

"Will this night ever end?" Bridget heard Lupita mumble once more just as the phone rang again. With the help of the lights from the parking lot, Bridget could see Gwen on her cell phone in the other car.

"Hello," Lupita said.

Bridget watched as the Whataburger manager went back inside out of the rain.

"Jane talked her into going in for some coffee," Lupita said as she closed her phone again. "Park over there before the manager calls the cops on us."

"Coffee?" Bridget repeated. "At this hour?"

"Let's make this short and sweet," Lupita said. "I'm tired and some of us have to be at work in a few hours."

Jane and Ola were already at a table in the back by the time Lupita and Bridget got inside. Gwen was headed toward the counter up front.

"Ola was on her way to the barn to kill that guy," Gwen whispered. "Jane convinced her not to. That's where we're at right now. You two want something?" she asked. "I'm getting a round of coffees."

"Nothing for me," Bridget and Lupita said at the same time.

They sat down at the small table Jane and Ola were at. *Oh, great*, Bridget thought. *More cold, hard plastic chairs.*

"I say we wait and move them tomorrow," Jane said. "It's raining, it's late, and we've all put in a hard day's work already. I don't think we should go anywhere *near* that barn until we're more rested and up for it. We can't take a chance on screwing this up."

Ola didn't say anything. As Bridget watched her, she saw Ola as a beautiful woman with kind, dark eyes. There was a sadness about her now that tugged at Bridget's heart. She couldn't imagine being in her position and having suffered such a devastating loss. Now that they were all together again, Bridget felt more compassion for Ola and all she had been through.

Gwen came back to the table with a tray full of tiny creamer containers, three coffees, a super order of French fries, napkins, and a pile of ketchup packets. She set the ketchup in front of Bridget and said, "Here. Just for you."

Bridget smiled, remembering the glob of ketchup that had landed on her favorite sweatshirt not that long ago. "Thanks."

Lupita crossed her arms over her chest and mumbled something under her breath.

"So what did I miss?" Gwen asked as she pulled up another chair and sat down at the end of the table.

"Ola's agreed to let us help her move the perverts tomorrow after we find a new place to put them," Jane announced.

Ola's eyes sprang open full of surprise. She seemed to wake up and snap out of the funk she had been in. "I never agreed to any of that!"

"Sure you did," Jane said lowering her voice. She leaned in closer to everyone. "You want to go to jail? Is that what your sister would have wanted for you?"

"No."

"Well, neither do we."

"We're willing to help you," Gwen added. "Each of us owes you. We owe you *big*! After we get these guys into the hands of the proper authorities, you never have to hear from us again and the police never need to know who or where you are."

"So it's important that you let us help you now," Jane continued. "We're all smart women. We can figure this out. We can find a way to take the spotlight off of you when the time comes."

"In the meantime," Gwen chimed in, waving a French fry, "I suggest we all get some sleep, set out tomorrow to find another place to move them, then we make it happen. Once they're all moved, we tip off the police and you're in the clear."

"It sounds so easy when I hear you say it," Lupita said. Bridget had just been thinking the same thing.

"It *will* be easy," Jane said. There was such confidence and conviction in her voice that even Bridget believed it might be possible. "Are they tied up good or just running around loose in the barn?" Jane asked.

"Handcuffed and shackled," Ola said without emotion. She sounded as tired as Bridget felt.

"Excellent!" Gwen said.

I'm getting punchy, Bridget thought. *In theory this sounds like a good plan. The part that's weird is how much Jane and Gwen seem to be enjoying all of it. Why isn't that worrying me more?*

"How much sleep have you really had lately?" Gwen asked Ola.

"I don't remember the last time I was able to sleep," Ola said.

"I have an extra room at my place," Gwen said. "Come back and stay with me and my kids. I have something that'll help you sleep."

"Yeah, I *bet* you do," Jane said with a smirk.

"No, I'm serious," Gwen said over the chuckles going around the table. "We need Ola fresh and rested tomorrow. It's gonna be a stressful, busy day."

"That's true," Jane agreed.

"Well?" Gwen said to Ola. "How about it?"

"Let me think about it."

"There's another problem," Lupita said. "One of those men knows me really well. I'm not sure it's a good idea that I'm around them. If this is going to work, none of us should be recognized."

"I've been thinking about all of that," Jane said. "You're right. One of those guys should remember me, too. Maybe we all need to wear ski masks or something. We also wouldn't want anyone in ordinary traffic to be able to recognize us while we're on the way to the barn. Oh, and we shouldn't be talking when we're around those guys either. Stuff like that."

On second thought, Bridget mused, *this whole idea is crazy. Where did I find these people?*

"Get us all some Richard Nixon masks," Gwen said. "I'm not a crook!" She shook her head and made peace signs with both hands. Jane laughed and reached for the French fry pile.

"You could do some of the driving," Ola said, pointing to Lupita. "No one in the barn would have to see you then."

Everyone was very still for a moment. Bridget could see it in her friends' eyes as each of them suddenly realized what had just happened. This was the first verbal indication they'd had that Ola was seriously considering letting them help.

"We could put pillowcases over their heads and they wouldn't be able to see any of us," Gwen suggested. "Ola could do that first. They've seen her already."

"Excellent idea," Jane agreed. She reached over for another French fry and used it to emphasize a point. "So we'll need twelve pillowcases and four ski masks. Is someone writing all of this down?"

"And duct tape," Bridget said dryly. "A good lesbian always has duct tape."

"Are we transporting them in the trunk of a car?" Lupita asked. "Or using the trunk and also loading them up in the backseat, too?"

"Eww!" Jane said. "I don't want them that close to me!"

"Each one fits nicely into the trunk of even the smallest car," Ola said. "We'll move them that way. With the help of a gun, you can get a man into almost anything."

After all the French fries were gone and the coffee cups were empty, they were ready to finally wrap things up for the evening. Bridget and Ola had classes to teach the next day and Lupita had to work until five, so it was decided that after Ola's morning class, she would take Gwen and Jane to the barn and leave it up to them to find another suitable place to move the men. Then later that afternoon, they would all meet again at Gwen's house and head out to the barn together to make the transfer.

Gwen began tidying the table as they all stood up to leave. "Have you thought about my offer?" she asked Ola. "I can give you something that'll help you sleep."

"I always have a change of clothes in my car," Ola said.

That's the closest thing to a "yes" we'll probably ever get out of her, Bridget thought. Gwen's radiant smile left no doubt that she was delighted to have Ola as a guest in her home.

"I'll ride with you back to my house," Gwen said.

In a bit of a huff, Jane barked, "Fine. Then I can take Lupita home."

"I have a ride home already," Lupita said as she glanced over at Bridget for confirmation.

Bridget nodded and thought, *What in the world is going on here?*

"Fine," Jane said again. "I'll see you all tomorrow."

Once they got outside, the rain had slowed down a little, but a

193

steady mist persisted. When Bridget and Lupita finally got back into her car again, it was a huge relief to be there.

"I think this night is about to end," Bridget said as she started the car.

"Why don't I believe that?" Lupita muttered.

They drove out of the Whataburger parking lot to the steady swish of the wipers.

"I'm sure Gwen will be doing the happy dance all the way home," Lupita said. She leaned her head back against the headrest and closed her eyes.

"Because Ola might be staying at her place tonight?"

"Might be? Gwen would probably throw a body block on her if Ola tried to get away now."

Bridget chuckled. "Maybe sleep has finally become important to her again. I'd like to think fatigue is one of the reasons we're all so wired and stressed out."

"It still surprised me that Ola would consider staying with anyone," Lupita said. "She strikes me as a loner, someone who handles things her way and on her own. Gwen might've slipped her a mickey in that coffee."

They shared a tired laugh together.

"It doesn't bother you that Ola and Gwen left together?" Lupita asked.

"No. Why should it? Do you think Ola is dangerous?"

"I liked her better before I knew so much about her," Lupita admitted. "When she was mysterious and bigger than life."

"And sped around town in her Kate-mobile," Bridget added. "Yeah, I know what you mean, but do you think she's dangerous now?" *Please say no*, she thought. *I'm too tired to do anything else but drop you off and just go home and sleep.*

"No," Lupita said. "At least not dangerous to us."

"Then why would it bother me that Ola and Gwen left together?"

Lupita shrugged. "It hasn't been that long ago since Gwen had her hands all over you in front of the computer. Now she's all dreamy-eyed over Ola."

"Hmm," Bridget said, a bit embarrassed.

"Hmm what?"

"Hmm yes, Gwen rubbed my neck and shoulders a few times, but I didn't really remember it until you brought it up."

"Oh, really?" Lupita said with a tinge of sarcasm. "A woman can't keep her hands off of you a few hours ago and you don't remember it?"

Surprised by Lupita's sudden anger, Bridget didn't know what to say. She focused on the sparse traffic and shook her head.

"Uh . . . I remember a few little neck rubs. That's about it."

"Oh, puhleeze."

Bridget shifted uncomfortably in the seat. *Why is she so upset?* she wondered as they drove on in silence. *What exactly just happened? Maybe Lupita's not used to seeing open displays of affection between women.*

After a while, Lupita said, "Jane wasn't too happy about the traveling arrangements this evening. By the way, thanks for driving me home."

Bridget felt relieved that Lupita didn't sound angry any longer. She vowed to make sure there were no more reasons to feel chastised over her behavior. "No problem. I enjoy the company."

After a moment, Lupita said, "Can I ask you a question?"

"Sure."

"At the table tonight . . . what was that little thing with Gwen and the ketchup packets?"

"Gwen knows how much I like ketchup. We had lunch the other day during our stakeout."

"I see."

The disappointed tone of her voice caught Bridget's attention again. "Why did you ask? No one really noticed the ketchup thing."

"I noticed."

Let's get it all out now, Bridget thought. *Lupita's current mood goes deeper than fatigue and stress.* "Are you upset with me about something in particular?" Bridget asked quietly. "Something besides the neck rub?"

"Yes. I mean no. I mean . . . oh, hell. It doesn't matter."

"Of course it matters. What's up? 'Splain yourself, Lucy," Bridget said, trying for a bit of humor in her best Ricky Ricardo voice.

Lupita turned her head and looked out the window. "I'm too tired to think about it right now. I might need a margarita or two before I'm even able to get into it."

"A margarita," Bridget said. "That could probably be arranged. The bars haven't closed yet."

Lupita laughed but continued looking out the window. "It's a nice thought, but I'm too tired. Please ask me again at another time."

There was a comfortable silence that followed before Lupita said, "I'm not looking forward to seeing Rudy tomorrow. I probably won't get much sleep tonight either."

"You don't have to see him. I'll make sure they move him first and you can be somewhere else while that's happening."

Lupita turned her head. "You're very kind."

"This doesn't have to be the goat-rope Jane and Gwen might try and make it into."

"It'll be all of that and more, I'm afraid."

Chapter Twenty-eight

Bridget was almost too tired to sleep. She took a hot shower and got into bed, but wasn't successful at shutting off her mind. As she tried to get comfortable, it surprised her to realize what exactly it was that seemed to be keeping her awake in the throes of exhaustion. There were so many things to be restless about—like eventually having to deal with a barn full of rapists, having friends with a stream of unfounded confidence, Ola with a gun, and Gwen with sleeping pills to hand out to whoever might need them.

Her mind was racing and the more she thought about everything, the more uncomfortable she felt. *You're not cut out for all this dyke drama. Up until two months ago, you led a very boring, uncomplicated life.*

Then there was the notion that they would be able to call the police once everything was taken care of and all would be well again. Bridget's newest fear was that these twelve men would somehow be seen as the victims when the police eventually found them. The possibility of some of them being set free to carry on with their badass ways continued to worry her. But even with all of that to consider and fret over, Bridget still found a faint flicker of light at the end of the tunnel. The one thing that was the most soothing for her was the amount of time she'd been able to spend with Lupita. Bridget was drawn to her gentle ways and sane outlook. Everything about her was appealing and refreshing. Out of the three other women in the group, Lupita was the one Bridget wanted to get to know better. She felt as though she already knew as much about Jane and Gwen as she cared to.

She turned her pillow over and was relieved to finally be settling down. Glancing at the clock on the nightstand, she saw that it was after two already. *I wonder what Lupita is doing right now?* she thought. Bridget stretched and liked the way the sheets felt against her bare skin. The next thing she knew, the sun was peeking in through the blinds.

Bridget's phone rang just as her Pop-Tarts jumped out of the toaster.

"Are you up yet?" Jane asked without waiting for a greeting.

"I am."

"Wow. What a night, eh? And today is just as busy. You should see this place!"

"What place?" Bridget asked. She hadn't been up long enough to be carrying on a conversation yet.

"The barn!" Jane said. "That's where we are now. Wow. Ola brought us out here, but she had to go back into town to teach another class. She couldn't find a sub. Even though this place is easy to get to, it's nice and secluded. It's also close to the county line just like we hoped it would be."

"So what are you doing now?" Bridget asked. "Is Gwen with you?"

"We both followed Ola out here this morning in separate cars."

"Are you *at* the barn . . . or *in* the barn?" Bridget asked. She had an alarming visual of Jane surrounded by bound and gagged rapists who were soaking up every morsel of information being inadvertently given to them.

"I'm *at* the barn. Ola has it all locked up. They can't get out and we can't get in."

"Well, you two be careful, and good luck finding a place to move them." *Thank the goddess it's not me out there now,* she thought with a shiver.

"We'll be in touch later," Jane said. "If not, meet us at Gwen's house after your last class."

Bridget hung up the phone and took her Pop-Tarts and coffee to the computer room to check her e-mail. Before she got settled, the phone rang again. This time it was Lupita.

"Gwen just called me," Lupita said. "Those two aren't the least bit nervous about any of this."

Bridget smiled. She liked hearing Lupita's voice on her phone. *Just the phone?* she thought. *Get real! You'd like hearing Lupita's voice anywhere.*

"I don't know about you," Lupita continued, "but I'd be terrified to know I was so close to all of that evil concentrated there in one place."

"Let's just be glad Gwen and Jane are willing to do this part. I don't think they're in it for the same reasons we are," Bridget said.

"I agree. I don't care to know what their reasons are any longer. I'll be glad when this is all over and those men are in police custody. Everyone will be able to get on with their lives."

Bridget heard the anger and frustration in her voice. "Maybe by tomorrow it'll all be over."

"I've gotta go," Lupita said. "I'll let you know if I hear anything else."

"Thanks. I'll do the same. I can pick you up after my last class if you like."

"That would be great. Thanks."

Bridget hung up the phone and sipped her coffee. In addition to the soothing warmth she felt at having spoken to Lupita, there was queasiness in her stomach that could only be attributed to the events that were to take place that evening. She felt apprehensive and afraid. Ever since her ordeal in the parking lot several weeks ago, she had gone to great lengths to convince herself that her attacker had been dealt with . . . that someone calling herself Kate the Lesbian had taken him away and punished him appropriately. But now that she knew none of that had been the case, Bridget could feel the fear and anxiety slowly building up inside of her again.

I just want this day to be over, she thought. *Putting this entire thing behind me is the only way to heal.*

Bridget gave a writing assignment to her afternoon class. While they stayed busy, she graded papers from another. Afterward, she grabbed something to eat in the cafeteria and checked her cell phone for messages. She had one from Jane and called her back while finishing a tuna sandwich.

"It's Bridget. What's up?"

"We found a place to move them," Jane said excitedly. "It's an old abandoned gas station. No windows in the place, the gas pumps are older than dirt, and there's a faded sign out front that has gas prices at fifty-three cents a gallon. We can stick those dirty-rat-bastards inside, call the cops, then drive like hell."

Bridget could feel her stomach getting upset all over again at hearing what they would be expected to do later.

"I got a call from Ola a few minutes ago," Jane said. "She has some other things she wants to go over with us. This is just too cool!"

"Cool? Uh . . . personally I think it's scary as hell."

"Scary? What's scary about it? We have Ola on our side."

"These are dangerous men, Jane, and they outnumber us."

"I'd put my money on four lesbians with duct tape any day."

"Oy," Bridget mumbled. "You know what else just occurred to me? Now that we know where these men are being kept, that makes us accessories to the crime. And once we help her move them, that also makes us guilty of kidnapping."

"Well, aren't you just a little ray of sunshine."

"To answer your earlier question," Bridget said, "there's a lot of things to be scared about."

"Yeah, maybe."

"Maybe?"

"It'll be fine, Bridget. Ola has them tied up. We're talkin' helpless here. They can't even scratch their butts right now."

"Being overly confident doesn't seem—"

"Overly confident?" Jane said. "That doesn't describe anyone I know. I'm excited about these bruisers getting what's coming to them. I'm also jazzed about helping Ola get out of the middle of this."

"Aren't you afraid?" Bridget asked.

"Afraid? Is that what this is about? You're afraid?"

"You mean you *aren't?* If that's the case, then I'm even *more* scared now!"

"No," Jane said. "I'm not afraid. Ola will be with us. Ola and her gun. The only people who'll be afraid will be those twelve assholes we'll be transporting, and *they* have every right to be afraid."

"OK," Bridget said, resigning herself to the fact that she was dealing with someone who obviously wasn't "getting it." She decided right then that helping out with the transfer might not be in her best interest. She would make a decision on whether or not to participate once she got to Gwen's house later that evening. At the moment she was leaning heavily toward bailing out of the whole thing.

After Bridget taught her last class of the day, she called Lupita to make sure their plans were still on schedule.

"Have you heard the latest?" Lupita asked.

"I guess not. What's going on now?"

"Ola has a new plan. Everything Jane and Gwen did today with finding a place to put the men is now out the window."

Bridget felt the relief overtake her. Now maybe they could get a nice dose of sanity back into their lives.

"What's the new plan?" Bridget asked.

"Ola hasn't said yet. We'll hear it when we all get to Gwen's house."

"Well," Bridget said, "the new plan can't be any worse than the old one was."

"Are you kidding me? The new plan is coming from the same woman who kidnapped twelve men and stuck them in a barn in the first place! Ola Cordician might be brave with a gun," Lupita said, "but she's no deep thinker."

Bridget chuckled and had to agree with her. "I'll be there to pick you up in about twenty minutes." Just as she hung up from that call, her cell phone rang again. It was Jane checking to see where she was.

"I'm on my way to get Lupita," Bridget said. "We should be at Gwen's house in about forty-five minutes."

"Did you hear the latest?" Jane asked. "All that work we did this morning is no good! Ola has a new plan!"

"So now what? Are we setting the barn on fire?" Bridget playfully suggested.

"Hey, don't tease me. I happen to like that plan!"

Holy cannoli, Bridget thought.

"Ola has us making tags for those dirty-rat-bastards," Jane said. "She wants each guy to have the name of the woman he attacked as well as where and when it happened. Gwen and I are matching up the names and numbers for all of that now."

Bridget nodded to herself. "That actually sounds like a good idea," she admitted out loud.

"Yeah, Gwen and I thought so, too, but we're still pissed off about all the time we wasted this morning. That old gas station was perfect. Well, hurry up and get here. We're still working on the tags. I can't wait to see what Ola's new plan will be."

Lupita was waiting for her outside when Bridget arrived at the apartment complex. It had been raining off and on for about an hour.

"Hi," Lupita said as she got in the car. "Thanks for picking me up."

"It's on the way," Bridget said with a smile. She liked the chocolate-colored pullover sweater Lupita was wearing. Bridget had also changed into darker casual clothes, since their activities that night would most likely demand it.

"Liar," Lupita said with a smile. "It's not on your way, but I really appreciate it. I'm not looking forward to this. I've been dreading it all day."

"Yeah, I know. Me, too."

"I'm tired. I didn't sleep well last night, and I was busy at work today."

Bridget pulled out of the parking lot. "Are you worried about seeing Rudy again?"

The heavy sigh that followed was all the answer Bridget needed, but Lupita's quiet voice and the carefully chosen words touched her unexpectedly.

"He would've killed me that night if Ola hadn't come along and stopped him. I've been afraid of Rudy for a long time now. The thought of him being back literally makes me sick."

Bridget didn't know what to say, but in her heart she knew that if there was ever anything she could do to help this woman, she would gladly do it without a second thought.

"I'm sure there are several things you can do tonight that won't involve getting close to those men," Bridget said in a determined, reassuring tone of voice. "In fact, I'll make sure of it. Just try and relax. It'll all be over in a few more hours. Once we get Ola completely off anyone's radar screen, we can put all of this behind us."

Lupita leaned her head back against the headrest. "You're beginning to sound like *them*."

Bridget laughed, knowing full well that she meant Jane and Gwen.

"You have a kind heart," Lupita said. "It's what I remember the most about you the first night we met."

Bridget smiled. "That seems like a long time ago now. Thank you. What a nice thing to say."

"What do you remember most about that night?"

"I remember how apprehensive I was about going to the meeting," Bridget said. "I still don't know why I went. I'm not much of a joiner."

"Dorothy Holt was very persuasive," Lupita said.

"What about you? What do you remember the most about that night?"

"I remember walking to the bus stop," Lupita said quietly. "Gwen and Jane both drove past me and each of them waved."

"They *saw* you and didn't stop?"

"I didn't think anything of it at the time. I've taken public transportation for a while now . . . ever since Rudy wrecked our car and lost his driver's license. I can get anywhere I need to be in this town on a bus. It's second nature to me now."

"It was dark," Bridget said. "We'd just been in a meeting about women being attacked. How could they see you and *not* stop?"

"Think of it another way," Lupita suggested. "You didn't know me, so why would you stop and pick up a stranger?"

"I *did* know you. We had just left a meeting together, and if my memory serves me right, I had to ask you twice to get in the car. You weren't all that willing to accept a ride from me either."

"Well," Lupita said with a shrug, "I don't get into a car with just anyone."

"All I knew at the time was that I didn't like you being out there at night that way. I would've worried about you all evening if I hadn't stopped."

"That's what I meant about your kind heart, Bridget. I don't feel judged by you and I appreciate your thoughtfulness."

Bridget could feel the heat spread up into her face. For the remainder of the drive over to Gwen's house, they talked about Ola's new plan and how glad they would both be to finally have this all behind them.

Chapter Twenty-nine

"There you two are," Gwen said when she answered the door. "Ola's on her way over. Come in. Can I get you something to drink?"

"Nothing for me," Bridget said. "I don't think any of us should be consuming that much liquid considering where we'll be and what we have to do tonight."

Bridget and Lupita both gave Gwen a pointed look.

"Yeah, yeah, yeah, I know," Gwen said. "I've got a bladder the size of a grape. I'm just trying to be a good hostess here already."

Bridget saw Jane in the living room and waved to her. Noting with amusement how all four of them were dressed in various shades of dark, drab clothing, Bridget decided they were about as ready for this night as they'd ever be.

"You should've seen how long it took me to convince Jane to *not* call those Lesbian Avengers from Austin."

"Yikes!" Bridget said. "That's all we need. More people involved who don't know what they're doing."

"Amen to that," Lupita mumbled under her breath.

"Come here and check this out," Jane called from the living room. "These are the tags Ola asked us to make. We had to use rubber gloves so there wouldn't be any prints on them anywhere. Have you ever tried to do anything with rubber gloves? They feel yucky . . . like putting a condom on your hands."

"Ewww!" Bridget said.

Gwen picked up one of the tags. "Check out our state-of-the-art work. Typed up, front and back, in a nice bold font," she said as if describing a model on a runway. "Laminated on both sides for easy reading in the rain, a nice hole punched at the top for convenience. White and black should match anything. Oh, and we have large safety pins to attach them to their clothing."

"Think of it as an accessory to their dingy outfits," Jane added.

"I think you two have been at this way too long," Bridget noted.

"Hey, I'm ready," Jane said. "I can't wait to see each one of those dirty-rat-bastards stuffed in the trunk of a car again. That visual alone cheers me right up."

"Who's putting the tags on them?" Bridget asked with a curled up nose.

"Not me!" Lupita said.

"I'll help Ola with that," Jane said. "She's supposed to have these guys blindfolded and tied up already. We'll brand 'em with a tag and toss 'em in the trunk. Sounds easy enough."

Bridget shuddered. Jane's description of how the evening should go instilled next to no confidence in this boondoggle as far as she was concerned. Bridget just hoped no one got hurt and that they would all be in the clear and forever disassociated from any of this once it was over.

"How did it go with Ola last night?" Lupita asked Gwen.

"She stayed in the spare room I have," Gwen said with a big smile. "I was too excited to sleep just knowing she was here."

"I'm still surprised she took you up on that," Jane said. "Wish I had thought of it first. I've got a king-size bed I would've gladly shared with her."

Everyone laughed just as the doorbell rang.

"That's her!" Gwen hissed. She adjusted her long-sleeved black sweatshirt over her matching sweatpants and scurried off to the door.

Ola came in dressed in her "Kate the Lesbian" outfit—a black long-sleeve silk shirt, black leather pants, black boots and a rolled scarf tied around each arm. The four women could do nothing but stand and stare at her. Ola was a formidable sight, and Bridget was reminded again why she was there. This was the woman who had saved her life. She would do whatever she could to help her.

"The tags are perfect," Ola said. "Good work. Now who has the largest car?"

The four women looked at each other and Gwen confirmed that her car was the biggest.

"Excellent. Then that's the car we'll use," Ola said. "In the bag here you'll find a pair of gloves for each of you. Put them on now and don't take them off until we get back here later this evening. I need two volunteers to put these on Gwen's car right now."

Ola pulled out a set of Texas license plates and two screwdrivers.

"I'll volunteer for whatever needs doing that doesn't involve being around the men," Lupita said. She put on her gloves and took the license plates and one of the screwdrivers.

"I'll help," Jane announced.

"Bridget can help me," Lupita said as she took the other screwdriver and handed it to Bridget.

"Also, here's a rag for each of you," Ola said. "Wipe things off as you go. We don't want to leave any fingerprints behind. Keep the rags and these flashlights with you at all times."

Ola passed around four flashlights and a set of batteries for each, all still in their original packages.

"Once we get out of the city," Ola said, "you'll also wear one of these." She took several ski masks out of the canvas bag and gave one to each of them.

"No Richard Nixon masks?" Gwen asked.

Ola smiled at her. "If you have one, wear it."

"You hold the flashlight," Bridget said as she knelt down on Gwen's concrete driveway with screwdriver in hand. Luckily, Gwen had a newer car and the screws holding the front plate in place came out easily.

"Gloves *and* rags?" Lupita said. "Why would we need both?"

"She's just being cautious, I think. So what's going on with you and Jane?" Bridget asked.

"Nothing," Lupita replied curtly.

"It sounds like something to me. I feel like I'm witnessing a lover's quarrel each time you two say anything to each other."

"Trust me. It's nothing."

"Oh, that was convincing," Bridget said dryly. She got the front plate off and the new one on. They moved around to the back of Gwen's car and had trouble getting the old license plate off. Bridget had to stand up and bend down for more leverage to get the first screw to budge.

"Have you two slept together?" Bridget asked.

"*Which* two?"

"You know who I'm talking about. You and Jane."

"No. Of course not."

"Well, something's going on."

"She's still in love with her ex."

"Ah, now we're getting somewhere. So something *did* happen between you two."

"We did a lot of talking," Lupita said. "I might've been interested in her at one time, but it was brief and I learned a lot from it. I'm in a different place now."

Bridget got the first screw out and knelt down again to work on the second one. It came loose with only a little pressure.

"What did you learn?"

"Jane was quick to remind me that I'm still married and very new to all of this."

"Well, she's right about that. What else?"

Lupita held the license plate up while still holding the flash-light. Bridget lined up the first screw.

"Jane is the kind of person who is impulsive and meticulous," Lupita continued. "She doesn't like loose ends dangling about. She's also self-centered and egotistical. Neither of those qualities appeals to me no matter how attractive she is."

Bridget tightened down both screws and stood up. "You might be just what she needs to mellow her out some."

"Sorry. Not interested."

"Jane is obviously still interested."

Lupita turned off her flashlight. "I told you already. She's still in love with her ex."

"Things change."

"Why are you doing this, Bridget? You're fishing and this fish isn't biting."

Bridget tucked Gwen's original license plates under her arm. "Life's too short to spend it alone. If you see something you want, you need to go after it. Jane can be reeled in and tamed," Bridget said with a chuckle. "She hasn't lost interest in you. She's doing all she can to recapture whatever it was you two had together."

"We didn't have *anything* together!"

Bridget stepped up on the porch first and reached for the door-knob. "If the plan is to use me to make her jealous, then it's work-ing. That impulsive Jane we know so well looks like she'd like to punch my lights out sometimes."

Once they were back in the house, Bridget saw Gwen and Jane sitting on the sofa carefully wiping off the laminated cards to fur-ther ensure there were no prints on them.

"It's a good thing Ola told us to use rubber gloves to make these with earlier," Gwen said. "I wouldn't have thought of that. This sticky stuff can yank a fingerprint off pretty easily."

Jane waved the other two over to the sofa and whispered, "Ola asked a lot of questions about Smokey, that reporter we didn't care too much for. She asked Gwen for Smokey's phone number."

"Why would she do that?" Lupita asked. They were all in a

huddle with their gloves on and new flashlights either attached to belt loops or stuck in their pockets. Lupita and Bridget were behind the sofa, leaning over watching the other two work.

"I don't know," Gwen whispered. "It's sort of nice having someone just come in and take over, but how do we know if Ola's plan is any good?"

"Maybe someone needs to ask her what the new plan is," Lupita suggested. "Where is she anyway?"

"On the computer," Gwen said.

"Where are the kids?" Bridget asked.

"Spending the night with friends."

"And what's the deal with us having rags if we're wearing gloves?" Gwen asked. "If we're wearing gloves, why do we need the rags?"

"I just asked Bridget the same thing!" Lupita said.

"Sounds kind of obsessive/compulsive if you ask me," Jane said. "She's all over the place."

"No shit," Gwen commented.

"Well, I was also wondering why we're having to switch license plates," Jane said. "The barn is in the boonies. There aren't any neighbors around it. What's up with that? No one's going to see us out there."

"She's being cautious," Bridget said again. "Paranoia does that to some people."

Ola came back into the room and all the talking stopped.

"Almost done with those?" she asked, pointing toward the cards on the coffee table.

"Yes," Jane said. "If not carefully wiped, then at least gleefully smudged."

"Is everyone ready?" Ola asked.

Bridget felt her stomach give a little lurch as the others began to mumble and move around.

"Attach the pins to the new tags and put the tags in this Ziploc when you're finished," Ola said as she pulled a plastic bag out of her canvas bag.

Bridget caught a glimpse of one of the tags and saw the name of

210

a woman she didn't know, where the woman had been attacked, and the date and time the attack had taken place. The same information was on the other side of the tag as well.

"Gwen," Ola said. "Go to your computer and delete all this information that's on it. We're leaving nothing behind in case something goes wrong."

Bridget felt her stomach twinge again. Having the vulnerability of their actions vocalized brought a little jolt to Bridget's psyche.

"So what exactly is the plan now?" Jane asked as she put the last tag into the bag.

Ola looked at her with an amused expression. "You don't really want to know."

"I don't?"

"No. You don't."

Bridget and Lupita helped clean up the coffee table as the silence surrounded each of them. When Gwen came back from the computer room, she had on a Richard Nixon mask that at first scared the bejesus out of everyone and then made each of them laugh until their sides hurt.

"Anyone wanna be Dubya tonight?" Gwen asked, holding up a mask of George W. Bush.

"I've never had the least bit of interest in being a Republican," Bridget said, "so I'll pass."

"I do! I do!" Jane said. "These ski masks look hot."

"There aren't any tiny little air conditioners in this thing either, kiddo," Gwen said.

"Are we ready?" Ola asked. "Do you each have the things I gave you?"

Bridget had her rag in one pocket, her flashlight in the other, and her ski mask tucked in the waistband of her pants. She saw the others also taking inventory of their gear.

"Give me the car keys," Ola said to Gwen. "I'll drive. We're all riding in one vehicle for now. Let's go."

They marched out of Gwen's house like good little lesbian mer-

211

cenaries. To Bridget's dismay, Jane got in the backseat with her and
Lupita, with Lupita ending up sitting in the middle between them.
There was a momentary distraction when Gwen began humming
the theme to *Mission Impossible* as Ola backed out of the driveway.
Before long they were all humming it.

"Who do you think she's calling?" Lupita whispered.

They were parked around the side of a 7-Eleven where Ola had
gotten out of the car to use a pay phone.

"It's long distance," Gwen said. "Did you see how much change
she poked into the phone?"

When Ola got back in the car, no one said anything and there
wasn't any humming. Bridget felt a bit apprehensive but no longer
afraid. She had no idea why or what had brought on such a new set
of feelings for her, but Bridget somehow instinctively knew that
she could trust Ola to help them all get through this and eventually
do the right thing.

Chapter Thirty

Ola drove them to a part of the city Bridget wasn't familiar with. She had so many questions, but Bridget didn't feel comfortable enough to say anything. Knowing Jane and her curiosity well, Bridget realized that sooner or later the right questions would be asked without her having to be the one to ask them. Finally after only a few minutes, Jane asked, "Where the hell are we?"

"No talking," Ola said.

"This isn't the way to the barn," Jane persisted.

"No talking!" Ola snapped.

So they all sat quietly, each trying to get her bearings by looking out the windows to see if there was something they were familiar with. About twenty minutes later, Ola pulled over into a Target parking lot.

"Where's the switch to turn off the inside dome light?" she asked Gwen.

"Up here," Gwen said as she reached up and flicked a switch.

"Very good," Ola said, then pulled out of the parking lot and continued on down the highway. Bridget saw enough vaguely familiar street names to at least know they were on the southwest side of town.

"Where are we going?" Jane asked again in frustration.

"No talking," Ola said, louder this time.

A few minutes later, Ola turned down a dimly lit street and switched off the car's headlights. About a quarter of a mile later she turned into the large parking lot of an assisted living facility. Ola stopped the car and put it in park.

"Gwen, you drive from here," she said. "When you see a van drive past you, make sure you follow it. Everyone put their masks on now and keep them on until we get back to Gwen's house later. Got it?"

"Got it," Gwen said in a trembling voice.

"Drive the speed limit and if the cops stop me, keep going. Don't stop. Abort the mission."

As soon as the word "mission" left Ola's lips, Jane began to quietly hum the *Mission Impossible* theme again. Bridget was momentarily horrified when she heard a nervous snort escape from her own throat.

Ola opened the door and trotted off into the darkness. Gwen got out of the car and went around to the driver's side and got in behind the wheel.

"I'm calling shotgun," Jane said excitedly.

"No talking!" Gwen said in her best Ola Cordician voice.

Over the subdued laughter, Jane said, "Oh, shut the hell up. I'm sitting up front with you!"

A few minutes later a white cargo van drove past them. It was too dark to see if it was Ola, but Gwen pulled out behind it anyway and kept a safe distance.

"Do you think she stole that van?" Jane asked.

"Nothing would surprise me," Gwen said.

Bridget felt silly sitting in the backseat with a ski mask on, but not half as silly as Gwen and Jane looked as Nixon driving and George W. Bush navigating.

"I think we're headed to the barn now," Gwen said. "If she plans to put these guys in a van to transport them, that's a much better idea than stuffing them in the trunk of a car one at a time. That was going to take forever."

Once they were on the highway, Bridget felt a heaviness return to the pit of her stomach. Soon they would be in the presence of evil, and all she could do was pray that this night would soon be over.

"Is it just me," Lupita said, "or is anyone else afraid?"

"No, baby," Jane said, "I'm sure we're all afraid. I know I am."

Bridget felt a tinge of irritation at Jane referring to Lupita as "baby." *Nope*, she thought. *It's not over for Jane.*

"Did anyone else get nervous when Ola turned off the head-lights on that dark road?" Gwen asked. "I thought I'd pee my pants."

"Goodness yes," Lupita said.

"Oh, crap," Jane said. "You don't have to pee again, do you?"

"Not yet," Gwen said.

"You two have no idea how weird it is to be sitting back here being chauffeured around by Nixon and Bush," Bridget said.

The peals of laughter helped relieve some of the tension that had been building all night. It was hard to stay irked at people who could make her laugh this much. *Maybe that's what friendship is all about*, she thought. *The ups and downs of human nature.*

"But I'll probably have to pee when we get there," Gwen said.

It started to rain as soon as they turned off the main highway out in the country. The bumpy dirt road forced the van ahead of them to slow down.

"Wow," Gwen said. "I think I might throw up. We're really about to do this."

"I thought you had to pee," Jane said.

"Oh, thanks for reminding me."

They traveled about a mile before Bridget saw the van up ahead turn off to the left. Gwen followed it down a long gravel driveway.

"We're here," Jane announced.

They all slowly got out of the car. Ola was waiting for them on the porch of a farmhouse about forty yards from the barn. There was a security light off to the far side of the house that cast a dim light where the women gathered. Ola set her canvas bag down and unzipped it.

"President Bush reporting for duty," Jane said as she gave a curt salute with the wrong hand. Ola smiled just before putting on her own ski mask. Bridget was amazed at the transformation. Ola looked dangerous and frightening with it on. Bridget took a deep breath and realized they probably all did at that particular moment.

"First off, no one talks but me," Ola said quietly. "Each of them has heard my voice, but I don't want them recognizing any of you. I need a volunteer who won't be afraid to use this," she said, holding up a metal rod.

"What's that?" Lupita asked.

"It's a stun gun thingy," Gwen said.

"Very good!"

"Oh! Me! Me!" Jane said as she waved a gloved hand in the air. "I'd love to stun somebody!"

"Can any of you use a pistol?" Ola asked as she gave Jane the stun gun.

"I can," Gwen said.

"Very good!" Ola took a pistol out of the bag and handed it to her. Gwen gave it back.

"I have my own." She reached into the top of her sweatshirt and pulled out a small gun. "After that bastard attacked me, I went to training classes and got a permit to carry."

"Are you nuts? You could shoot a boob off with that thing!" Jane said.

216

"You carry that with you all the time?" Bridget asked.

"All the time," Gwen confirmed. "The only time it's off my body is when I'm in the shower, but I keep a water gun in there just in case I need it."

"Oh, puhleeze," Jane said before she joined the others in a little group chuckle.

The wind picked up, but the rain was nothing more than a light drizzle. Ola instructed them to sit down on the porch as she explained how she wanted things to go over the next few hours.

"I'll bring the men out of the barn one at a time," she started. "If they offer any resistance whatsoever, they get a stun gun surprise."

"Oh, goody," Jane said.

"The men already have numbers on them," Ola continued, "so we'll just have to attach the right tag to each person. Who wants to be the one to put the new tags on them?"

Ola was looking at Bridget and Lupita, neither of whom was eager to say anything.

"I can do that part," Gwen said. "I helped make the tags with those extra long safety pins. I'd like to be the one to get close to these guys with a sharp object."

"OK," Ola said. "That'll work. Then you two can be wiping down the van and the barn door and getting rid of whatever old prints are on there now," she said pointing to Bridget and Lupita.

"Are we ready?" Jane asked.

"Not yet," Ola said. "We need to go over what will happen once we get them in the van. I need someone to ride along with me and make sure no one gets out of line on the way back to San Antonio."

"San Antonio?" Jane said. "What about the gas station we found?"

"Change of plans," Ola said. "We're parking the van with the men in it about a block away from a police substation in San Antonio. You'll pick up me and whoever else volunteers to go with me. We all leave the scene in Gwen's car, get back to Gwen's

217

house, and I'll call the police on my way home from a pay phone. The police find the van, and hopefully all twelve of them will eventually be in police custody."

"Wow," Lupita said. "That sounds like a great plan."

"All that running around we did this morning here in the boonies was for nothing?" Jane asked incredulously.

"Of course not," Ola said. "It kept you busy and out of my hair for a few hours."

Bridget, Ola and Lupita were the only ones who found that amusing.

"Ha ha," Jane said dryly.

"Who wants to volunteer to go with me in the van?" Ola asked.

"I will," Jane said. "I get to use the stun gun on them if they act up, right?"

"I don't think you'll be able to stay quiet that long," Ola said. She looked right at Bridget—the eyes behind the ski mask were dark and piercing. "How about you?" she asked. "Bridget, isn't it?"

"Yes," Bridget said in a near whisper. She thought her heart had stopped beating, but there was no pain in her chest.

"You're quiet. I like that. Are you afraid to use the stun gun?"

Bridget cleared her throat to make sure her voice would still work. "I wouldn't be if I had to."

"Just remember that night in the SAC parking lot," Ola said in a soft, kind voice. "Turn your fear into courage. We have the upper hand tonight. These men are at our mercy." Ola moved directly in front of her and said, "I would appreciate it if you'd be the one to volunteer to ride along with me on the way back."

What else could she say other than yes? Ola had never asked anything of her, and Bridget felt as though she owed her something. She nodded and uttered the words, "I'll do it," and was surprised at how unafraid she felt and sounded.

"Let's get started," Ola said. "Remember—no talking. Just follow my directions. We keep them subdued, tag them, shove them in the van and off we go. Got it?"

"Got it," they all said together.

218

Bridget tried to prepare herself for everything imaginable, but the one thing she hadn't been ready for was the smell. Bridget, Jane, Gwen and Lupita were busy wiping down the inside of the van with their rags when Ola opened the barn door. The smell of human waste permeated the crisp country air and made them all gag.

"Holy shit!" Jane mumbled in between gasps for air.

"Shush! No talking!" Gwen hissed. "Great. The smell of urine makes me have to pee."

"Shush!" Jane said to her. "No talking!"

Bridget stayed busy with her rag, wiping off the steering wheel and door handles. It made no sense to be doing it because Ola had been wearing gloves the whole time, but Bridget was glad to have something to do to stay busy. She moved around to the back of the van where Lupita was working on the door handles. Bridget could hear Ola talking to the men in the barn.

"It's your lucky night, boys. If you're good, you might live long enough to tell your friends about your little ordeal. I've got a gun and a joy stick I like using. If you don't want your balls fried off, I suggest you cooperate."

Shortly, Ola came out with the first one. His shirt was dirty and tattered and his pants had stains all over them. He had a scraggly beard and took small steps because of the chains on his ankles. His hands were cuffed behind him, and there was a blindfold covering his eyes. He stood at the back of the van and whimpered as Gwen pinned the tag on him.

Things went smoothly for the first six, and Bridget was getting accustomed to the stench. Lupita had made herself scarce at the side of the house where Ola had the Kate-mobile parked. Everything was going fine until Ola came out with the man who had attacked Jane. He was tall and big and kept trying to yell through the duct tape over his mouth. Jane handed the stun gun to Bridget and walked around to the side of the van to vomit.

Ola looked at Bridget standing there holding the stun gun and said, "Give him one zap to the testicles, please."

The guy whimpered and bent over to protect himself. He grew quiet at just the mention of the words "zap" and "testicles." It was obvious to everyone there that he had experienced it before. Gwen pinned a tag on him.

"Much better," Ola said. "Now get in the van and shut up."

He sat down on the edge of the van and scooted in.

"Move closer together!" Ola barked. "It's gonna get crowded!"

By the time they got to the judge, Jane was feeling well enough to help them with him. He was older and wasn't able to walk easily. Once she was inside the barn, Bridget noticed the huge pile of fast-food bags, cartons, pizza boxes and wrappers on the floor all around them. Their meals had come from Wendy's, McDonald's, Pizza Hut, Taco Cabana and Jack in the Box. *At least she didn't starve them*, Bridget thought.

She and Jane helped get the judge on his feet and out of the barn. His once-expensive suit was soiled all over, and he smelled as bad as the rest of them. Gwen pinned the tag on him, and they helped him into the van. By the time they got to the last one, the van was full and the women heaved him in and slammed the door.

Chapter Thirty-one

Ola gathered them all together away from the van to quickly go over once again what would happen next. Everyone but Bridget seemed to be anxious to get out of there. At the moment, Bridget was happy to postpone having to get in that smelly van any time soon!

"We're going back to town the long way," Ola said. "Once we get there, we're going to a drive-thru car wash on West Commerce Street. We run the van and Gwen's car through it to get all this country dirt and mud off. We can't leave any evidence of where the van has been. After the car wash, we head over to the police sub-station on Babcock Road. That one is nestled in a quiet neighborhood. When you see me put on my flashers, that's where you park," she said, pointing to Gwen. "Bridget and I will find you once we stash the van, then we'll all leave the scene together. Got it?"

"Got it," the four women said quietly.

"One more thing," Ola added. "If the van gets stopped by the cops on the way into town or anywhere else along the way, you just keep going like you never knew us, OK?"

Bridget felt a chill scamper through her body. The last thing in the world she needed was to get caught in a van with twelve kidnapped men. *Oh, great, you dumb shit. Why did you volunteer for this part?*

"Everybody ready?" Ola asked. Not waiting for an answer, she said, "Let's go."

To Bridget's surprise, Gwen and Jane both gave her quick hugs and wished her good luck. That didn't help her feel any better about what she was about to do, but she appreciated their parting words. But when Lupita grabbed her by the hand and pulled her to the side of the van, Bridget's heart began to race. Lupita took off their ski masks and kissed Bridget tenderly on the mouth. The kiss was an unexpected surprise that sent a warm rush of emotion swirling through her body. Bridget wanted to stay that way forever, encased in a cloud of soft lips and newly discovered passion. Lupita took Bridget into her arms and hugged her. *If riding along with Ola and her captives was what prompted this kiss,* Bridget thought, *then I'm more than willing to be Ola's little volunteer!*

Lupita finally pulled away from her and whispered, "I don't want you going with them."

Bridget couldn't think. All she wanted was one more kiss, one more chance to feel alive again and to mean something to someone.

"Let Jane do it," Lupita said. "She already told Ola she wanted to."

"I can't do that," Bridget whispered. "Ola asked me to go. She's depending on me."

Lupita bowed her head in disappointment. "Please be careful."

Bridget's stomach was off doing cartwheels all on its own. "I will," she said in a low, breathless voice.

Lupita leaned forward and kissed her again before handing Bridget her ski mask back.

222

Bridget and Ola got in the van after Ola locked up the barn and checked the van's back door. In sign language, she cautioned Bridget not to speak.

"If you see anyone moving back there, just zap 'em," Ola said loud enough for everyone in the van to hear her. A few of the men began to whimper at the mention of that magic word "zap" again, but there was next to no movement and no mumbling through duct-taped mouths.

The smell in the van was terrible, but after the first five seconds of being in there, Bridget learned that breathing through her mouth was the only way to tolerate it. Unfortunately, she was too nervous about being in charge of the zapper to concentrate much on the two kisses she had shared with Lupita. *What a brave woman she is,* Bridget thought. *And what a great kisser!*

"Shut up back there!" Ola yelled.

Bridget jumped and realized she hadn't been paying attention. She did notice, however, that they were going back to town a different way. They were still traveling on a dirt road, but there were signs posted for a highway she didn't recognize coming up.

"You boys might finally get some decent food and maybe a shower tonight," Ola said.

Why doesn't she just drive? Bridget wondered. *What good is all this chitchat? All this taunting?*

One of the men raised his shackled feet and slammed them down again, making a loud racket. Before Bridget knew what was happening, several more men started doing the same thing.

"Hold on," Ola said just before she swerved the van from side to side on the dark country road.

Bridget could hear a few heads in the back hitting the side of the van as Ola shook them up like bound rag dolls.

"Reach back there and zap one of them," Ola said. "They'll straighten up when they hear the sound it makes."

Bridget turned to look in the back of the van, but it was too dark to see anything. She got her flashlight out of her pocket and switched it on. Everyone was right where they were supposed to be.

"Ahh," Ola said. "See? Just hearing the word 'zap' and they're all nice and quiet again."

It took them well over an hour to get back to San Antonio. The city lights made Bridget leery of wearing the ski mask as they rode along in the van, but she kept it on anyway. It didn't seem as though anyone out there on the streets was paying attention to them anyway.

One of the scariest parts of the entire evening for Bridget was being in the drive-thru car wash. The noise it made inside the van with the high-pressure spray hitting them all over gave her a bad case of claustrophobia. She had to close her eyes and pretend they were caught in a storm in order to keep herself from opening the door and bolting. Once the car wash was finished, Ola pulled up out of the way so Gwen could wash her car as well. *It's almost over,* Bridget thought. *Two more steps and we're in the clear.*

Once both vehicles were clean, Ola drove the speed limit and carefully followed all traffic laws. They were close to where Lupita lived when Ola finally switched on her flashers and turned down a dark street. She stopped the van about fifty yards away from where they turned and motioned for Bridget to hand her the stun gun. Ola put it in the canvas bag she had in the seat between them and tucked the van keys up over the visor. There were newspapers on the floorboard that Bridget hadn't noticed before. Ola opened her door and carefully collected the paper on the driver's and passenger's side of the van. She stuffed the newspapers in her bag and zipped it up.

"Let's go," she said, and started to run. Bridget followed her around the block where they saw Gwen's car parked at the end of the street.

Slowing their pace, they caught the three women inside off

guard. As Ola tapped on the front passenger's side window, two of the women inside screamed while Gwen accidentally honked the horn with her elbow. Bridget yanked off her ski mask and hissed, "Open the door! It's us!"

Lupita was alone in the backseat and scrambled to unlock the door.

"Jesus, Joseph and Mary!" Jane yelped. "You scared the living shit outta me!"

"Are we sure we want to get in a car with two Republicans?" Bridget asked Ola.

Lupita put her arms around Bridget's neck and pulled her inside the car. "Ohmigod! It's you," she said just before pulling off her own ski mask and kissing Bridget on the mouth.

"Maybe I should drive," Ola suggested.

"Yes," Gwen said from the driver's seat as she struggled to speak. "You drive. You scared me so bad I think I peed my pants."

As Ola drove them back to Gwen's house, the chatter in the car was constant and animated. The three women who had followed the van had a stream of never-ending questions for them.

"Did you get to zap anybody?" Jane asked excitedly. She was turned around in the front seat so she could see in the back better.

"No," Bridget said. "I didn't have to. Each time Ola suggested I do it, they got very quiet again."

"What happened when the van started swerving?" Lupita asked. She had her arm laced through Bridget's and was leaning close to her.

"Yeah!" Jane said. "We were so worried! We thought one of them got loose and was fighting for the wheel or something! Just like in the movies!"

"Nah," Ola said. "They started making some noise—"

"So she tossed them around like watermelons back there," Bridget added.

"Well, it scared the crap out of us!" Gwen said. "We were screaming like girls!"

"Did it scare you as much as when Ola tapped on the window?" Bridget asked.

"Hey!" Jane said. "Not funny!"

They laughed all the way to Gwen's house.

"OK," Ola said when she pulled into Gwen's driveway. "Keep the flashlights and the gloves, but put the rags and ski masks in my bag. Someone also needs to put Gwen's license plates back on."

"I can do that," Bridget said.

"OK. After that's done," Ola continued, "everyone go home and sit tight. I'll call Smokey on my way and then I'll call the police and tell them where they can find the van. The local news stations should be all over it by morning."

They were out of the car and Bridget got started on the front license plate while Jane worked on the back one.

"Also," Ola whispered, "we all need to go on about our business and not be in contact with each other for a few days. Let the dust settle first."

"What if Smokey gets in touch with any of us?" Gwen asked.

"Be cool," Jane said as she handed over one of the bogus license plates to Ola.

"Say nothing and be unavailable," Ola suggested. "The police might come around, too. Just do like Jane said. Be cool."

Bridget handed the other license plate to Ola, who stuck them both in her canvas bag.

"Thank you, ladies," Ola said. "I appreciate all you've done for me."

"No," Lupita said. "We're the ones who wanted to thank *you*. I know for a fact that you saved my life." She was the first to give Ola a long, warm hug.

Once Ola left, the four women exchanged hugs of their own on Gwen's porch.

"At least I got my car washed tonight," Gwen said.

"So we can't call each other and stuff?" Jane asked. "I'm missing that already."

"If the police suspect any of us," Gwen said, "there's a lot of things they can do to us that we don't even want to think about."

"We'd better all get going," Lupita said. "Ola still has a lot to do, and we need to be someplace else. It also wouldn't hurt for us to work on an alibi for tonight."

Bridget was nervous as she slowly drove away from Gwen's house. It took every ounce of self-control she had in order to just keep driving instead of parking the car and taking Lupita into her arms.

"What do you think is happening in that van right now?" Lupita asked quietly.

"A lot of kicking and yelling. It smells so bad the owners might not want that van back once this is over."

"Can we turn the radio on? We might hear some news about it."

Bridget switched on the radio and glanced at the clock on the dashboard. It was almost ten.

"Why am I still so nervous?" Lupita asked. She held out her hand, but it was too dark for Bridget to see if it was shaking or not.

"If no one knocks on my door over the next few days," Bridget said, "I'll certainly feel a lot better. But I don't think we're out of the woods yet."

"You know," Lupita said, "that police substation where Ola parked the van is close to my apartment. Maybe it's better if you drop me off at my mother's house."

"Where does your mother live?"

"Not far from where Consuelo is. Over there in that area."

Bridget didn't like the idea of Lupita being someplace so easily known to Rudy, whether it be her mother's house or Lupita's own apartment. *What if the police let Rudy go?* she thought. *What if they come looking for Lupita to let her know her husband has been found?*

"I have a better idea," Bridget said suddenly. "You can stay with me tonight. I have two spare rooms and no one has to know where you are. If Rudy gets out tonight, he might go looking for you. Or even his family could be looking for you."

"Ugh," Lupita said with a heavy sigh. She leaned back against the headrest. "Ola's troubles might be ending, but mine could just be starting up all over again."

"That settles it then. You're staying with me." Bridget turned the car around and headed toward her house.

Chapter Thirty-two

As soon as she arrived home, Bridget turned on the television. The ten o'clock local news hadn't been on very long and she and Lupita stayed glued to the TV waiting for information about the van. Finally, a commercial came on and they both managed to relax a little.

"Do I have ski mask hair?" Bridget asked, patting the top of her head.

With a tired smile, Lupita said, "Not at all. You've got really nice hair."

"You want something to drink? Did you have dinner?"

"I'm fine. Thanks."

Bridget took off her shoes and socks. "Well, we did it. We got them all back without incident. I think right now is the first time I've realized this whole crazy plan might actually work."

"It was awful seeing you get in that van with them tonight," Lupita admitted. "It made me see a lot of things more clearly."

"What things?"

The news came back on and they both sat up and were immediately engrossed in each new story. It wasn't until the weather came on that they were able to relax again.

"Are you feeling some mixed emotions about Rudy?" Bridget wondered out loud.

"Not really. Why do you ask?"

"It's no different than breakups between gay couples. I don't want to live with any of my exes, and with some of them I'll be just fine if I never see them again, but I wouldn't want anything bad to happen to them. You can't love someone that way once and not want them to be safe and happy somewhere else."

"Did any of your exes ever beat you?"

Bridget was shocked by the question. She knew that domestic violence occurred in all classes and every family structure mix imaginable, and no one was immune to it. But just the thought of one of the women she had shared her life with ever raising a hand to her was unthinkable. As bad as things had gotten with any of her partners, physical abuse had never been an issue for Bridget.

"Well?" Lupita said. "Did they?"

"No."

"The first time he hit me, we'd only been married a short time. I left him, but he begged me to take him back. His mother even begged me. She probably didn't want him living with her either. Anyway, I gave him another chance, and he cleaned up his act for a while, but he couldn't hold a job. Two years or so went by before he hit me again. I had him arrested and filed a restraining order against him. Restraining orders are such a joke. Do you have any idea how many women with restraining orders are killed each year? The numbers are staggering."

"This just in," the TV anchor said. "There's been a van found on the northwest side containing several illegal aliens. More on this breaking story as it becomes available."

"*What!*" Lupita and Bridget said at the same time.

"Illegal aliens?" Lupita repeated.

Bridget changed the channel.

"The van appears to be abandoned," the reporter from another station said. "As you can see behind me, several EMS units are on the scene. Our sources tell us there were twelve men found in the van and they had obviously been there for some time. This man lives nearby. Tell us, sir. What did you see?"

"A lotta lights and police sirens," the elderly man said. He appeared to be in his pajamas covered with an overcoat and his thinning hair standing straight up in the wind.

"Any idea who this van belongs to?" the reporter asked him.

"No, sir, but it wasn't there earlier when I came home from work."

The reporter nudged the man out of the way and addressed the camera. "We'll have the complete story at five a.m. Now back to—"

Bridget changed the channel, but other stations had already started their late night programming.

"My father has a police scanner," Bridget said, "but I don't want to call and get him suspicious."

"We'll just check out the news in the morning," Lupita said. "I could sure use a shower."

"Me, too. I feel like I still have that barn stench all over me." Bridget got up from the sofa. "One of the guest rooms has its own bathroom. Let me show you where it is. I'll get you some clean towels and something to sleep in."

She led the way down the hall and turned on the light in the first room on the right.

"I can't even remember the last time I was in here," Bridget said. "Looks like it's way past time to dust, though."

"It'll be fine," Lupita said. "I really appreciate this. Thank you."

"I'll be right back with those towels."

Bridget went to her room down at the end of the hallway and came back with some shorts, a T-shirt, and two clean towels. She set them on the end of the bed in the guest room.

"Everything you need should be in here somewhere," Bridget said. "Toiletries and a new toothbrush. I'm just down at the end of the hall. What time do you need to be up? I'll set my alarm."

"I'd like to be up by five to watch the local news."

231

"Oh! That's right." *How could you forget that?* Bridget wondered. "Then five it is. I'll see you in the morning."

She left the room and went to turn off all the lights in the house. Bridget was tired and emotionally drained from all they'd been through that evening. There was a great sense of warmth and satisfaction knowing she had helped the woman who had saved her life. If she never accomplished anything else as long as she lived, Bridget felt as though she had done something truly remarkable that night.

As she went down the hallway to her room after locking up the house, Bridget could hear the shower in the guest bathroom. It had been a long time since someone had stayed over. Just knowing Lupita was there made her feel less lonely.

Bridget came out of her bathroom in a terrycloth robe, drying her hair with a towel. She switched on the TV in her room and found some clean shorts and a T-shirt to wear to bed. Usually she slept nude, but with someone else in the house she didn't think that was wise. *You'll probably start out in these,* she thought as she took a pair of orange shorts and a purple T-shirt out of the drawer, *but you'll end up naked anyway by morning.*

The clothes she had been wearing that night didn't smell nearly as bad as she imagined they would. She was sure that the smell of that barn would be etched in her memory for years to come, though. She combed her hair and dressed for bed. After setting the alarm for five, she wondered what was happening at the scene where the van had been found.

Bridget slipped into bed, turned off the lamp on the night stand, and propped herself up on a stack of pillows. Her evening routine usually involved surfing the TV channels and finding nothing to watch. Occasionally she graded papers in bed, which was an excellent cure for any insomnia she might otherwise experience.

She heard a light knock on her bedroom door and saw Lupita

standing there. The T-shirt and shorts she had on were about two sizes too big for her and made Lupita look adorable.

"Is the TV too loud?" Bridget asked as she reached for the remote and hit the mute button.

"No. Not at all," Lupita said. "I was wondering if I could stay in here with you."

"Oh," Bridget said. "Sure!" She pulled back the covers on the bed in an inviting way and moved one of the pillows back on the other side of the bed.

"I just don't want to be alone tonight."

"I understand," Bridget said. *It's Rudy*, she thought. *He's back in town and could be out on bail by morning.*

"The TV doesn't bother me," Lupita said. "I fall asleep with it on all the time."

Bridget hit the mute button on the remote, turning the volume on to the theme music to *Cheers*.

At first Bridget thought she would be too nervous to relax and sleep with someone else in her bed, but the next thing she knew, the credits for *Cheers* were flashing on the TV. The program was over, which meant she had been asleep for about thirty minutes already. She turned the TV off and set the remote on the night stand. It wasn't until Lupita turned over that Bridget remembered she wasn't alone.

"Will you hold me?" Lupita sleepily whispered.

"Of course."

Bridget opened her arms and welcomed Lupita's soft, warm body. She couldn't remember anything ever feeling so right. It wasn't long before she heard Lupita's even, steady breathing. Bridget fell asleep quickly, too, and didn't wake up again until the alarm went off.

She wasn't accustomed to getting up so early, but Bridget's eyes popped open at the sound of the alarm clock and as she reached over to turn it off, she found the remote to turn the TV on. Lupita was on the other side of the bed, but moved over to be closer to her.

"Houston Judge Logan Harold, missing since November third, has been found in the back of a stolen van with eleven other men," the local news anchor said. "Judge Harold was the victim of a kidnapping and is at University Hospital listed in fair condition. With more on this still-breaking story is our Ken Rable. Ken?"

"Thank you, Fred. The van was found here on the northwest side of San Antonio in a quiet neighborhood. Our sources tell us there were twelve men inside who had been handcuffed and shackled. No one knows for sure how long these men had been in the vehicle or who left them there. All twelve men were taken to area hospitals suffering from severe dehydration. The van appears to have been stolen from a nursing home facility on the Southside. The Texas Rangers have been called in to help with the investigation. Authorities aren't releasing any details yet. We'll have an update on this story at noon. Back to you, Fred."

Bridget turned the channel to another local station.

" . . . eleven of the men appear to be local. Judge Harold is the only one from outside the San Antonio area. Police tell us the van was wiped clean of prints, and they have no clues as to who is responsible for leaving these men here this way. As I said earlier, this is still a breaking story and as soon as we know more—"

Bridget turned to another local news station.

" . . . Judge Harold is in fair condition suffering from severe dehydration. The Texas Rangers have been called in to help with this investigation. There was never any ransom offered for the Judge or any of the other victims, so the authorities are puzzled by this chain of events. We'll have more on this story at noon as it develops."

Bridget turned the volume down as the station returned to its regular morning news.

"Did you hear what they referred to those perverts as?" Lupita asked. She was sitting up in bed, her dark hair scrambled and her eyes still a bit squinty from sleep.

"Victims?" Bridget said. "Yes. I heard."

"Sounds like the media doesn't know about the tags on them yet," Lupita said. "We're sure putting a lot of trust in the police. I hope they don't let us down."

"If all twelve of those perverts are released from the hospital and get to go home," Bridget said as she threw the covers off and got out of bed, "then everything we've all been through was for nothing."

Lupita got up and helped her make the bed.

"The police might be keeping the media in the dark about a lot of things," Lupita commented.

Bridget had to smile at how cute Lupita looked in a T-shirt that hung down past her knees and shorts that were so big they would barely stay up.

"I need to go over to my place and get some clothes," Lupita said. She held up her hands. "I can't go to work like this."

Their silly laughter put them both in a good frame of mind to start off what would become a very tedious, difficult day.

Chapter Thirty-three

It was nearly six a.m. by the time Bridget and Lupita got to Lupita's apartment. Bridget had convinced her to stay with her for a few days—at least until things settled down. Lupita needed clothes for work and enough personal items to last for a while. Bridget wasn't surprised at how strange it felt to be so close to where they had left the van only a few hours earlier.

They climbed the stairs together, slowing their pace when they saw the notes stuck all over the apartment door. Lupita snatched them off, barely even glancing at any, and then unlocked the door.

"Who are the notes from?" Bridget asked. If they were from Rudy, she wanted to make sure they were out of there in a hurry.

"Rudy's brother," Lupita said, "and some reporters."

For some reason that didn't make Bridget feel any better. They went inside the small, tidy apartment. Bridget turned on the television to see if the local news had changed while she waited for Lupita to pack and get ready for work. Bridget heard the shower running and then a few minutes later the rustling of hangers in a closet. When Lupita finally came out of her bedroom, she was wearing a long rust-colored skirt, a tan sweater and beige boots with tall heels. She looked stunning, and luckily for Bridget, Lupita was oblivious to the effect she had on her. *Roll your tongue back in before you step on it,* Bridget reminded herself as she took a deep breath.

"Eight messages since yesterday afternoon," Lupita said, glancing over at the telephone. The red light on the answering machine blinked angrily.

"Are you going to check them?"

"No." Lupita went into her bedroom again and came out with a large suitcase. "Let's go. I don't want to be late for work."

"Here. I'll take that." Bridget got the suitcase from her while Lupita collected her cell phone charger, purse and a rust-colored blazer that matched her skirt.

She's not curious about the phone messages, Bridget thought. *She probably already knows who they're from.*

"I'm kind of looking forward to going to work today," Lupita said as she opened the door. "Hopefully, I'll be too busy to think about any of this."

All Bridget knew was that Lupita worked somewhere downtown on Flores Street. It wasn't until she was told to stop in front of the Frost Bank that Bridget knew where they were going. The sidewalk in front of the bank was crowded with men in suits as well as some dressed in jeans and T-shirts. Most had cameras or microphones, and upon closer inspection, Bridget noticed a TV camera from one of the local news stations.

"Do you work at this bank?" Bridget asked.

"No," Lupita said with a sigh. "I work next door at the Mexican Consulate's office."

"Well, what's going on here at the bank?"

"I'm hoping they're all waiting to cash a check, but since the

bank doesn't open for another hour and a half, that's not likely."
Lupita opened the car door. "I'll call you later. Let me know if you
hear anything of interest on the news."

"I'll pick you up after work," Bridget said. "What time do you
get off this afternoon?"

Before she could answer, one of the men on the sidewalk
opened the car door all the way and asked if she was Lupita Ochoa.
Lupita got out of the car and turned to Bridget and said, "Go."

Bridget didn't want to leave but noticed several of the men
coming around to her side of the car. She drove off slowly and
watched in her rearview mirror as Lupita disappeared into the
crowd of reporters.

She drove around the block and parked illegally across the one-
way street where she could see what was happening. When a car
behind her started honking, Bridget went around the block again.
The next time she saw Lupita, she was being escorted into the consulate's office by two security guards. Within less than a minute,
the crowd of reporters had dispersed.

On her way back home, Bridget called Lupita's cell phone.

"Hello."

"Are you OK?" Bridget asked with alarm. "Please tell me
there's been some sort of international incident involving us and
Mexico."

Lupita's soft, tired laughter made Bridget's heart skip a beat.

"We should be so lucky," Lupita said. "Actually, Rudy has told
the police and the media all he knows about me, where I work and
where I live. He's also told them all he knows about the woman
calling herself Kate the Lesbian."

There was something about the way Lupita spoke and the
things she said that put Bridget on instant alert. Could it be possible that their phone calls were being monitored?

"What all does he know about her?"

"He knows nothing," Lupita said, "but Rudy loves attention
and he's finally getting some."

"Is he out of the hospital?"

238

"I don't know."

"Are you sure you're OK?"

"I'm fine. This is the best place for me now. I'll call you later."

Bridget drove home and listened to the radio to see if she could get any news about the van and the twelve men. A while later when she turned down her street on her way home, she saw five cars parked in front of her house.

"Isn't it a little early for you to be up?" Mrs. McBee asked when she found Bridget standing on her parents' front porch. Her mother was well aware of her sleeping habits.

"Have you been listening to the news?"

"Your father has it on. Have you had breakfast yet?"

Bridget couldn't think of a better distraction than being with her parents, but she still couldn't put Lupita out of her mind. *If there are cars in front of my house,* she thought, *I'm sure Jane and Gwen are getting the same kind of attention along with all the other women known to have been attacked. At least let's hope that's what the situation is,* she thought. *If all twelve women aren't being sought after by police and reporters now, then the four of us might have screwed up somewhere last night!*

Bridget felt fear dart through her body at the possibility of the police knowing exactly what all had gone on the evening before, as well as how involved the four of them had been.

Bridget sat down to breakfast with her parents but didn't have much of an appetite. She was just starting to wake up a bit more when her father asked, "Are you going with us to Dallas for Thanksgiving?"

"Uh . . . I haven't thought about it," Bridget said.

"It's next week. We're considering flying instead of driving. The rates will be through the roof, but at our age a forty-minute flight beats a five-hour drive any day."

Bridget's cell phone rang—it was Lupita. She excused herself from the table and went outside on the patio to take the call.

"I had about fifteen messages waiting for me here when I got to work," Lupita said. "All from Rudy's family telling me he's in the hospital. They expect me to go see him today."

"Oh."

"I'm not going."

Bridget felt the relief slowly begin to seep out of her body.

"I have a call in for my lawyer," Lupita said. "Rudy violated the restraining order when he attacked me the last time I saw him. I want to make sure the police remember that."

"Do you think they'll take him to jail once he's out of the hospital?"

"I hope so."

Bridget told her about the cars that had been in front of her house that morning. "I'm here at my parents' place now."

"Smokey said it would be easy to find out all kinds of things about us, so nothing would surprise me anymore, at least not after that fiasco here at work this morning."

"I'm thinking about going home and seeing what they want," Bridget said. "And getting all of that out of the way before I pick you up later."

"This thing with Rudy could get nasty, Bridget. It might be best if I call my sister and have her pick me up after work. I can stay with my mother for a while."

"No, please," Bridget said quickly. "I've got your clothes and other things already. You'll be safe at my house. I promise."

"I'm not worried about being safe. I'm worried about getting you involved in all of this—"

"I'm already involved," Bridget whispered. "I *want* to be involved. It'll be OK. Really."

There was silence for a moment. Bridget held her breath as she waited to hear what Lupita would say next. *Geez, you suck at this,* she reminded herself, but to her immense relief, Lupita said, "Then pick me up at five."

❧

On Bridget's way home after breakfast with her parents, she had an overwhelming urge to call Gwen and Jane to see what was happening with them, but she remembered Ola's suggestion about laying low and keeping to themselves. She turned down her street and saw only one car in front of her house now. Bridget made up her mind right away that she wanted this over with.

She pulled into her driveway and a man got out of his car. He appeared to be in his mid-thirties and was dressed casually in black slacks and a gray tweed sport coat.

"Ms. McBee?" he called.

"Yes?"

"My name's Alan Harper. I'm a reporter for the *Dallas Morning News*." He showed her his press credentials. "Can I ask you a few questions about a woman calling herself Kate the Lesbian?"

"No comment," Bridget said. "I've already told the police all I know."

"Vigilantes are of great interest to the public."

Bridget stayed close to the driver's side of her car. No way was she inviting this man into her home no matter what kind of credentials he had.

"Are you aware of a van that was found last night?" he asked.

"It's been all over the news this morning," she said calmly. "Something about illegal aliens."

Alan Harper's smirk did nothing to endear himself to her. "It seems as though the twelve men who were in the van were taken by force from separate crime scenes. They were taken by the woman known as Kate the Lesbian. One of those men is the one who attacked you, Ms. McBee."

Even though he wasn't telling her anything she didn't already know, the shock of hearing someone actually say the words out loud stunned her for a moment.

"Ms. McBee?"

Bridget blinked a few times and took a deep breath. "No comment," she whispered.

"Is there anything new you can tell me about this woman?

Anything at all that you've been able to remember since you last spoke with the police?"

She didn't say anything else and started walking toward her front door.

"Thank you for your time," he called.

She reached her front porch and stopped and turned around. "Mr. Harper," Bridget said. "Do you know anything about the man who attacked me?"

Alan Harper was still standing in the same place. "He's been released from the hospital and he's now in police custody."

Bridget breathed a sigh of relief at hearing that bit of good news.

"The police might be able to tell you more," he said.

Chapter Thirty-four

Bridget had five phone messages waiting for her. She checked them and was surprised at how many were from reporters from around the state. The last message, however, was from the San Antonio Police Department. They wanted her to come down to the station and identify the man who had attacked her.

As she drove back downtown, Bridget had mixed emotions about seeing her attacker again. Last night she had made herself scarce when it had been time to get him in the van. She wanted him to be locked away for a long time, and Bridget knew she had to do everything possible in order to make sure that happened. The next woman he attacked might not be as lucky as she had been.

Bridget drove around the police station and eventually found a parking place. She wasn't far from where Lupita worked and Bridget couldn't help but wonder how she was doing now. Getting out of her car and climbing the grungy steps to the police station, Bridget saw Jane coming out of the building.

"Ohmigod!" Jane said as she threw her arms around her. "It's so good to see you! Are you here for a pervert lineup, too?"

"I think so," Bridget said. "They called and wanted to see me."

"I just got finished with all of that," Jane said. "Like I could ever forget that dirty-rat-bastard's ugly face. Anyway, I need to get back to work. I'm supposed to be in a meeting right now."

Bridget went inside the building and asked for the officer who had left her the message. The whole process was quick and painless. *This is just like what I've seen on TV,* she thought. Everything about the inside of the building looked worn and tired. *A coat of paint would do it a world of good,* she thought. *What a depressing place.*

Bridget was taken to a room where one entire wall was all glass. Six men were brought in and lined up—all dressed very similar and with features that were surprisingly alike. She knew immediately which man had approached her, grabbed her and pressed a knife to her throat. A shiver darted through her body, and she thought she might be sick.

I bet he looks a lot better now than he did when they put him in the van last night, she thought. *Probably smells better, too.* There were things in her life she would never forget, and this man's face was one of them. Bridget identified him, wrote a statement and was ready to go. The officer explained that charges would be filed and the perpetrator would be in jail shortly.

But for how long? she wondered on her way back to her car. *What if that scumbag makes bail? If reporters can find my address, why can't this guy find it too if he gets out? Face it,* she thought as she unlocked her car door. *You felt safer when Ola had them all tied up in a barn.*

Bridget drove to the main post office and bought a Houston paper. The headline read: "Judge Harold Found In San Antonio." Smokey Wells had written the article, which Bridget thought to be alarmingly accurate. Details such as the tags pinned to their clothing were mentioned, and the article strongly implied that Judge

Harold was guilty of attempting to sexually assault an escort he had arranged to have dinner with. Nothing like that had been reported by the San Antonio media. Bridget thought Smokey had done a good job on the article, covering the basics of Judge Harold's hospital stay and his claim of being a kidnap victim. *She has her story,* Bridget thought. *Hopefully, Smokey's sniffing around will stop soon.*

While at the post office, she also purchased a San Antonio paper in which the articles concentrated more on the van, where it had been stolen from and the condition of the twelve men. It was apparent that Smokey had either done more homework on her story or she had some excellent sources. The San Antonio reporters had obviously spent more time on the details of the van because that was about as much information as the local police had released so far. *Maybe with Smokey's help,* Bridget thought, *Judge Harold won't get away with this. He needs to pay for his crime just like those other eleven losers.*

It was a little after three when Bridget heard a knock on her door. She had been grading papers and was contemplating taking a nap before going to pick up Lupita from work. She peeked out around the drapes and saw a limo in front of her house. There was another knock on her door and Bridget found Lupita there on the porch.

"Hi. My boss let me off early," Lupita said. She turned to wave at the limo driver who then slowly drove away. "He also offered me a ride. We were trying to beat the afternoon rush of reporters."

"Wow. Come in!" Bridget held the door open for her. "What a nice surprise. Can I get you anything?"

"Just hold me."

Lupita stepped into her arms and they held each other while Bridget's stomach did a few somersaults of joy. Lupita smelled dreamily of Escape perfume and her jet-black hair was soft against Bridget's cheek. After a moment, she pulled away from Lupita just enough to find her lips. Their kiss began as innocent exploring before eventually melting into a slow, simmering hunger for more. Bridget felt as though she were floating, and she couldn't remember the last time she had felt this way, the last time someone had wanted her or cared about her with any semblance of passion.

Their kiss deepened into a heated exchange of breathtaking emotion and desire. When Lupita reached for the buttons on Bridget's shirt, she felt such a rush of urgency and longing that she wasn't sure if she could remain standing.

Once her shirt was open, Bridget slipped Lupita's blazer off and let it fall to the floor.

"So soft," Lupita whispered as she kissed the side of Bridget's face, making a slow trail of kisses up to her earlobe and into her neck. "You're so much softer than I imagined you would be."

She's imagined this already, Bridget thought as she leaned her head back so Lupita could explore her throat with that wonderful mouth.

"You're making my knees weak," Bridget said in a trembling voice.

"Right now my everything feels weak," Lupita whispered. "Take me to bed."

Their lips met again in a ravishing burst of heat and desire. Bridget was certain she had never felt this way before. Something new and primal had been released inside of her. As long as she lived, Bridget would never forget this moment. She would never forget how wild and happy the words "take me to bed" had made her feel.

She grabbed Lupita by the hand and led her down the hallway to her bedroom. The usual concerns about making love for the first time with someone new weren't there this time. Bridget wasn't afraid of anything that involved this woman. Nothing in her life had ever felt so right.

The first time they made love was as hot and clumsy as one would expect from two people who knew nothing about each other, but the desire to please helped them overcome whatever initial awkwardness there had been between them. Lupita seemed fascinated with Bridget's breasts, which was more than fine with both of them.

"So soft," Lupita kept muttering over and over again. "I can't touch you enough."

Bridget smiled and kissed her on the forehead. "Take your time. There's no hurry."

Lupita was also avidly curious about Bridget's naked body, and she took great pleasure in kissing her all over as well as rubbing her own wonderful breasts against Bridget's. Having an orgasm had become more of an afterthought and a nice surprise once Lupita's urge to explore led them in that direction. Lupita was eager to show her what she liked, and Bridget felt comfortable enough to do the same. Then as if they knew all they needed to know, fingers easily slipped into the right places and they were off on a new, incredible adventure. They rolled on top of each other and kissed until the next level of intimacy became nothing less than an emergency.

Afterward, Lupita kissed her with such passion that it left them both ravenous for more. They made love for hours and napped off and on, entwined in each other's arms.

Bridget woke up to tiny kisses on her bare shoulder. The bedroom was dark except for a sliver of light coming from the bathroom. She tightened her arms around Lupita and kissed her sweetly on the lips.

"I'm starving," Lupita said.

"What time is it?" Bridget turned her head to look at the clock. It was eight-thirty and already dark outside.

Lupita propped herself up on an elbow and slowly pulled the sheet down, uncovering Bridget's breasts.

"I adore these," she said, and bent down to lightly run the tip of her tongue around Bridget's left nipple.

"They're quite fond of you, too."

"Do you have anything to eat?" Lupita asked. "I'm starving. I didn't have lunch today." She took one of Bridget's nipples into her mouth. "Never mind," she whispered. "I found something."

Bridget laughed and touched Lupita's face with the back of her hand. She kissed her and pulled her into her arms.

"I'd better get some real nourishment in you," Bridget whispered. "You'll need it for later."

Dressed in baggy shorts and T-shirts, Bridget and Lupita sat around the dining room table with chips, dips, a fresh loaf of bread and cold cuts. Bridget had a bottle of wine ready to open when the doorbell rang. She saw the instant apprehension and uneasiness register in Lupita's eyes.

"Maybe if I don't answer it they'll go away," Bridget suggested.

"The lights are on and your car's in the driveway. Go see who it is."

"And *then* get rid of them," Bridget added.

She turned on the porch light and peeked out through the drapes. Smokey Wells was standing there by the door.

"It's Smokey," Bridget called over her shoulder.

"And the Bandit?" Lupita added. They both chuckled. "Is she alone?"

Bridget knocked on the window to get her attention. "Are you alone?"

"Yes," Smokey said.

Bridget opened the door and let her in. "I read your article on the judge today. I liked it."

"Thanks," Smokey said. She had on a denim jacket and jeans and looked a little ragged around the edges. It was obvious that the wind had been playing havoc with her hair.

"Come in," Bridget said. "We're having dinner, sort of. Let me get another plate if you don't mind sandwiches."

"I'm glad to find you two here," Smokey said as she took off her jacket. "Gwen's working, and Jane isn't home."

"So I was your third choice?" Bridget asked dryly. Lupita smiled at her as they both seemed to enjoy Smokey's momentary discomfort.

"What's up?" Lupita asked.

"I need some advice." Smokey sat down at the table, and Lupita handed her the wine bottle and a corkscrew. As they made sandwiches and drank wine, Smokey began to talk.

"She's been in touch with me."

"She who?" Bridget asked.

"Kate the Lesbian."

"Holy shit," Bridget said in her best attempt at a "surprised" voice. "For real?"

"For real. She calls me from a pay phone and doesn't let me ask many questions. She talks and I take notes."

"Why you?" Lupita asked. "Why not a San Antonio reporter?"

"I attempted to ask her the same thing," Smokey said as she looked at both of them with a slow, steady once-over. "I have no idea why she picked me or even how she found me. That's part of the reason I'm here. Do you two have any ideas about why she would choose me for her story?"

"Maybe it's because you claim to be a lesbian," Bridget said.

"Claim to be?"

"I don't think you are. You sort of dress the part, but there's something missing. I think you'd claim to be anything that would get you a good story."

Smokey stuck a knife into the mustard jar and had a little smirk on her face.

Ha! Bridget thought. *I'm right!*

"That doesn't explain how she found me," Smokey said.

Bridget didn't really like this woman and now wished she hadn't invited her in. *She's only here to pump us for information*, Bridget thought, *so I'll just make sure I don't give her any.*

"You told us yourself that it's easy to find out anything on anyone," Lupita reminded her.

"Yeah, well—"

"And you've done other articles on the missing judge," Bridget said. "This Kate the Lesbian person has probably read everything written on this story—even in its early stages. Maybe she liked what she saw in you compared to whatever else she was reading."

"Yeah, you could be right," Smokey said, a bit reluctant to be influenced by flattery. "And here I was all ready to think the four of you had figured out who she was."

"You give us way too much credit," Bridget said with a laugh.

"We would *love* to know who she is!" Lupita chimed in. "What does she sound like? Was it like talking to an angel? That's how I'll always remember her."

"Not really," Smokey said. "But then I have no idea what an angel would sound like. She's a pain in the ass, if you want the truth. She gives me just enough new information each time to make a mediocre story a great one. The info is so good I think the cops are starting to get suspicious."

"Can you blame them? You seem to know a lot more than the cops do," Bridget noted.

"That's why I'm here in San Antonio now. The police in Houston want to see me, so I'm here doing more research and trying to get an interview with the judge. He's still recovering in the hospital."

"What does Kate talk about when she calls you?" Lupita asked.

"She's adamant about wanting to see justice served," Smokey said with a bit of irritation in her voice. "It's like that's the reason she's giving me all this information. She expects me to write articles to help sway public opinion. If any of those men get out of jail, she wants me to hound them in print, keep the public aware and riled up that these guys are sex offenders." Smokey took a healthy swig of wine from her glass. "She's giving me the story of a lifetime. Reporters would kill to be in my position right now."

"So what kind of advice do you need?" Bridget asked. "Sounds like Kate the Lesbian has you by the *huevos*. You either do what she says, or she'll find another reporter."

"I have a story coming out in tomorrow's edition of the *Houston Chronicle* and the *San Antonio Express-News*. It states specific details about what happened to each of those men after Kate took them. I expect the police to be looking for me as soon as the papers hit the stands."

"Reporters don't have to reveal their sources, right?" Lupita asked.

"I couldn't reveal this source anyway," Smokey said. "She gets in touch with *me* each time, and she's careful about how long she stays on the phone. I wouldn't be surprised if I didn't spend a few days in jail over this, though, but that would only give the stories more publicity."

"You know what they do to nice-looking women in jail?" Lupita asked with a teasing wink. Her hair had that "I've just been ravished in bed" look that made Bridget's stomach do a little flip.

"I just *love* those 'women in prison' movies," Bridget added with a laugh.

"Well, you two sure aren't any help!"

"Seriously," Lupita said. "It sounds to me like we all want the same thing Kate the Lesbian wants. We all want justice. These scum-buckets who go around attacking women need to be punished whether they happen to be bums under a bridge or a judge on the bench. Kate's asking you to help her accomplish that. If it means you have to spend a few nights in jail, then maybe the publicity will help benefit our cause."

"I agree," Bridget said. "Let these twelve weenies tell their stories. All the way to the part where a beautiful woman stuffs their ugly butts in the trunk of her car. Maybe that'll make a few of them out there think twice before hurting someone else."

"Talking about this jail thing makes me very uncomfortable," Smokey said, shaking her head as she took another bite of her sandwich.

"Then maybe you're not the right reporter for the job," Bridget suggested. She looked up and met Lupita's gaze. They smiled at each other.

"Maybe Bridget's right," Lupita agreed.

"Oh, no!" Smokey said. "No one's taking this away from me! Just because I don't like talking about jail-time doesn't mean I won't give this story a hundred percent."

"Ever been strip searched?" Bridget asked. "Or even better, have you ever had a body cavity search?" She took a leisurely bite of her sandwich and enjoyed seeing Smokey's wide-eyed look. *That's what she gets for pretending to be a lesbian,* Bridget thought.

"By a jail matron called Big Bertha?" Lupita added.

"Cut it out, you two," Smokey said with a nervous laugh. She slowly took the last bite of her sandwich.

"So what kind of advice do you need?" Bridget asked. "Or did we cover that already?"

"I think I just needed a break," Smokey said, "and maybe some reassurance that I'm doing the right thing."

"You're reporting the truth," Lupita said. "The truth should always be the right thing."

"If all Kate the Lesbian wants right now is justice," Smokey said, "then there might be a problem. I can't promise her justice. No one can. The only thing I can promise is a good story as long as she keeps talking to me."

"How long will you let her keep you dangling this way?" Bridget asked.

"Dangling?"

"Yeah, dangling," Bridget said. "She calls and you drop what you're doing to jump on the next angle of this story. She's throwing you a few crumbs and you write something up until the next phone call."

"I'll keep doing this until the whole story's told."

Bridget put her napkin on the table. "How will you know when that happens?"

Smokey shrugged. "I'll know."

"Tell us why you really came here," Bridget said. "You don't need our advice or a pat on the back for the good job you're doing. And if all you needed was a break, then you could just as easily have gone for a walk or to see a movie."

"You're hoping we know more than we're telling you," Lupita said. "Since neither one of us was your first choice for a little visit this evening, I bet you expected to get more out of Gwen or Jane. Am I right?"

The smile Smokey tried to hide behind her napkin told them what they wanted to know. "Gwen and Jane are usually more eager to talk than ask questions. You two like picking things apart. I have to think too much when I'm around you."

"What does that mean?" Bridget asked.

"Let me ask you this," Smokey said. "If you did know something, would you tell me?"

"But we don't know anything," Bridget said.

"That wasn't the question." Smokey shrugged. "I appreciate you taking the time to talk to me." She stood up and the other two got up as well. "Thanks for dinner."

"The women who were attacked deserve your attention, Smokey," Bridget said. "If you can help put those men away, then you're another kind of hero to all concerned. That's probably all Kate the Lesbian wants from you now."

"I'll do what I can to help make that happen. Just don't get your hopes up."

"One more thing," Bridget said. "The next time Kate the Lesbian calls you can you thank her for us? She saved my life. She saved a lot of lives."

"I'll do that."

"And we promise to visit you in jail if it comes to that," Lupita added.

"How thoughtful of you!"

Bridget opened the front door for her. As Smokey put on her jacket and stepped off the porch, Bridget said, "For your sake, I hope Big Bertha has small hands."

Chapter Thirty-five

Bridget woke up each morning feeling truly blessed to have Lupita beside her. Even though Lupita had only been staying there with her less than a week, they had already settled into a nice routine. They spoke on the phone several times during the day when Lupita was at work, and Bridget got up with her early in the morning so they could have coffee and breakfast together. When Bridget wasn't teaching in the afternoons, she picked her up from work.

Lupita's husband remained in jail, and his family was upset that Lupita had filed charges against him. None of them knew where she was staying, so the harassing phone calls from Rudy's family stopped in the evenings when she turned off her cell phone.

"What do you want to do about Thanksgiving?" Lupita asked as they sat down to dinner Tuesday evening. Bridget had put a roast in the crock pot that morning.

"My family is meeting in Dallas at my brother's house this year," Bridget said. "I already told them I couldn't make it."

"Rudy's brother has been watching my mother's place," Lupita said with a sigh. "My sister approached him yesterday and he eventually moved on, but I don't think they are giving up on trying to find me." She scooped potatoes, onions, mushrooms and carrots from the steamy, brimming bowl and passed it over to Bridget. "Maybe if we went over early to my mother's house we could—"

"Have you thought about us just staying here for Thanksgiving and doing something?"

Surprised, Lupita looked up from her plate. "You mean have Thanksgiving dinner here?"

"Why not?"

"We couldn't get a turkey thawed in time. At least not safely."

"You can buy them thawed already, or we can buy one already cooked with all the trimmings," Bridget said, getting excited about the idea. In her mind there was no better way to gauge the seriousness of a new relationship than by spending a major holiday together. It seemed a little early to be meeting family members already, but the thought still made Bridget happy.

"I think I'd feel better about things if I stayed away from my family for this holiday," Lupita said. "It would be just like Rudy's mother to show up with some people to try and cause trouble if they knew I'd be at my mother's house. I'll explain it to her. She already knows how worried I am about all of this."

Bridget reached for Lupita's hand and gave it a light squeeze. She didn't like knowing there were still people out there wanting to hurt her.

"Maybe you should get a restraining order against other members of Rudy's family."

"I've thought about it. If things keep up this way I will."

The phone rang, and Bridget went to check the caller ID. It was Gwen.

"Hello! How are you?" Bridget asked.

"I'm fine. I miss you," Gwen said. "I was wondering what you were doing for Thanksgiving. I'm actually off that day."

"Lupita and I were just discussing that."

There was a moment of silence before Gwen said, "Jane's

ordering a turkey and all the extras from a caterer she knows. We're throwing this together pretty much at the last minute. So can you and Lupita make it?"

"Just a minute." Bridget put her hand over the phone and asked Lupita what she thought of the idea.

"Whatever happened to that 'keeping a low profile' thing?"

Bridget shrugged. "We kept kind of low for a few days there. Hey, it's Thanksgiving!"

Lupita smiled. "OK. Sure."

Bridget put the phone up to her ear again. "We'd love to. What time?"

On Thanksgiving Day, as soon as they got up, Bridget could tell that Lupita was not her usual agreeable self. Bridget went to make coffee and let her have some space. A few minutes later Lupita shuffled into the kitchen and came up behind her to put her arms around Bridget's waist and rested her head against her back.

"I feel whiney today," Lupita confessed.

Bridget chuckled and poured two cups of coffee. "You do? Any idea why?"

"No."

"Could it be that even though Rudy's in jail, he's still managing to screw up your Thanksgiving?"

"Maybe." She let go of her and took the cup Bridget offered. "Will Christmas be like this, too? New Year's Eve? All those holidays are usually spent with my family."

"We'll get the Rudy-thing worked out before Christmas," Bridget said. "I promise." She turned around and kissed her lightly on the lips. "You should call your mom's house today and talk to your relatives. Maybe Rudy's family is having their own holiday dinner and leaving everyone else alone."

"Oh, great," Lupita said as she hugged her. "Get the Ochoas together with a few beers and no telling what all could happen. Those people are just flakey enough to try and storm the jail and cause a scene there, too."

"Then what could be better than having them all in jail at the same time?"

Lupita smiled. "You're just trying to cheer me up."

They took a shower together, and Bridget was glad to see that Lupita's gloomy mood was lifting.

"Just being with you," Lupita said. She sat on the side of the bed with a towel around her wet hair and a bottle of lotion in her hand. "Just being with you here . . . like this . . ."

Bridget pulled out a pair of underwear and a sports bra from the drawer and stopped to look at her.

"What about being with me here?" Bridget asked.

Lupita shrugged and squeezed lotion onto her palm.

"I don't know how I ever thought I could be happy with a man. What in the world was I thinking back then?"

Bridget smiled and slipped into her underwear. "Some lesbians never figure that one out. They just go through their lives wondering what the problem is. You're lucky to have saved yourself a lot of time and heartache. I have a friend who was married three times before it occurred to her that something just wasn't right. Then the moment she kissed her first woman, things fell into place."

"You know when it all really began to make sense for me?" Lupita had a shapely leg on the bed, slightly bent at the knee, slowly rubbing lotion over her soft, brown skin. Bridget couldn't take her eyes away. Lupita looked up and a slow smile spread across her face. "Are you listening to me?"

Embarrassed, Bridget got busy again getting dressed. "Of course I am."

"What was the last thing I said?"

"You asked if I was listening to you."

"No. Before that."

Bridget laughed, still embarrassed. "You've gotten me all distracted. I'm sorry. What was it you were saying?"

"Never mind. I don't even remember now." Lupita finished putting lotion on one leg and started on the other.

"Something about when all of this started to make sense to you," Bridget said.

"So you *were* listening."

My God she's beautiful, Bridget thought.

"All of this started to make sense to me when I began to notice how much attention Gwen was giving you. I couldn't understand why it always made me so pissy."

Bridget laughed hearing her use such a word.

"I would go home at night and couldn't sleep," Lupita confessed. "I kept wondering what you two were doing. I had an awful time with it."

Bridget slipped on some tan corduroy slacks and zipped them up. She still couldn't take her eyes off Lupita.

"Then that night we were talking to Ola on the computer," Lupita said as she pulled the towel off her hair and gently rubbed it dry. "Gwen was playing with your hair and rubbing your neck. I wanted to scratch her eyes out," she said with a laugh. "Well, maybe nothing quite that drastic, but it was close."

"I never got *any* signals from you," Bridget said. "Not one. You and Jane were all wrapped up in your own little world."

"Jane gave it a few good tries," Lupita admitted, "but she couldn't get past the fact that I was married and that her girlfriend was still in love with her. Jane is an emotional mess. She doesn't see any of it, but if you get her talking about anything personal, it all comes tumbling out quickly."

Lupita stood up and started to get dressed. She wasn't shy about her body, which made Bridget's heart swell.

"I'm glad you took a chance on me," Bridget said quietly. "It wasn't easy seeing Jane whisk you off after every meeting. Or seeing the two of you arriving somewhere together."

"But you wouldn't have done anything about it."

"No," Bridget admitted. "You seemed happy with the arrangement."

"I've learned a lot these last few weeks," Lupita said. She

tugged on a pair of tight jeans. "If you don't go after what you want, you'll never get it. You as much as told me that once, and you were right."

Bridget felt a little tumble in her stomach. "I've never been known to take my own advice. So . . . uh . . . I was something you wanted?"

Lupita turned around and looked at her. "You were," she whispered, "and you still are." The emotion in her voice brought a lump to Bridget's throat. "No one's ever made me feel the way you do. No one. I can't even begin to explain it to you."

Bridget couldn't speak and her eyes clouded over with tears. She managed to nod and then finished dressing.

Gwen's house had the most wonderful Thanksgiving smells waiting to greet them. When they arrived, Bridget handed over a pumpkin pie and closed her eyes to inhale roasted turkey while her stomach growled.

"You should see the spread Jane's putting together in there," Gwen said. She wore a tall pilgrim hat with a buckle on the front. She had one for each of them and upon closer inspection, Bridget could see that the hats were plastic, but very authentic-looking.

"Do we have to wear these?" Lupita asked with a curled-up nose. "My people came from across the river. There's not a drop of pilgrim blood in me anywhere."

"There's none in me either," Bridget said, "but I'll wear one." She took the hat Gwen offered and stuck it on her head.

Jane came out of the kitchen with an apron that had a winking turkey on the front of it. Her pilgrim hat was perched on the back of her shaggy red head.

"Good to see you both," Jane said and gave them each a hug. "They say that pilgrims have to wear suspenders because they keep their buckles on their hats."

It was fun laughing with them again. Bridget reluctantly admitted that she had missed these two. They followed Jane into the kitchen and Gwen set the pie down on the counter. There was already enough food in the kitchen to feed a dozen people.

"Where are the kids?" Lupita asked.

"With their father for the next few days," Gwen said.

"The police are tripping all over themselves to get more evidence on that guy who killed Ola's sister," Jane said. She dried her hands on the bottom of her apron. "He made them look bad when he escaped the first time, so now they're throwing the book at him. He'll go away for a long time for her murder. That's helped calm Ola down considerably."

"You've been in touch with her?" Lupita asked.

"Just briefly." Jane laughed. "She called me from a pay phone. She must've gotten me confused with Smokey."

"Oh, have you two heard the latest about the judge?" Gwen asked.

Bridget was a tad nervous when Lupita reached for her hand in front of their friends, but when she squeezed it and laced their fingers together, Bridget felt as though a surge of energy had raced through her body. She gathered strength from just touching Lupita, and whatever brief bit of apprehension there had been initially was now gone.

"What about the judge?" Lupita asked. She leaned closer to Bridget, allowing their shoulders to touch.

Bridget could hear Gwen talking, but the only thing that really mattered was the connection she felt with the woman she loved. No matter what obstacles were ahead for them, whether those obstacles included divorce issues for Lupita, family issues with Lupita's current in-laws, or just ordinary relationship blues, Bridget knew they were in this together.

"So the judge is having a little mental breakdown?" Lupita asked.

"Our Smokey has been busy!" Jane said. "She's been in touch with escort services in other Texas cities where he's been on business trips, and she found four women he's slapped around and tried to beat up."

"Now all of a sudden he goes into a catatonic state anytime someone asks him a question about it," Gwen said.

"Will he go to jail?" Lupita asked. She let go of Bridget's hand in order to get a clump of grapes off a fruit tray.

"Once he gets out of the loony bin," Jane said.

"Out of psychiatric care," Gwen said, giving Jane a disapproving look.

"Hey, he's been caught with his pants down," Jane said. "He's the one we were worried about getting away with it. As it stands now, it won't just be Number Ten's word against his. Now we've got four other women who will testify against him."

"Pictures of all twelve men will be in the paper soon, too," Gwen announced. "I betcha once *that* happens, more women will come forward with new charges against all of them except Rudy. I find it hard to believe that we were the first and only women these perverts had ever attacked."

"Wow," Bridget said. "It looks like things are finally coming together."

Lupita smiled and poked a grape into Bridget's mouth.

"Speaking of coming together," Jane said with a grin, "how are you two doing these days?"

Bridget nearly choked on the grape, but as she was coughing and being slapped on the back by her friends, she knew things would be just fine.

Epilogue

Waikiki Beach

Ola Cordician watched the sun set over the ocean—it had a very calming effect on her. She needed this rest but was torn between returning to her job in San Antonio and everything else that was familiar there or perhaps remaining in this paradise of blue until she was ready to move on again. The dreams had stopped, and Ola embraced that with both relief and a bit of sadness. She was able to finally get the sleep she needed in order to function, and she no longer feared whatever the night might bring. But the dreams had also been a constant reminder that she and her sister, Kate, were still in touch. Ola missed that connection to her sister, even if it was only in her dreams, and it was hard for her to let go of that.

She had been able to come to terms with the fact that it wasn't possible to save all women from whatever evil lurked in the darkness. As fate and her sister would have it, Ola had been able to help several women for a brief period of time, and for that she would always be grateful. Knowing that she had made a difference in some women's lives helped her cope with all the violence and pain Kate had been through at the hands of a murderer. In many ways, justice had already been served, but in other ways there was nothing that could ever be done to vindicate what so many had lost.

Ola would never forget the terror that had surrounded her during the first dream. Kate's message and the visions forced on her that night had been bone chilling and frightening. Ola could hear Kate's voice inside her head as street signs, buildings and huge clocks branded places and times into her brain. Kate urged her to go to these places and even sent her visions of someone in black arriving on the scene in a car just like the one Ola had recently purchased. Because she had never experienced such a vivid dream before, that alone had been enough to make Ola want to forgo sleep as long as possible.

Kate's resourcefulness even after she was gone still amazed Ola to this day. Even though Kate did everything she could to get her on the scene to help those women, it was Ola's idea to put the attackers in the tiny trunk of her car and take them away. Letting them go while knowing what these men were capable of made no sense to her at the time. Putting each of them back on the street again to hurt someone else was certainly not an option. The single most important thing that drove Ola to commit such brutality was the thought of Kate being so alone when she died. If only someone had arrived and pointed a gun at her attacker, both of their lives would have been changed forever.

But no one had been there for Kate. No one had come to her rescue. It became obvious to Ola that Kate didn't want that for the others, and she chose her to be that "someone" for them. The dreams made it impossible for Ola to say no to her.

That first night as she drove to the location Kate had shown her in the dream, Ola was shocked to see a man there slapping a woman as he yanked her around by the hair. The scene was exactly as she had witnessed it in her dream just nights before. Ola was shaking all over at the realization that her sister had contacted her and brought her there to help that woman. She was still in shock as she got out of the car and pointed the gun at him. Ola remembered her relief at seeing the fear in his eyes when he finally noticed the gun. She knew she had the advantage, and it was obvious to them both that he was no longer in control of anything. Ola wanted to be sure he wouldn't hurt anyone else ever again.

After getting him in the car, she decided to take the would-be rapist to Kate's barn in the country. Once they arrived there, Ola knocked the coward out and put him in handcuffs and shackles. She left him there but went back the next day to check on him. She was relieved to find him right where he was supposed to be. It eventually got easier once Ola began bringing more of them there. She would go to the barn once a day and bring them food and water. They had what they needed to survive. She saw her actions as being more humane than theirs had been and at times even more humane than they deserved. Each time she brought a new one to the barn, Ola wondered whether or not she had captured Kate's killer. It occurred to her more than once that perhaps this was the reason Kate was asking for her help.

She felt a deep, intense rage at having lost Kate in such a violent way. It was truly a miracle that Ola never shot and killed one of those savages while he was beating up on a woman. There was so much hatred inside of her, fueled by a sense of loss and devastation at having her younger sister taken away from her, that grief and anger persisted to taint her judgment as she continued to collect the attackers and bring them to the barn. How does a person recover from a loved one dying at the hands of a killer? How could she get past knowing how Kate must have suffered? Ola thought her heart would always ache just thinking about how alone Kate had to have been those last few minutes of her young life. Ola imagined spending the rest of her own life emotionally wrapped around those gut-wrenching thoughts forever.

But then she remembered Consuelo, the gifted woman who

had brought Kate's words to her after she was gone. There were times in our country's history when women like Consuelo had been burned at the stake. Now Ola sought Consuelo out to help guide her back from despair, and her life quickly became much different because of her.

Even though the dreams had stopped, Consuelo had helped her get in contact with Kate one last time. Through Consuelo, Kate told her that she was at peace, and she urged Ola to find the same within herself. Ola was trying to do that now—trying to let go of her as best she could.

After a while, Kate's words slowly seeped into Ola's consciousness to the point where she could still hear them clearly. Her final words were what Ola had needed to hear in order to help her begin to heal inside. That never seemed possible before, and she had Consuelo to thank for that. For the first time since Kate's death, Ola felt a sense of hope. Her dreams lately had been more normal and full of the usual nonsense people dream about. She could finally see a way to get her life back.

Now that sleep came more easily and the smell of the ocean and the sound of the waves were so soothing, Ola wasn't sure she could ever leave this place. It was time she started taking care of herself again. That had become her new goal.

And tomorrow, she would go shopping for a boogie board.